MAYDAY!

THE JUNIPER JUNCTION HOLIDAY MYSTERY SERIES: BOOK FIVE

AMY M. READE

BOOKS BY AMY M. READE

THE JUNIPER JUNCTION HOLIDAY MYSTERY SERIES

The Worst Noel

Dead, White, and Blue

Be My Valencrime

Ghouls' Night Out

MayDay!

THE MALICE SERIES

The House on Candlewick Lane

Highland Peril

Murder in Thistlecross

STANDALONE BOOKS

Secrets of Hallstead House

The Ghosts of Peppernell Manor

House of the Hanging Jade

BOOKS BY A. M. READE

THE CAPE MAY HISTORICAL MYSTERY COLLECTION

Cape Menace

Pau Hana Publishing

Print ISBN: 978-1-7355221-3-5

Ebook ISBN: 978-1-7355221-2-8

Printed in the United States of America

❀ Created with Vellum

ACKNOWLEDGMENTS

I wish to thank my husband, John, who is always my first reader. Thanks also to Anneli Purchase, Holly Bolicki and Patti Linder, each of whom helped make this a better book. And finally, I would like to thank Celie Roberts, who won a contest to name one of the characters in the book (can you guess which one?).

CHAPTER 1

*L*illy Carlsen slammed the phone down. "The caterer is giving me fits."

"What's wrong?" Her daughter, Laurel, glanced at the clipboard on the kitchen counter next to Lilly. It was covered with sticky notes in every color of the rainbow.

"Now she says she won't be able to provide shrimp cocktail for the wedding. Bill and Noley specifically requested shrimp cocktail."

"Why can't she provide it?"

"Because she's allergic to it. Just yesterday she called to say that she's going to be short-staffed. And since she won't have enough employees there, she's afraid that will increase her chances of having to be near the shrimp. Apparently they give her hives and she swells up like a tick."

"Eww."

Lilly wondered aloud for the hundredth time whose idea it had been for her to organize the wedding of her brother and her best friend.

"Mom, why do you keep asking that? It was your idea."

"It's way more work than I realized. My only experience was

planning my own wedding, and that was a hoedown compared to this."

"I don't know why you couldn't just hire someone on Juniper Lake Manor's approved list of caterers."

"I told you why. Noley was adamant that I hire a caterer who graduated from the culinary program at the community college. She's always looking for opportunities for the graduates."

"You couldn't have talked her out of that?"

Lilly gave Laurel a look. "Hardly. Besides, I haven't even tried. She's had enough on her mind lately. And I would think, being in that program yourself, that you'd agree with her."

Laurel shrugged. "I guess. But if the caterer isn't doing a good job, you should be able to hire someone more reliable."

"Well, it's too late to hire someone else now anyway. With the wedding only a few days away, we're just going to have to cross our fingers and hope for the best."

Lilly's next call was to her son, Tighe. He was nearing the end of his sophomore year in college and had the honor of being Bill's best man. Lilly hadn't seen him in several months, so she couldn't wait until he arrived on Friday.

"Hi, honey."

"Hi, Mom."

"I just want to make sure you know the plan."

"Yup. I'll go after my last class tomorrow and pick up the tux. I'll be home by around two on Friday afternoon. What time is the rehearsal?"

"Four. As long as you're home by three o'clock, you'll be fine."

"The only problem is that I'm going to miss a review session that afternoon for my hardest class."

"Can someone tape it so you can watch it?"

"I guess so. The thing is, I wanted to ask the professor some questions."

"I'm sorry, Tighe. Is there another session you could attend?"

"Yeah, but it's on Saturday. I'm really worried about that final."

"When's the final?"

"Next Monday."

"Want me to get in touch with the professor and explain what's going on?"

"God, no. I'm not in second grade. I'll deal with it. Thanks, anyway."

"All right. Let me know if you change your mind. I'm looking forward to seeing you Friday."

"Love you, Mom."

Lilly hung up and dialed Bill's number. She knew he was at work, but she needed to run a couple of last-minute details by him. He and Noley had wanted an April wedding, but Noley's publisher had other ideas—namely, they wanted her to appear on television and radio shows in the weeks leading up to the publication of her new cookbook. May Day was the first Saturday she'd be available after the first of March. Scheduling the wedding before she began her travels had been logistically impossible, so they had chosen the first available date. With Noley unavailable so much, Lilly had no choice but to make Bill her point person for wedding questions.

Lilly and Bill's mother, Bev, was the real reason Bill and Noley wanted to have the wedding as soon as possible. With Bev's worsening dementia and the associated physical impediments that went hand-in-hand with the disease, Lilly had a sinking feeling that time was not on their side; Bev had fallen several times over the past couple of months. Luckily Nikki— her regular nurse—or another nurse had always been nearby to assist immediately, but Lilly and the rest of the family feared that it was only a matter of time before Bev seriously hurt herself.

When Lilly arrived at the shop the next morning, her assistant, Harry, was already there taking down the Easter decorations.

"Good morning, Harry."

"Morning, boss. I know you wanted to get the May Day stuff up, so I thought I'd get the Easter things out of the way as soon as I got in this morning."

"Thanks, Harry. That's a huge help. I'll get the May Day swag from my office."

Harry was a godsend. He and his fiancée, Alice, were getting married later in the year. It was a big year for weddings: Harry was getting married a couple of months after Bill and Noley, and a couple of months after Harry's wedding, Lilly's ex-husband, Beau, was marrying her mother's nurse, Nikki. She still wasn't sure how she felt about being a guest at Beau's wedding to his second wife, but she had resolved months ago to face it like a grown-up and be happy for them.

She rummaged in the closet where she had stored the decorations. With Laurel's help, Lilly had constructed several mini maypoles out of PVC pipe and ribbons. The ones for the shop had turned out so cute that they had made enough little maypoles to put one on each table at Juniper Lake Manor in addition to the flower centerpieces and floral cones that would hang on the back of each chair.

When she returned to the front of the store, her arms laden with her crafts, she was pleased to see her boyfriend, Hassan Ashraf, standing by one of the jewelry cases talking to Harry.

Hassan immediately walked toward Lilly with his arms outstretched. "Here, let me take those, Lil."

She stood still while Hassan took several maypoles, and then she kissed him on the cheek around the pile still in her arms.

He grinned, the dimple in his chin deepening. "Only a few more days," he said.

"I can't wait until Saturday," she said. "Even though the wedding is being planned in sort of a rush, I think it's going to be beautiful. I hope it goes off without a hitch. Well, one hitch. Get it?" She threw her head back and laughed at her own joke.

Hassan smiled and shook his head. "That was awful, love."

Harry looked at them in confusion.

"Bill and Noley are getting hitched," Lilly explained.

Harry laughed suddenly, snorting coffee out his nostrils. "I just got that!" He hurried into the office, returning a moment later with paper towels and glass spray. He cleaned up the mess on the counter, laughing all the while.

"Hassan, have you picked up your tux from the dry cleaner?" Lilly asked.

"Yup. I even tried it on just to make sure it still fits." He patted his stomach. "It's a tiny bit tighter than it used to be, but I can still squeeze into it."

"I can't wait to see you in it. After all the time we've dated, I've never seen you in a tux."

"I guess you're not supposed to see me in my tux before the wedding," he said with a wink.

Lilly smiled. Wedding talk between the two of them had

been inevitable since she was in the midst of planning one, but they had continued to dance around the subject of getting married themselves. She recalled the previous Valentine's Day with great embarrassment: she had been convinced that Hassan was going to ask her to marry him, and at the time she hadn't been ready. She blushed at the memory of choking on her bread and gulping down a glass of wine to cover her dismay. As it turned out, Hassan hadn't even planned to ask her that night.

She changed the subject. "Can you take a couple of these maypoles and put them on each end of that counter?" She gestured toward the counter closest to the door as she handed Hassan two of the mini maypoles.

He arranged the maypoles artfully and grabbed his coffee from one of the other counters. "I need to get going. I just stopped in to say hi. I've got a ton of work waiting for me at home. Have a good day, hon." He leaned close to Lilly and she kissed his lips. She wouldn't have done that if the store had been open, but as long as the door was still locked to customers, she didn't mind the public display of affection.

There was a knock on the window shortly before opening time and Mallory Abbott stood on the sidewalk wearing a wide smile. Mallory, a newcomer to Juniper Junction, had purchased the decorate-your-own-pottery shop on Main Street following the death of its previous owner, the odious Ivy Leachman. She was so new to town that she hadn't even found a place to live yet—she was living with her sister while she house-hunted.

Harry, knowing Mallory and Lilly had become friendly, opened the door to her.

"Good morning," Mallory said in her singsong voice. "I came to drop off the flowers you painted, Lilly. I glazed them over the weekend and I thought you'd like them for your May Day displays."

"Ooh, thanks!" Lilly hurried over to peek in the bag that Mallory handed her. After meeting Mallory, Lilly had tried her hand at decorating pottery and, to her surprise, realized what a great stress reliever it was. She had painted a couple of dozen small flowers for May Day decorations and she had been eager to see the finished products. "I love them! Thanks for bringing them over, Mallory. I hope you didn't fire these specially for me."

"Nope. I had a huge batch of stuff to fire. I think these turned out so cute. Where are you going to put them?"

Lilly reached into the bag and withdrew several of the small flowers. She divided them between Mallory and Harry. "You two choose where they should go. I'll defer to your judgment."

Mallory beamed and looked around the shop for several seconds. Then she strode over to one of the windows and nestled her flowers among the folds of velvet and tulle around the base of the display. She stood back and surveyed her work. "What do you think?"

Lilly and Harry joined her to look at Mallory's arrangement. "That looks great," Harry said. "I'll put these in the other window."

"Thanks, guys. Everything looks just right," Lilly said.

"I have to run. I'll see you two later," Mallory said. She waved and left, disappearing down the sidewalk in a matter of seconds.

"She's so different from Ivy," Harry said.

Lilly chuckled. "You can say that again."

CHAPTER 3

*L*illy unlocked the door to the shop and within a few minutes she and Harry were both waiting on customers. Business was brisk until mid-afternoon, when they had the store to themselves for a little while.

"Will you be here on Friday?" Harry asked.

"No. I decided to close the shop on Friday and Saturday. That way I can concentrate on my wedding planner duties without worrying about what's going on at work. I'll pay you for those days, though, obviously."

"Sounds good to me. Alice and I are really excited to go to the wedding. We're hoping to mooch some ideas for our own wedding."

"Mooch all you want. I think it's going to be beautiful, but simple at the same time. We haven't had a ton of time to plan it and Bill and Noley wanted to keep it low-key."

"That's what we want, too. Low-key."

The next couple of days flew by in a flurry of preparations, appointments, and to-do lists. Lilly needed to run out to Juniper Lake Manor on Thursday evening, the night before the rehearsal, to take care of some last-minute details, and she invited Laurel to go with her. She drove home quickly after work on Thursday and Laurel was waiting for her. They grabbed dinner at the diner outside Juniper Junction and ate quickly so they could get to Juniper Lake Manor before it got too dark.

"What time are we supposed to be there?" Laurel asked.

"Darla Smithers, the venue manager and my contact up there, is going to meet us at seven thirty. They have a big event tomorrow night, too, so the place will be hopping."

"I can't wait to see it in person. I looked up their photo gallery online and it looks gorgeous."

"It is. It's a breathtaking place for a wedding."

"Maybe I'll get married there."

Lilly shot her daughter a look. "Let's not be in a hurry to pick out wedding venues, please."

"Don't worry, Mom. Can't have a wedding without a boyfriend."

"Let's not be in a hurry for that, either."

"I'm not in a hurry."

"Good."

The sky was growing dusky by the time they arrived. A half mile off the main road, a big, rambling building clad in weathered cedar shakes rose up before them.

"Wow. This is so pretty," Laurel said.

"Isn't it gorgeous? Noley said she's always dreamed of having her wedding at a rustic place like this. Wait until you see inside."

"I'm so going to post a thousand pictures on social media."

Lilly smiled. "Me, too. I think the May Day decorations are going to be perfect with the décor."

The manor was a barn-like structure with big double doors in front and softly lit sconces which welcomed guests to the magnificent property. People in casual dress bustled around inside, carrying chairs, fabric, flowers, and candlesticks from one room to another.

"Ready? Let's head in and I'll show you around. We'll try to stay out of everyone's way."

They walked up the wide stone steps and into the large foyer of the manor, where employees continued to hurry to and fro. One young man stopped and smiled at them. "What can I do for you?"

"We're looking for Darla," Lilly said.

"I saw her a couple of minutes ago," he said, looking over his shoulder. He scanned the room. "There she is." He pointed to a petite woman disappearing through a door in the rear of the room.

"Thanks. Let's go, Laur." She tugged on Laurel's arm and Laurel turned away from the young man to follow her.

"He's cute," Laurel whispered as they made their way to Darla.

Lilly grinned. "I agree."

Lilly hailed Darla as they approached her. "Hi, Darla."

Darla spun around and smiled. "Lilly! Good to see you."

"This is my daughter, Laurel. She'll be making the mini cakes for the wedding favors." Lilly gestured toward Laurel, who held out her hand to Darla.

"Nice to meet you," Laurel said.

Darla shook her hand enthusiastically. "I've heard so much about you, Laurel. Your mother is very proud of you. I can't wait to see those little cakes."

Laurel blushed and smiled shyly. "Thank you. I study culinary arts at the community college."

"I hope you'll save a cake for me."

"Definitely," Laurel said.

"I wanted to show you what we're doing for tomorrow evening's wedding reception, Lilly, just so you get a good idea of what the space looks like when it's decorated. Then, after that event, of course we'll break down the rooms and start again with the decorations for Bill and Noley's wedding." She beckoned for Lilly and Laurel to follow her into the bar at the rear of the building.

"The bar will be set up in here before and during the reception." She turned around and pointed to an empty space near the door. "This is where the coffee bar will be set up after dinner."

"Perfect."

The ceiling around the bar area was festooned with strings of white lights, giving the space a party vibe. One bartender dressed in a brown leather vest was busy wiping wine glasses so they sparkled and another was examining the bottles behind the bar and making notations in a small book.

"Come on. I'll show you how we've decorated the bridal lounge."

CHAPTER 4

"What's a bridal lounge?" Laurel asked.

"It's where the bride and her attendants get to hang out and relax until the ceremony starts. They can get dressed in there, do their hair and makeup if necessary, whatever they want." Darla led the way upstairs and into a cozy room above the bar.

"This is adorable!" Laurel exclaimed. Lilly, who had seen the room already, smiled at Laurel's reaction. There was a long sectional sofa against one wall, underneath a window framing a wide grassy lawn that led down to the shore of Juniper Lake. The lawn was shrouded in shades of deep lavender in the dusk, but Lilly could picture it vividly. She was eager for Laurel to see it again in all its sun-drenched beauty on Saturday. At least, Lilly hoped it would be sun-drenched.

Tasteful furniture was placed around the room and a big-screen television hung on the wall. On the screen, a peaceful mountain stream tumbled over rocks in a burbling rush. Darla saw Laurel watching it, mesmerized.

"We've found that ambient sounds really help relax the wedding party, and especially the bride and groom. There's a

TV playing almost the same thing on a loop in the groom's lounge."

"I love it in here. It's so relaxing." Laurel peeked into the ensuite bathroom. It was huge, as Lilly recalled. Laurel would be jealous. As if on cue, Laurel turned to her mom, her mouth agape. "Have you seen the size of this bathroom? We need this at home."

"The groom's room is practically identical, so we'll skip that tonight. Let's head back down," Darla said.

In the large main room where the reception would be held, Juniper Lake Manor employees moved about in what looked like controlled chaos, moving tables and chairs, and consulting a large white board that hung on one wall. The young man who had greeted Lilly and Laurel at the door came up to them.

"Are you thinking of hosting an event here?" he asked.

"Drew, meet Lilly and Laurel. Lilly is planning the wedding of Bill Merriweather and Noley Appleton on Saturday."

"Great! It's nice to meet you. See you on Saturday, then." He smiled at Laurel and then excused himself to get back to work.

"Drew is the owner's son, so he's more than just your average employee." Darla glanced fondly at Drew's retreating back. "He takes a keen interest in everything."

Laurel's eyes twinkled. "And he's so cute!"

Darla laughed. "You're not the only young lady who has noticed that, believe me."

Laurel's smile disappeared. *I do not need this tonight*, Lilly thought. She turned to Darla quickly. "Um, so, can you tell me a little about the wedding tomorrow?"

"Sure. The wedding is at a church at five o'clock, so the reception won't start until six o'clock or so. You'll have plenty of time to have the rehearsal and clear out before they get here. The bride is a rancher's daughter and the groom is the son of a rodeo owner. It's a real Colorado-cowboy wedding. The bridesmaids are wearing boots with their dresses and everything."

"That sounds fun!" Laurel exclaimed.

"I think it'll be a real hoot," Darla said. "Of course, I'll be in business attire, just like I will be on Saturday for Bill and Noley's wedding." She turned to Lilly. "Do you have any questions?"

"Actually, yes. I need to check a few details with you." Lilly pulled her clipboard out of her shoulder bag and glanced at Laurel. "Do you want to look around while I talk to Darla?"

"Sure." Laurel walked further into the room where the reception would be held, and Lilly turned to Darla.

CHAPTER 5

*L*illy had a litany of questions: what time to have the decorations at the manor, how many heaters would be outside for the ceremony if it was chilly, whether there would be wine in the bride and groom lounges for pre-wedding jitters, and many more. The women spoke for several minutes, until Laurel returned to her mother's side wearing a wide smile.

"Just a sec, Laur." Lilly made one final checkmark on her clipboard and held out her hand to Darla. "Thanks so much, Darla. You've made my job so much easier."

"Lilly, I can't believe you're not a full-time wedding planner."

Lilly laughed. "No way. Too much stress for me. I planned my own wedding over twenty years ago—"

"Really? That's great!"

"Not really. He left after three years and only recently came back to town."

Darla frowned. "Sorry to hear that."

"It's okay. He was my starter husband." Lilly laughed and Darla joined her.

"Anyway, you're good at this. If you ever sell your jewelry store, let me know. We could use you here."

Lilly could feel the flush on her cheeks. "Thank you, but my jewelry shop is where my heart is."

Drew passed Lilly and Laurel as they exited the building, and he gave Laurel a wink. She blushed.

"What was that all about?" Lilly asked as they made their way to her car.

"I was just talking to him while you spoke to Darla. He's really nice."

"And that's all?"

"That's all." Laurel grinned. Lilly didn't have to ask any more questions. Obviously Drew had made quite an impression on her daughter.

On Friday morning Lilly drove over to Noley's house as soon as she finished breakfast. Noley had finally gotten home from her book tour in the middle of the night. She greeted Lilly with a big hug at the front door.

"I've never been so glad to see anyone," Noley said. "I had forgotten how hard it is to be on the road constantly."

As a nationally renowned chef, Noley was used to being in demand by television and radio show producers. She also had a syndicated cooking column in newspapers across the United States and worked as the head of recipe development for a cooking magazine. But this cookbook tour had been physically and mentally draining, even for her.

"Have you seen Bill yet?"

"He's still at work. He'll be over as soon as he gets off shift at noon."

"Are you ready?"

"To see Bill? Of course!"

"No, not to see Bill. For the wedding."

Noley took a deep breath. "I've got one last appointment with the seamstress this morning and I have to confirm my hair and makeup appointment for tomorrow."

"Good. As long as you have that stuff under control, I'll call the bakery, the florist, the caterer, the minister, the rehearsal dinner restaurant, and my contact for the band." Lilly ticked off her fingers as she listed her chores. "Everything is coming together!" She gave a little squeal.

Noley let out a nervous laugh. "All that's left is to actually get married."

Lilly cocked her head and looked intently at Noley. "Have I told you how happy I am that we're going to be sisters?"

"You have. Have I told you how much I appreciate you doing all this work for me and Bill? The planning, the leg work, the worrying, everything. We'll never be able to repay you."

"You don't have to repay me. I wanted to do it. Especially with you on the road, you needed a planner who knows you and Bill really well. Who knows you both better than I do?"

Noley held out her arms and Lilly hugged her best friend. When they separated, Noley's eyes were glistening.

"No crying, now."

"They're happy tears. And I wouldn't be crying if I weren't so exhausted."

"Go to your appointment, make your calls, and then take a long nap. You need to be rested up for the rehearsal this afternoon. I've got to run."

"All right. Thanks again, Lil. I'll see you later."

CHAPTER 6

*L*illy left and drove straight to her mother's house before heading back home to make all her calls. Nikki greeted her with a smile.

"Ready for the big wedding?" Nikki asked. She held the door open so Lilly could come inside.

"Do you think Mom'll be all right? If there were a way to do this without making her leave the house, you know I would have done it."

"I know. But I think she's actually looking forward to it."

"Great. How is she doing today?"

"Confused, as usual, but nothing we can't handle. She seems eager to get dressed up."

Lilly nodded. "I'll go talk to her."

She walked into the living room, where Bev sat in her favorite chair, her new walker on the floor right in front of her. She was listing a bit to one side, but she looked up at Lilly with a smile.

"Good morning, dear. Are you ready for the wedding?" Bev's speech had become harder and harder to understand of late, but Lilly usually got the gist of her words.

"I sure am. I'll be glad when it's over."

"Remind me where you're going on your honeymoon."

Every time Bev was confused like this, Lilly fought the urge to explain reality. She longed to remind her mom that she wasn't getting married—Bill and Noley were. But she played along.

"Aruba."

"Ah, yes. Aruba. I've never been there. Nikki showed me pictures on the computer. It's beautiful."

"It sure is. And speaking of beautiful, Mom, you're going to be amazed by the place where the wedding and reception are going to be. And tonight the rehearsal dinner will be at The Treetop Inn. You love it there." Indeed, Bill and Noley had chosen that particular restaurant because it was Bev's favorite.

"Nikki helped me choose a lovely dress."

"I know. You showed it to me, remember? The lilac color goes so well with your eyes."

"Thank you, dear. You should go so you get everything done. Nikki and I can manage, can't we, Nikki?" Nikki had come into the room and was standing next to Lilly.

"You bet, Bev. Lilly, we'll be at Juniper Lake Manor for the rehearsal by three thirty."

"Great. I'll see you there."

Lilly left and sped back to her house, where she poured her second cup of coffee and sat down with her phone.

The minister was ready, as were the band, the florist, and the bakery. The caterer, Maureen Davies, was her last call.

"Were you able to find temporary employees to fill in for the staff who can't be there tomorrow?" Lilly asked.

"Here's the thing, Mrs. Carlsen. I have to pay temporary employees more than my regular employees. And obviously I can't eat that charge, so I have to pass that cost along to you."

"I don't see why. We signed a contract. We pay you for a service and you agree to provide the service. How you choose to staff it is up to you, but you have to staff it according to the contract."

"The contract states that we make 'reasonable efforts' to execute our responsibilities. It is unreasonable to ask me to take a haircut on my profit because I have three employees out sick."

"I would say it's entirely reasonable to ask you to do that. If we had to cancel the wedding at the last minute and asked you to make adjustments, would you?"

"Of course not."

"You see?"

"That would be a completely different circumstance. I require forty-eight hours' notice for a cancellation. That deadline has passed. All I have to do is make a reasonable effort to staff the event. Don't worry, Mrs. Carlsen. The guests will not even notice, I promise you."

"Somehow I doubt that."

"Well, I have one more thing I need to discuss with you. I need to substitute all the beef entrées with fish," Maureen said.

"Are you kidding me?"

"Unfortunately, no. There's an issue with my supplier and I simply won't have the beef in time. But don't worry. The fish is really good."

"It won't taste good to the people who ordered beef."

"Well, I'm afraid there's nothing I can do about it. You'll never find a caterer to make that many beef entrees in time for the reception."

"What if I pick up enough beef at a grocery store and drop it off to you?"

"I can't guarantee its quality."

"Can you at least sub chicken instead?"

"I wish I could, but most of my chicken is already in a huge batch of salad I need for a brunch I'm catering on Sunday. Don't worry, the fish will be delicious. Listen, I need to get going. I'll call you if there's any change." Maureen hung up without waiting for a reply.

"Aaargh!" Lilly yelled.

"Mom! Are you all right?" Laurel called from upstairs.

"No. Did you order the beef for tomorrow night?"

"Yes. Why?"

"I hope you like fish."

"Oh, no. The caterer again?"

"The caterer again."

"This is going to be awful," Laurel said.

"I wish I had never heard the name Maureen Davies."

CHAPTER 7

*L*illy took a quick nap after lunch and woke up a little before two o'clock to the sound of Tighe coming upstairs.

"Tighe!" She rushed out of her room and hugged him. "I'm so glad you're home. Have you eaten lunch? Are you tired? Do you want to rest before we leave?"

Tighe laughed. "Slow down, Mom. I grabbed lunch and a coffee on the road, so I don't need to eat or sleep. I'm gonna study until it's time to go."

While Tighe studied, Lilly took her time dressing. She had chosen a lime green and pink dress with three-quarter length sleeves and a mid-length skirt and paired it with silver earrings and a necklace. Hassan called just as she was slipping into her high heels.

"Hi, love. Are you ready to enjoy the fruits of your labor?" he asked.

"You bet. I'll just be glad when this is over."

Truer words were never spoken.

Lilly went downstairs, where Laurel was waiting for her in the kitchen.

"Wow, Mom. You look fab!"

Lilly spun around so her flared skirt swirled around her. "Thank you. So do you! I love that dress." Laurel was dressed in a light blue long-sleeved dress with a short skirt and a V neckline. It was perfect for her age and her complexion. Laurel, too, had chosen silver jewelry and wore a pretty bracelet with a couple of dangly blue charms.

"Do you need to take anything with you to the rehearsal?" Laurel asked.

"I don't think so. I'll be busy tomorrow, but tonight all I have to do is practice being Matron of Honor and make sure everyone gets to the restaurant on time. And hand out these schedules for tomorrow." She waved several sheets of paper as she spoke.

"It's pretty cool that Noley picked you over her own sister to be the Matron of Honor."

"I know. Noley's sister will play a role in the ceremony, though. She's going to do a reading."

"Are they close?"

"Not as close as Noley and I are, so she understands why Noley chose me."

"That's good. Are you ready?"

"I'm ready." Lilly went to the bottom of the stairs and yelled up. "Tighe! We're ready to go!"

A few seconds later Tighe joined them in the kitchen. He wore a navy suit jacket, a white Oxford with a pink tie, and khaki pants.

"Do I look okay?" he asked.

"Very handsome," Lilly said. Tighe rolled his eyes.

On the drive to Juniper Lake Manor, Lilly and Laurel discussed the things that needed to be done the next day before the wedding ceremony. Laurel had brought a notebook and pen, so she took copious notes as Lilly spoke.

"If you need help decorating the mini cakes tomorrow

morning, just let me know. I can help before I head off to get my hair done," Lilly said. Laurel had offered to make the wedding favors, which were going to be mini Bundt cakes. With Noley's input, Laurel had decided on two delectable-sounding treats: red velvet cakes with a cream cheese frosting and decorated with red velvet crumbs, and dark chocolate cakes with a raspberry curd filling, a vanilla buttercream frosting, and decorated with dark chocolate curls.

"I should be fine. Really, there aren't that many cakes to do. I've made fifty and they're expecting forty-six guests, right?"

"Right."

"Okay. It shouldn't take much time at all to frost and decorate them."

"Tighe, are you going to be able to help out tomorrow?"

"I doubt it, Mom. Sorry. I'll be studying for my final until the wedding."

"That's fine."

When they arrived at Juniper Lake Manor, Laurel got out of the car and looked around.

"Looking for someone?" Lilly asked, her eyes twinkling. "Someone named Drew, perhaps?"

Laurel blushed. "I don't even know if he's supposed to work tonight."

"Well, if he isn't here tonight, you'll see him tomorrow. Come on," Lilly said. "Let's go inside and see if anyone else is here." She led the way into the manor.

CHAPTER 8

*D*arla was the first person they saw. Lilly introduced Tighe and they shook hands. "You're the first ones here for the rehearsal. I'd give you the lounges to relax, but they're being prepped for the wedding party coming in this evening. I can give you another room to hang out in if you'd like."

Lilly looked at Laurel and Tighe, who nodded. "Lead on," Lilly said. Darla led them up the rustic wooden staircase to a large sitting area on the second floor overlooking the foyer and reception hall. There were two sofas in the space, along with a tea service and small basket of snacks.

Laurel and Tighe made themselves comfortable on one of the sofas. Tighe whipped a textbook out of the backpack he was carrying.

They all sat in silence for a short time, and then Lilly glanced at her watch. The rest of the wedding party would arrive at any moment. "Guys, we should go downstairs so no one has to come looking for us." Tighe groaned.

"I could really get used to staying in a place like this," Laurel said. She stood up and put her heels back on. "All right, I'm ready."

Downstairs, a few members of the wedding party were already gathering. Lilly introduced herself and the kids, and they all chatted while they waited for Noley and Bill, who arrived together a short while later. There were hugs and handshakes all around and a few of the groomsmen availed themselves of the bar while everyone waited for the minister to show up. They didn't have to wait long. Bev and Nikki arrived just after the minister, followed immediately by Noley's parents, Melissa and Russell.

Nikki walked behind Bev, who pushed her walker slowly up the ramp in front of the manor. Bev didn't like to admit that she needed the walker, so it was a big deal when she had agreed to use it at the wedding events.

The groomsmen, many of whom Lilly remembered from Bill's high school days and visits home from college, were all solicitous of Bev and swarmed around her like there was no one else they would rather have seen at the wedding rehearsal. Of course, Bev had always invited them into her home when they were boys and young men, and they remembered her fondly. She had been quite a hostess in those days.

"Of course I remember you, George," Bev was saying to one of the groomsmen. Her words were slightly garbled, but everyone seemed to understand her. "You used to love my macaroni and cheese. And you, Ray, you used to spend the night after every football game." The men beamed as Bev spoke, and it was wonderful to watch her face light up with joy every time she recognized one of the men who used to spend so much time in her house.

"Oh, Tom, I remember you. You were such a cute little thing."

Tom Toole, who had grown up on the next block and had been Bill's first partner on the police force, rolled his eyes and smiled. "I finally had that growth spurt," he said. Indeed, he and Bill were about the same height.

Lilly glanced outside. The minister was already down at the lakeshore with Bill and Noley, deep in conversation. "Nikki, let's take Mom outside and get her situated so she can see the whole rehearsal," Lilly suggested.

Once Bev and Nikki were comfortably seated in chairs that had been placed on the lawn for them, Lilly returned to the manor to request that everyone make their way down to the lakeshore. But before they departed, she distributed the wedding-day schedules to everyone in the wedding party. Darla had helped her plan the wedding day down to the minute, and Lilly intended to stick with the schedule so that there wouldn't be the usual chaos over wedding party photos and protracted receiving line conversations. Once everyone had a schedule and Lilly had made sure there were no questions, they all followed Lilly out the back door of the manor and down to the water's edge.

The minister gathered the entire wedding party around him and asked for the best man to step up.

Tighe stepped forward. The minister showed him what to do and where to stand. Lilly watched the exchange wistfully. Her little boy, all grown up.

The minister directed Noley and her father to start down the path to the lake when they heard the first notes of "Trumpet Voluntary," which he would cue with a thumbs-up, since there would be no music at the rehearsal. Russell started to blink rapidly. Noley swallowed hard and followed suit. Before long all the women in the group were sniffling and fighting back a full onslaught of tears.

"This is supposed to be happy." Bill rolled his eyes.

That broke the momentary silence and Noley gulped out a laugh. "It is! These are happy tears. Aren't they, Dad?"

Russell nodded, wiping his eyes on the sleeve of his jacket.

Melissa, her eyes glistening, too, walked up to Russell and handed him a tissue. He and Noley, followed by all the women in the wedding party, made their way back up to the manor.

While the women were getting in place, the groomsmen took their places to the side of Bill. Seeing that everyone was ready, the minister beckoned for Lilly and the bridesmaids to start down the aisle. When they were in place down by the water, the minister gave the thumbs-up. Noley and her father emerged from the back of the manor and made their way to the shoreline. The minister held out his hands in a "slow down" gesture and they slowed the pace. When they arrived at the water's edge, the minister smiled at everyone.

"Noley, I know this is exciting, but you might trip running down the aisle."

That broke the nervousness in the group and everyone laughed. Russell, who appeared to have a death grip on Noley's arm, relaxed and smiled. He kissed Noley on the cheek and made his way to Melissa's side in the front row of chairs.

CHAPTER 9

The ceremony was over in just a few minutes. Noley's sister, Cynthia, read beautifully, as did Hassan, and Bill and Noley exchanged imaginary rings. Lilly could almost hear the recessional play in her mind as the party made their way back to the manor after the ceremony concluded. Most of the wedding party reconvened a bit later at The Treetop Inn, though groomsmen Tom and George were on duty that night and had to return to work.

Dinner was a festive affair, despite the staid atmosphere of The Treetop Inn. The wedding party had a small banquet room to themselves, so they didn't have to worry about bothering other diners with their noise and enthusiasm.

It came as no surprise to Lilly that Bev was holding court at dinner. Though Lilly had harbored a fear that people would be uncomfortable trying to understand Bev's distorted words, everyone seemed to catch on to what Bev was saying. After that, Lilly was just afraid of what family secrets Bev might spill while she enjoyed being the center of attention.

She told the story of the time Bill tried to teach himself to fly by jumping off a picnic table on the patio. Lilly remembered waiting for him in the emergency room. Then Bev told the story of the time Bill got caught cheating on a physical fitness test in gym. "He took so long walking around the track that he finished two laps as most of the other kids were finishing four laps," she said.

"Mom." Bill rolled his eyes.

"Oh, pooh. These are the stories one tells at weddings."

"This is only the rehearsal."

"Good. Then I'm rehearsing."

The woman was remarkably sharp sometimes.

Then she shifted gears and began a story about one of Bill's old girlfriends.

"Mom." This time Bill's voice held a warning.

"Billy, I'm sure Noley knows you have old girlfriends. Even beautiful ones, like Tisha."

"Mom, that's ancient history. No one wants to hear about Tisha."

"Who's Tisha?" asked Noley. Lilly glanced at Bill, who was pleading with his eyes to get her to stop Bev from saying anymore.

"Mom, let's go to the ladies' room," Lilly said.

"I don't have to use the ladies' room."

"Yes, you do. Nikki, care to help me?"

Nikki pushed her chair back and helped Bev stand up, and they made their way to the restrooms, out of hearing of the others. Bev was scowling. "I am not a child, Lilly."

"You're acting like one, Mom. Tisha is not an appropriate topic for Bill's wedding rehearsal. Or his wedding, so don't tell me you're rehearsing."

"Tisha was a beautiful girl. Remember her?"

"Yes, I do. The one with boobs out to here and not a brain in her head. Yes, I remember her."

"You're being awfully grumpy, Lilly."

"Mom, please lay off the stories about Bill's girlfriends. It's not nice to do that to Noley."

"I don't think I like that Noley very much."

"What?? You love Noley. You've loved Noley since the moment you met her years ago."

"She's not good enough for Billy."

Lilly sighed. "Bill loves her, Mom. She's perfect for him. Everyone can see that. He comes alive when she's around."

"A mother never thinks her daughter-in-law is good enough for her son."

Lilly wanted to ask, *But Beau was good enough for me?* But she didn't. She didn't want to make matters more uncomfortable. And with Nikki standing right there, it was probably best not to drag Beau's name into the fray.

"I still don't have to use the ladies' room," Bev said.

"All right. Fine. But you have to promise that you're going to keep your mouth shut about Bill's old girlfriends while we're here tonight. It's inappropriate."

"All right." Bev wore a pout that any toddler would be proud to sport.

Lilly shook her head and looked at Nikki, who was smiling. "This is hard for her," Nikki whispered. "Her son's getting married." Bev was washing her hands and couldn't hear them over the sound of the running water.

"I get that. But to talk about Tisha, really? It's not fair to Bill and it's certainly not fair to Noley."

"I'll try to keep her quiet."

Lilly thanked Nikki, though she didn't see how Nikki was going to accomplish that. No one had figured it out for nearly eight decades. It was unlikely Nikki was going to crack the code at Bill's rehearsal dinner.

Then her heart twisted. How could she be mad at her mom? The poor woman was powerless to stop what was happening to her. It wasn't her fault she had lost her filter. Could Lilly really be so callous as to be angry that her mother was trying to dredge up ancient history?

She sighed. Yes. In fact, she could be that callous. She wished she weren't. She just wanted everything to be perfect for Bill and Noley. She knew perfect wasn't possible, of course, but she hoped to come close. Dementia interfered with that.

She placed her hand on Bev's arm as they made their way back to the table. Bev's lips had been set in a thin line, but they softened a bit as Lilly helped guide her to her seat.

"I'm sorry," Bev whispered.

Lilly hugged Bev's shoulders. "I know, Mom. Let's just enjoy dinner, shall we?" Bev nodded and smiled. When she sat down she winked at Noley and Noley grinned at her. It was clear that Bev had been forgiven for her *faux pas*. Bill was lucky to have a woman as confident in herself as Noley was. Bev's comment about an old girlfriend might have rattled a lesser woman.

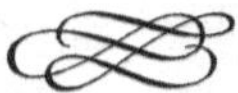

CHAPTER 10

After dinner Lilly, Laurel, and Tighe went home. Nikki took Bev home so she could get a good night's sleep before the big day, and the rest of the wedding party, including the bride and groom, went out to a bar in Lupine.

May Day dawned bright, sunny, and warm. Lilly couldn't have asked for better weather. She was up at the crack of dawn, bustling around the house, gathering decorations, making lists, drinking coffee, and trying to keep Barney from getting underfoot. He knew something was different because Lilly was more harried than usual. He whined constantly, trying to get her attention.

"Barn, it's fine. I'm only going to be gone for a few hours. You'll stay with Mallory."

He stopped whining and cocked his head and stared at her. She smiled and handed him a dog biscuit. "You eat your treat and let me get things done."

Laurel was downstairs pretty early, too. She took the mini Bundt cakes from the freezer and set them on the counter to thaw just a bit before frosting them. She mixed up the two kinds of frosting and Lilly watched in fascination as she transferred the frosting to two piping bags.

"I don't understand how my body created someone who is so good at cooking," Lilly said.

"Maybe I get it from Dad."

"Hmm. Could be."

Not a chance, Lilly thought. But she wasn't going to spoil the day by sniping about Beau.

Laurel glanced at Lilly out of the corner of her eye and grinned. "But you're a good cook, Mom. I probably got it from you."

That's much better.

Lilly was transfixed by Laurel's skill at frosting the cakes. There were little rosebuds on the red velvet cakes, and rich, glossy swirls on the chocolate cakes. After Laurel had frosted all the cakes, Lilly watched as she carefully sprinkled red velvet crumbs on the red velvet cakes and then took a vegetable peeler and a big hunk of chocolate and made little chocolate curls to put on top of the chocolate cakes.

"These are going back into the freezer so the chocolate curls don't melt before we get to Juniper Lake Manor," Laurel said. She put the cakes in the freezer and spent the rest of the morning helping Lilly with the lists and the last-minute preparations.

Noley called mid-morning in a panic. "I need help!" she cried.

"Slow down. What's wrong?" Lilly asked.

"I ripped my dress."

Lilly gasped. "How did that happen?"

Noley was sobbing. "I tried it on one last time with heels and I tripped. What am I going to do?"

"Is it bad?"

"It's awful!"

"I mean, is it a big rip?"

Noley gulped. "I don't know. It's in the back of the dress and I can't see it very well."

"All right. Leave it on and I'll be right over. In the meantime, call the seamstress and see what she recommends."

"I will. Hurry, okay?"

"I'll hurry." Lilly hung up. "Laurel, I'm going to need you to take care of a few things on this list. Noley ripped her dress."

"Oh, no!"

"She's a mess. I've got to run over there and see if I can help. Can you just make sure this stuff gets done?"

Lilly raced over to Noley's and found her best friend sitting in her wedding dress on the bedroom floor, her head in her hands.

CHAPTER 11

"All right. Let's see this rip," Lilly said. "Where's your mom?"

"She and Dad are over at your mom's house. They wanted to visit with her before the ceremony. They were afraid it would be too busy and noisy at the reception to chat with her then."

"That was so nice of them," Lilly said. Her mind was racing. *What if Mom doesn't know who they are and she freaks out? What if she's mean to them? It wouldn't be the first time she was mean for no reason at all.*

Lilly shook those thoughts out of her head so she could focus on the problem at hand. "Did you call the seamstress?"

"Yes." Noley sniffed loudly. "It went to voicemail. I left a message, but we have to do what we can without her just in case she doesn't call me back."

"Okay. Stand up and turn around so I can get a good look at it."

Noley stood up while Lilly looked at her—really looked at her—for the first time. "What happened? You look awful!"

Noley responded with a fresh cascade of tears. "Thanks."

"I didn't mean it the way it sounded."

"Yes, you did."

"Your face is all puffy. You have vampire eyes."

"I know," Noley said. "I was out too late last night and I didn't get much sleep. I drank too much, Lilly! I look terrible!"

"Okay. The rip really isn't that bad. I brought a sewing kit that I found in my bathroom. I can try to stitch up the rip. While I'm doing that, I want you to go soak your face with cold water. We need to get that puffiness down. Do you have any cucumbers?"

"They're not in season."

"Nol, I don't often wish you weren't a chef, but this is one of those times. Who doesn't eat cucumbers year-round?"

"Me."

"I'll call your mother and ask her to stop for cucumbers on her way home from my mom's house. You need to put them on your eyes. They take down swelling."

"Don't call it that. You make it sound like I've gone fifteen rounds with Big-Boned Bertha."

Lilly couldn't help laughing, though it was clear Noley didn't think this was a laughing matter. "Okay, not swelling. Puffiness. How's that?"

"A little better."

Noley shimmied out of the dress, which was a gorgeous ivory silk A-line creation with long sleeves, a bateau neckline, a slim ribbon belt, and a chapel train. The rip was in the hem of the dress right near the spot where the train began.

"This shouldn't be a problem at all," Lilly murmured to herself. Noley was splashing water on her face in the bathroom. It sounded like a fire hydrant was being flushed. "Nol, you don't need to douse your face. Just press lightly on it with a cold washcloth."

By the time Lilly had sewn up the hem, she had been reminded why she had gotten a D in high school home economics. The hem was crooked and the stitches looked like they had been put there by a drunk in the dark.

"How's it look?" Noley called from the bathroom.

"Well, it's not ripped anymore. The good news is that no one is going to be looking at the hem. They're going to be looking at you. How do your eyes feel?"

"Better." Noley appeared in the doorway and her eyes did, in fact, look better.

"I'm still going to call your mom. Cucumber eye patches never hurt anyone, even though the puffiness has gone down."

"Lilly, what if Bill and I aren't happy?"

Ah, there's the real source of the tears, Lilly thought. She stood up from her spot on the bed and placed her hands on Noley's shoulders. "You listen to me. You and Bill are two of the best people I know. You know how happy you make each other. These are just jitters talking. You're going to be happier than you ever thought possible, and that's a promise. No more sulking. The rip is fixed, you and Bill are going to live happily ever after, and if I don't call your mom soon she's going to drive right past the grocery store and you won't get your cucumber."

Noley smiled and looked at her feet. "You're right. I'm just nervous." She took a deep breath. "Thank you, Lilly. I don't know what I would do without you."

"You'd still get married to Bill, but the wedding wouldn't be nearly as magical as it's going to be," Lilly said. "Now I've got to stop at the hairdresser and then get back to my house. There are still a million things to do. I'll see you later on." She embraced Noley and the two women held onto each other for several long moments.

When she got home Laurel was on the phone. "Oh, here's my mom," she said. Lilly shut the back door and gave Laurel a questioning look.

"Caterer."

Lilly closed her eyes. *Not now. I can't handle it.*

"Hello?"

"Mrs. Carlsen, I'm calling about this evening's event."

"Yes, I figured. How can I help you?"

"I've just gotten off the phone with the manager of the venue. Darla something-or-other. She is very rude. I am going to have to ask that you intervene to make sure she knows I am the one in charge of the food."

"She knows that."

"She seems to think the venue staff will not be assisting me in any way."

"Is that a problem?"

"Yes. I've already told you I'm short-staffed."

"The employees of Juniper Lake Manor do not work for you."

"I know that. But I am going to need their assistance to make everything work today."

"Then you need to take that up with Darla, not me."

"As I've already told you, Darla is very unpleasant to work with."

"She's always been perfectly fine with me."

"I can see I'm getting nowhere. Fine. I hope this reception isn't a total disaster."

"If it is, you'll be hearing from my lawyer."

"Do not threaten me, Mrs. Carlsen."

"You would do well to remember that I received special permission from Darla to allow you to work at Juniper Lake Manor. If you want to be added to their approved list of caterers, you'd better hope the reception isn't a total disaster."

Maureen hung up.

"Grr," Lilly said through gritted teeth. "She is going to get such a bad review from me."

CHAPTER 12

$\mathcal{I}$t was mid-afternoon when Laurel said, "You should start getting ready, Mom."

Lilly looked at her watch. "You're right."

Lilly tapped on Tighe's bedroom door before going into her own room to dress.

"Come on in."

Lilly cracked the door open and stuck her head into the room. She was surprised at the look on Tighe's face. His mouth was pinched and his eyes were worried. "What's wrong?"

"It's this test. Mom, I'm going to have to do my best man thing at the wedding and just leave right afterward. I have to study or I'll never pass this final."

Lilly went into the room, closing the door behind her. "Whatever you need to do, that's fine. Just let me know. I'd love for you to stay because your uncle is only getting married once. But if you need to leave after the ceremony, that's okay."

"The quicker I get back to campus, the happier I'll be."

"Oh. You want to go all the way back to campus after the ceremony? I thought you'd just come home."

"No. There's someone at school who can sit down with me and show me what I need to know."

"You'll be getting back awfully late."

"That's okay."

"All right. For now, don't worry about it. Just get into your tux. We have to head out to Juniper Lake Manor."

"Already? The wedding isn't for three hours!"

"I have to be there early to make sure everything is being done the way we want it."

"All right. But I'm bringing my stuff to study."

"That's fine."

Lilly showered and slipped into the dress Noley had chosen. It was pale green and it made Lilly's face look sallow. She had to remind herself it was only for a few hours.

She put on a pair of nude high heels and chose dangly earrings to complement her chignon. Laurel knocked on the door.

"Hi, Mom. You look nice."

Lilly turned and fixed her with a wry smile. "Thanks. I know you're lying. This shade of green is the worst possible color on me, except for maybe yellow. You look great in it, though." It was true—Laurel was lovely in her bridesmaid dress.

"It's too bad we can't just wear what we want."

"Laur, you'll have your revenge when you get married. You can force your bridal attendants to wear any color you want." Laurel laughed. "Are we ready?" Lilly asked.

"I'm ready."

"Tighe!" Lilly called. "Ready?" She and Laurel went down to the kitchen to wait.

When Tighe clumped down the stairs in his tux, Lilly's breath caught in her throat. Visions of her little boy flashed before her eyes. Tighe starting Kindergarten, holding her hand when he got a vaccination, playing with one of his stuffed animals while she made dinner. She couldn't speak for a second.

"What's wrong?" he asked.

"Nothing. You look nice in that tux."

"Thanks. These shoes are a nightmare."

His comment broke the train of nostalgia speeding through Lilly's mind and threatening to derail in a puddle of tears and ruined makeup. "Those shoes are a rite of passage, my dear."

Tighe chuckled. Without the frown, he looked more like he was going to a wedding and less like he was going to a funeral.

They dropped Barney off at Mallory's house first. Barney was beside himself with excitement to get into her house.

After they had watched Barney bound into the house behind his new friend, they left for Juniper Lake Manor. Bill was planning to get there an hour or so before the wedding and Noley was planning to get there before that. She wanted to be in the bridal lounge to dress and put on her makeup before Bill even arrived. She was adamant that he not see her before the ceremony.

The catering staff, minus their missing employees, was already at work when Lilly arrived at the manor. The first person she saw was Darla.

"I'm going to kill that Maureen Davies," Darla said.

CHAPTER 13

"What's wrong?" Lilly asked.

"She's bossing around my staff like she owns the place. Mark my words, Lilly, she and I are going to be at each other's throats before tonight is over."

Lilly sighed and went upstairs to the bridal lounge. Noley and her mom were already there. She must not have hidden her disgust with Maureen very well because Noley took one look at her and asked, "What's wrong? What happened?"

"Nothing."

"Bill's backing out, isn't he?"

"Noley, why on Earth would that be the first thought that leaps into your head?"

Melissa stood behind Noley and shook her head, her eyes wide open. She even made horizontal X-ing motions with her arms. But it was too late—Lilly had already gone down the slippery slope.

Noley burst into tears. "Because of Tisha!"

Lilly was confused, but only for a moment. Tisha. *Mom.* If she could have snorted fire through her nose, she would have set the whole room ablaze.

"Noley, you know Mom. She loves you. She may not love me anymore when I'm through talking to her, but she loves you. You know that. And Bill loves you. Tisha was an old girlfriend and absolutely nothing more. She was as dumb as they come. Mom didn't mean anything by what she said. I'll bet you Bill hasn't given Tisha a thought since the day he dumped her. Do you hear me? *He* dumped *her.*

"The reason I'm mad is because of the caterer." She managed to stop herself before saying any more—she hadn't mentioned the beef debacle for fear of freaking out Bill and Noley. Better to let them learn about it with the rest of the guests, when they couldn't go ballistic.

"How did she make you mad?" Noley sniffled.

"Oh, she's just got an attitude. I'm fine now. See?" Lilly offered her best smile to Noley and her parents.

"If you're sure...."

"I'm sure. Nol, this is supposed to be the happiest day of your life. Why are you so weepy?"

Melissa put her hand on Noley's arm. "Come on, sweetheart. Why don't you lie down for a little while? You've got a couple of hours before the ceremony."

"I don't want to lie down." But Noley followed her mom into the bedroom and Melissa came out a few minutes later. Russell had excused himself to go to the rest room. Lilly was quite sure he didn't have to use the bathroom at all. Being in a room with emotions running this high would be enough to scare any man away.

"She's exhausted from the traveling," Melissa explained quietly when she joined Lilly again. "She's also upset about the rip in the dress. She just wants everything to be perfect. And, you know, the Tisha thing." Melissa had the grace to look sheepish for mentioning it.

"I told my mother yesterday she needed to stop talking," Lilly said. "I'm so sorry it upset Noley. I had no idea it would affect her the way it has."

"Oh, Lilly, it's not your mom's fault. She can't help it when things escape her mouth."

"That's usually how I feel, too, but this time her words have really upset Noley."

"Noley is usually stronger than this," Melissa said. "I'm sure a little nap will set her straight. You know, it didn't help that she went out last night after the rehearsal dinner. She came home so late. She had had a few too many, if you know what I mean." Melissa shook her head.

"She was drunk?" Lilly asked.

"To say the least. I think she was just trying to unwind after her trip and she didn't realize how many she had had. And she was having fun catching up with her friends in the wedding party. Bill brought her home. He warned me that she was weepy —he was right."

"Has she talked to Bill today?"

"Yes. He called to see how she was feeling. He's so sweet."

"He is. He must have been worried about her."

"I'm sure he was. She was threatening to throw up when he brought her into the house last night."

Suddenly both women turned toward the bedroom. Retching sounds could be heard coming from the bathroom. Russell walked into the parlor and, upon hearing the noise, blanched and walked right out again.

Melissa hurried into the bedroom and Lilly could hear her knocking on the bathroom door. "Noley, are you all right in there?"

Lilly couldn't hear Noley's reply. A few moments later Melissa came back into the parlor. "I think she's going to be fine. She's brushing her teeth and taking a shower."

Lilly took a deep breath and held up two crossed fingers. "Let's hope she's fine."

CHAPTER 14

*I*t wasn't long before Noley appeared in the parlor wearing a sheepish smile. "I'm sorry about that. I'm so embarrassed."

"That's all right, Noley. It's perfectly normal to be a mess on your wedding day."

"I'm not a mess anymore. I feel much better."

Lilly let out a sigh of relief. "I'm glad you're back. I didn't recognize the woman who was in here before you threw up."

Noley smiled. "I should know better than to have more than one or two glasses of wine, at the most. But I'm back and better than ever, as they say. When do you think I should start getting dressed?"

"How about now?" Melissa asked.

Noley beamed. "Okay. Can you guys help me?" She spun around and headed back to the bedroom, where she flung open the windows to air out the space and let in the warm spring breeze.

A short while later, Noley stepped out of the bedroom, followed by Lilly and Melissa. Russell, who had returned to the lounge after Melissa sent him a text that all was well, turned around and got his first look at his daughter in her wedding dress.

His Adam's apple bobbed up and down as he blinked back tears.

"My baby girl." His eyes shone. "You look beautiful."

"Thanks, Dad." Noley spun around slowly so everyone could admire the dress. Everyone could hear the bridesmaids clamoring down the hallway outside and when Noley opened the door to let them in, they took one look at her and burst into a chorus of catcalls, applause, and exclamations of delight.

"You look *gorgeous!*"

"I love the dress!"

"Perfect!'

Noley was all smiles as she gestured the women into the room. The bridesmaids, except for Laurel, who was already dressed, hurried to the bedroom, the bathroom, and every other available space to change. Russell hightailed it out of there fast. Laurel came into the room shortly, a smile on her face.

"What have you been up to?" Lilly asked.

"I found Drew."

"Oh? Do you think he'll be allowed to dance with you?"

Laurel looked horrified. "Mom, I will *not* be dancing. And frankly, I don't want to see all the old people dancing, either."

"Are you calling me old?"

"Sort of. I mean, you're old compared to me and everyone here is about your age, aren't they?"

"Yes. Even us geriatrics deserve to cut a rug once in a while, Laur."

"That's not what I meant, and please don't say stuff like that around other people."

Lilly chuckled and turned to Noley, who was wondering if it was possible to get some food in the room.

"I'll go ask Darla," Lilly said. "There's supposed to be cold stuff available for the wedding party in the bride's and groom's suites. And wine, though that might not be the best idea."

"No way," Noley said with a shudder. "I'll drink the champagne toast later on, but that's the only alcohol I'm having tonight. Or maybe ever."

Lilly hurried downstairs in search of Darla and found her in the kitchen of the manor, preparing several large trays to be delivered to the suites upstairs. "The men have already sent word that they're starving," Darla said. "I figured the women could use some food now, too."

"Perfect timing," Lilly said. "Shall I help carry them upstairs?"

"No need. We have wait staff to do that. Besides, I wanted to talk to you for a minute."

CHAPTER 15

*L*illy was on high alert. "What's wrong?" she asked.

Darla frowned. "I just wanted to talk to you about Maureen. She really lit into one of my staff for moving one of the tables she planned to use. I had to step in and tell her to stop. She was not pleased with me."

Lilly shook her head. "I'm so sorry. If I had known she'd be this bad, I would have forced Noley to choose someone else. Is there anything I can do to help?"

"I don't think so. We have it under control. I just want you to be aware of the backstory if she tries to tell you that I was mean to her."

Lilly could feel her cheeks redden. Darla had been so sweet and so easy to work with, and she had gone out of her way to ensure that Noley and Bill's wedding was going to be magical. Lilly hated the thought of making Darla's job harder because of the pig-headed caterer.

"Seriously, Lilly. Don't worry about it. I told her she'll work within my rules or she won't be allowed back here. She won't be coming back here in any event, but that can be our little secret." Darla winked at Lilly, who smiled with relief.

"Just a few more hours and you won't have to deal with her anymore," Lilly said. "I may have to, but you won't." She accepted a glass of wine from Darla, willing away the thoughts of lawsuits swimming around in her head.

She returned to the bridal lounge, where everyone was in high spirits. Bridesmaids were snapping photos, taking selfies, posting on social media, and chatting. Lilly had warned Bill that this would happen and she had warned him to stay off social media the day of the wedding. The last thing she wanted was for him to see Noley in her wedding dress before the ceremony.

The time sped by. At quarter after six, the women all used the restroom one last time, checked hair and makeup, slipped into their high heels, snapped a few more pictures, and headed downstairs. They all crowded around the door at the back of the manor.

The guests were assembled in the white chairs on the lawn leading down to the shore of Juniper Lake. Bill, Tighe, and the rest of the groomsmen were standing in a tight knot, talking. Once in a while one of them would look toward the manor and the women would shrink away from the door so they wouldn't be seen.

Just before six thirty, the trio of musicians began to play. The bridesmaids walked sedately down the aisle as the final stanzas of "Jesu, Joy of Man's Desiring" rang out. When the women were in place, the musicians paused dramatically before beginning "Trumpet Voluntary."

At the first notes of that song, the guests all stood and turned around. Bill, Tighe, and the groomsmen lined up alongside them stood still, all eyes on the back door.

Noley and Russell smiled at the congregants as they made their way forward. Russell looked like he hadn't loosened the tourniquet grip on his daughter's arm, and she leaned over and whispered something to him. They both laughed. Lilly glanced at Bill, who was staring at Noley transfixed, a smile on his face and his eyes full of joy. Then she glanced at Bev, who was wiping her eyes with a tissue. Nikki held her other hand.

Russell kissed Noley's cheek at the altar, sat down next to Melissa, and the minister began speaking.

The ceremony was over in less than a half hour. Lilly recalled the same feeling from her own wedding to Beau—for all the work that went into planning such a huge event, it was over awfully fast. Noley's sister and Hassan read beautifully and with just the right amount of emotion, and Noley and Bill's handwritten vows brought tears to the eyes of everyone present.

When the celebratory sound of the recessional rang out, the wedding party paired off, arm in arm, and made their way back to the manor. The guests stood up and began to file slowly toward the manor, where the bar and tapas tables were already set up.

Once the guests had been through the receiving line, Lilly joined Hassan, who took her hand and kissed it. "You look gorgeous," he said.

She laughed. "You're so sweet to lie to me like that." He laughed and she knew he agreed that green was not her best color.

Lilly had requested that the caterer set up a few tables of food outdoors, on the rocky outcropping just above the surface of the water, as soon as the ceremony had concluded. It was forecast to be a lovely evening, so Lilly figured some guests might want to stay outside. As the guests were wending their way through the receiving line, some of the catering and Juniper Lake Manor staff were moving tables and platters of food down to the water's edge.

The photographer was snapping photos of the guests while he waited for everyone to get through the receiving line. Afterward, he asked the bride and groom, their families, and the rest of the wedding party to go down to the lakeshore with him to get some more formal pictures. Laughing and chatting, the entire wedding party accompanied him down to the lake.

The mood was festive and joyful. Bill and Noley looked happier than Lilly had ever seen them. They looked relaxed, too, and *that* was the look Lilly had most wanted to see. It made all the work and all the stress of planning the wedding worth it.

Nikki helped situate Bev in each photo and even got in a few photos herself. Bev looked beautiful in her dress. She insisted that the walker be stashed out of the photos, and managed to stand tall next to Bill in some photos and next to Noley and her parents in others. Her smiles for the photographer were genuine and filled with joy.

The first thing that Lilly hadn't foreseen happened as the wedding party was regathering after the family photos were taken.

CHAPTER 16

Tighe heard it first. The photographer had asked for big smiles when Tighe squinted up into the sky.

"You, there, best man, I need a smile from you," the photographer was saying.

Tighe straightened up, smiled, and the photographer clicked away. Within a few seconds, though, everyone was looking up. Even the photographer. A buzzing sound coming from the sky was getting louder and louder, but no one could see anything.

A few bridesmaids covered their ears as everyone looked skyward. The noise was deafening. Lilly looked around in alarm and could later recall vignettes of activity. All the guests standing around on the lawn were looking up. Nikki was moving swiftly toward Bev. A look of confusion crossed Hassan's face.

Moments later, a small plane appeared over the roof of the manor, its nose pointed toward the wedding party. It flew shockingly fast and low as it made a beeline for the people standing by the edge of the lake. Fear and surprise rooted Lilly to the spot where she was standing, but most of the wedding party and the guests scattered, several of them screaming. As if

it were happening in slow motion, Lilly could see Nikki knock
Bev to the ground and cover her with her own body. Beau came
running from the back of the manor, eyes wild and bewildered.
The catering staff hit the ground and covered their heads with
their arms. Lilly finally managed two words, which erupted out
of her mouth like cannon shot: "Tighe! Laurel!"

The terror and noise only lasted a few seconds, but then the
pilot made a tight circle in the air over the middle of the lake
and headed back in the direction of the manor. As the plane
approached, Hassan came rushing up to Lilly, grabbed her arm,
and yanked her behind him, running toward the manor.

"Stop! Where are the kids?" she yelled.

He pointed to where they were standing, clutching hands,
under the eaves behind the manor. Lilly looked around wildly.
Guests were still running. Bill had scooped Bev up in his arms
and Noley had grabbed her parents by the arms and was pulling
them toward the manor with her. Beau had reached Nikki and
was pushing her under one of the tables set up with food.

Lilly ran alongside Hassan while the plane rushed toward
them again. She let out a scream as it buzzed the lakeshore
again, this time coming even closer to the building and the
people. Hassan flung her to the ground and threw himself on
top of her. It looked like the plane was going to hit the manor.

But at the last possible second, it banked sharply skyward
and just missed grazing the top of the manor as it flew off into
the distance. Lilly dared to glance around; most people stayed
right where they lay on the ground, their heads covered, though
a few brave souls were already on their feet, running toward the
manor for safety. Nikki and Beau were among them, and they
rushed up to Bill, who was still carrying Bev. He set her down
and they ushered her into the manor, Beau practically carrying
her himself.

Darla erupted from the back door of the manor.

"What happened?" she yelled. "What's going on?"

"A plane! It buzzed us!" Bill thundered. He motioned for Noley and her parents to come to him and yelled for Lilly.

"I'm here!" Lilly called. Hassan helped her to her feet.

"Do you have any idea what that was all about?" she asked, panting.

"No. No. I've never heard a noise like that in my life. I didn't see it happen, though. I was busy inside," Darla replied. She raised her voice and yelled out, "Is anyone hurt?"

Most people were shaking their heads, and a few called out "No!" as they made their way toward the manor. Everyone's clothes were covered with grass and dirt stains. Lilly stood still, listening, wondering if the plane was coming back. Several people had pulled out their cell phones and Lilly presumed they were dialing nine-one-one.

But half the Juniper Junction police force was already on the scene, in suits and dresses and nice shoes. They quickly formed a knot, beckoning Bill to join them. He stalked over and buried his head with theirs.

Only seconds had passed since the plane buzzed the group a second time. Then a terrific *boom* came from the forested slopes that surrounded the valley where Juniper Lake Manor was located. Everyone stopped what they were doing and stood still. It only took a few more seconds for black smoke to darken the sky in the direction of the noise. It was obvious: the plane had crashed.

CHAPTER 17

Noley ushered her parents into the manor and Lilly could see them collapse in chairs near the back door. Tighe and Laurel came rushing over to where she still stood outside with Hassan and the four of them embraced in a tight circle. Lilly disentangled herself from the kids and ran to the back door of the manor, searching the reception room for Bev. There she was—safe on the other side of the room, sitting between Nikki and Beau, both of whom looked disheveled and astonished. Lilly hurried over to them and sat down. People who had been inside were helping herd the other guests into the manor. Choruses of "What happened?" and "Is everyone okay?" could be heard over and over. Darla and the Juniper Lake Manor staff were going around the room, checking on each guest to make sure no one needed medical assistance.

"What happened, Lilly?" Bev asked. She held her hand over her chest and was still breathing heavily. Nikki already had a small blood pressure monitor on Bev and was staring at it intently, waiting for a reading.

"I don't know, Mom. I can't think what must have happened." She glanced outside and could see the members of the Juniper Junction police force running toward the parking lot. "I'll be right back." She jumped up and ran out the front door of the manor. "Bill! Where are you going?"

"That plane crashed, Lil. We're going to check it out."

"Be careful!"

"We will. Tell Noley I'll be back as soon as I can. Backup is coming from Lupine." He looked toward the entrance of the manor and saw Tom and George running down the steps. "Can you two guys stay here?" Bill shouted. "Just in case there's trouble." Tom and George stopped, nodded, and headed back inside. And with that, Bill ducked into one of the cars that had screeched to a stop next to him. The next moment they were off, followed by several other cars full of police officers.

Noley appeared at Lilly's side quickly. "Are they leaving? Did Bill go with them?"

Lilly nodded. "Welcome to the family."

Darla had taken charge inside the manor, where all the guests were now gathered. "Ladies and gentlemen, it looks like the drama is over. Please, sit down and we'll get some staff in here to take drink orders. The coffee bar, which is normally set up after dinner, is in the process of being set up now. The catering staff will go ahead with the meals, so you can all eat as soon as possible."

Lilly threw Darla a grateful look. She wasn't capable of organizing her thoughts enough to ensure the guests had food and drink, so she was glad Darla's professional instincts had kicked in. Frankly, Lilly was amazed that anyone wanted to stay for the meal. Lilly walked over to Noley, who looked shell-shocked.

"Are you all right?" she asked.

Noley turned to her, tears in her eyes. "My wedding is ruined."

"Your wedding was gorgeous, and that's the most important part. And look at it this way: who's ever going to forget this party? You'll have the most talked-about reception for decades!"

Noley smiled and let out a wry chuckle. "That's looking on the bright side. My groom is off chasing a downed plane, my guests probably can't wait to leave, and I look a wreck."

"You still look beautiful. Darla is rounding up staff to serve drinks and dinner. Do you want the band to stay?"

"I guess. We're paying them whether they stay or not, right?"

"Yes. Might as well make this as normal an experience as possible."

Tom, George, and several other groomsmen had disappeared and were now back, talking among themselves. "We were just watching the news in the groom's lounge and the plane crash is all over the television," Tom said.

Lilly grimaced and spoke to the groomsmen. "Guys, you might as well go sit with your dates. Drinks and food will be coming around before too long."

The other men, nodding and talking among themselves, moved away into the reception area, searching for their plus-ones. Tom asked the bartender for a beer, and then made his way over to a woman Lilly hadn't noticed in the congregation during the ceremony. She was buxom and had long, unnaturally blonde tresses and her dress clung to her in all the right places.

Tisha.

CHAPTER 18

*L*illy did a double-take and groaned inwardly. *What are the chances she would be his date? And why would she agree to attend the wedding of a man who had dumped her? And how do I keep Noley from finding out she's here?*

She looked around to locate Bev, who was still sitting between Nikki and Beau. She needed to know if Bev had seen and recognized Tisha. If she knew Tisha was there, it was only a matter of time before she tried to strike up a conversation with the woman and, knowing Bev, demand that Tisha be introduced to Noley.

The band had struck up a lively dance tune that was completely incongruous under the circumstances, but Lilly was grateful for it. She went over to the table where her mother sat. "Nikki, Beau, why don't you go dance? The first dance will obviously have to wait—maybe we'll make it the last dance—so I want everyone to have a good time, if that's even possible at this point. Nikki, I'll sit with Mom for a while."

"Thanks, Lilly," Nikki said. Beau smiled and held out his hand to Nikki. They moved over to the dance floor and melted into the small crowd already dancing.

"Well, Mom, are you feeling better? That was quite a scare."

"I'm feeling a little better. What happened?"

"I don't know yet. Bill and a bunch of the other police officers who were here went to see if they could find the plane that went down. If they find it, maybe they'll be able to figure out what happened."

"Who would have wanted to ruin the wedding reception?"

"I—" Lilly stopped mid-thought. She had assumed, until now, that the pilot of the plane had lost control and had just managed to avoid hitting the manor and the wedding party down by the lake by performing super-human maneuvers in the air.

But was it possible, as Bev suggested, that someone had done this terrifying thing on purpose?

It was unthinkable. Besides, who would do something like that, and why?

"It had to have been an accident, Mom. I can't believe that anyone would do something so drastic to ruin someone else's wedding."

"Well, I think—" Bev was cut off as a scream from outdoors echoed through the manor. Lilly whipped her head around to see what was going on and yelled for Nikki, who came over to sit with Bev as Lilly hurried toward the back door. Tom was only a couple of steps behind her.

They reached the back door at the same time as Darla, who was running in from outside. Lilly and Darla locked eyes and Lilly knew something awful had happened.

"What's wrong? Who screamed?" Lilly asked in a rush.

"What's going on?" Tom asked at the same time.

Darla leaned in so no one could overhear her. "I screamed. It's the caterer. I think she's dead."

Lilly gasped. She stood there, staring at Darla, a million thoughts running through her head. That couldn't be. Maureen? Dead? It wasn't possible.

They were all under a lot of stress and clearly, Darla had lost her mind.

But Tom leapt into action. He took off running toward the lake while shouting behind him to keep all the guests indoors.

Darla grabbed Lilly's arm and led her outside, demanding that the rest of the guests stay indoors. She shouted for four of the Juniper Lake Manor employees to guard all the building exits and to keep all the guests indoors.

"Tom told us to stay inside," Lilly fretted.

"He said to keep the guests inside. We're not guests."

Hassan had joined the women by that time and he gave Lilly a questioning look.

Lilly stumbled along behind Darla. The sky had turned a dusky orange and once the sun went completely behind the mountain to the west, it would get dark very quickly.

Tom was on his cell phone when Darla, Lilly, and Hassan caught up with him. Darla pointed. There, in the shallow water only a few feet below the outcropping of rock, lay Maureen, her eyes staring upward. Water lapped along the sides of her face and over her uniform. Her hair was splayed around her in a grotesque light brown halo. A trickle of blood could be seen on her lips, though it was quickly being washed away by the clean water of Juniper Lake.

CHAPTER 19

*L*illy covered her mouth and turned to Hassan, burying her face in his chest. "I don't believe this."

Tom stopped talking and turned to Darla. "Are you in charge here? What's your name? What happened?"

Darla's response came out high-pitched and taut. "Yes, I'm in charge here. My name is Darla Smithers and I came down here to make sure the table set up on the rocks, right over the water, was being disassembled and brought inside after the incident with the airplane. I wanted the keep the guests indoors. I saw the woman in the water and screamed and ran up to the manor."

Lilly's phone rang and she stepped away to take the call. It was Bill.

"Everything okay there?" he asked.

"Hardly. The caterer is dead. At least, I think she's dead. She's lying in the water and there's blood trickling out of her mouth."

"My God. I was worried because I couldn't get in touch with Noley. She must have her ringer off. Okay, I'll be back as soon as I can get there. We've called for a team to help here and we'll assemble a team there, too. Tom's there, isn't he?"

"Yes. Hurry, Bill. The guests are starting to wonder what the heck kind of wedding this is."

He hung up without another word and Lilly's phone rang again. This time it was Noley.

"What's going on, Lilly? The guests are frantic. The Juniper Lake Manor staff isn't letting anyone out!"

"Don't let on that you know what's happening, Nol, but the caterer is dead. She's down here lying in the water." She heard Noley gasp. "Nol? Are you still with me?"

Noley answered in a shaky whisper. "Yeah. I'm here. Are you sure she's dead?"

"Pretty sure. I've already talked to Bill and he's on his way back with the officers who left the reception with him. They've called another team to help wherever they are."

"Where are they?"

"I didn't think to ask."

"This is officially the worst wedding reception in the history of weddings."

Despite the horror of the evening, Lilly had to smile. Noley was probably right. This had been pretty bad, as wedding receptions go.

"What we need is to keep everyone inside for now. We don't want anyone outside fouling up what might be a crime scene."

Noley gasped again. "A crime scene? You think someone *killed* her?" Her voice was a high-pitched whisper.

"Shh. I don't want any of the guests to overhear you. They're going to know what happened soon enough, but let's try to keep things as light and calm as possible. Can you go out there and suggest a line dance or something? Get everyone moving and keep their minds off what's going on out here. I'm sure we'll be in soon. The food should be served any minute. And turn your ringer on." She hung up and stared at Maureen's body. Tom was on the phone again, issuing terse orders.

"Well, all the classes I took for event planning never

prepared me for a night like this." Darla blew out a long breath, puffing out her cheeks.

"I can't imagine death and aircraft mishaps were part of the curriculum," Lilly said. "Bill's on his way back here with the officers who were at the wedding."

"Did he say what they found?" Tom had come over to the small group and heard Lilly's last statement.

"No. I didn't ask. I was just focused on getting him back here." She shook her head. "So much planning went into this wedding. How could it have gone so wrong?"

Hassan put his arm around Lilly. "You've had a tough night. Don't make it harder by beating yourself up over something you couldn't possibly have controlled or foreseen."

"All three of you need to head back inside," Tom said. "I'll stay out here to secure the scene." He cocked his head. "Why are you out here, anyway? Didn't I tell you everyone needed to stay indoors?"

"You said 'guests' and we're not guests," Darla said.

Tom grimaced and pointed toward the back of the building. "Go."

CHAPTER 20

*L*illy and Hassan walked on either side of Darla. "You're in charge here, Darla. Maybe you should make an announcement explaining that there's been an accident and we're waiting for the authorities."

"You're right. What do you think I should say to Maureen's staff?"

Lilly shrugged. "I suppose you should tell them that she's not able to come back right now and they should continue doing whatever they need to do to get the food on the tables."

"All right."

Darla left and Lilly turned to Hassan and spoke in a low voice. "Do you think the plane and now Maureen's accident have anything to do with each other? It's so strange that they took place so close in time."

Hassan replied in a tone that matched hers. "I have no idea. I guess that's the question of the hour. If they're related, that would mean the plane buzzing the wedding reception wasn't an accident. It would also mean that Maureen's 'accident' wasn't really an accident."

Shivers traveled up and down Lilly's arms. "I don't even want to think about the possibility."

"We'll know more once Bill and the others get here."

Just a moment later they heard the wail of sirens in the distance. Guests looked around in alarm, no doubt wondering what in the world was happening.

"Thank God someone's coming to take care of Maureen," Lilly said.

"Are you going to tell the police about the problems you had with her?"

Lilly sighed. "If they ask. She got under Darla's skin, too. I'm not the only one she annoyed." She knew she sounded defensive.

"It sounds like she's the type who gets under the skin of lots of people."

Lilly scoffed. "I wish Noley hadn't insisted on hiring someone who graduated from the community college. There are plenty of caterers who are easy to work with. Juniper Lake Manor has a long list of caterers they recommend. But Noley was adamant."

Another minute passed, and then Darla ushered two paramedics through the reception space and out back to where the body still lay in the water. Guests murmured among themselves and pressed against the back windows to see what was going on. Someone, probably directed by Darla, had set up portable spotlights so emergency personnel could see better. Thankfully, Maureen's body wasn't visible from the back of the building.

Lilly could see that Bill and the other officers had returned and they, too, had gathered on the lawn behind the manor. Several of them, including Bill, rolled up their pant legs and waded into the water to take a closer look at the body. The paramedics supplied them with gloves to protect the scene from contamination and they pulled the body onto the rocks lining the shore. At least, Lilly knew it was a body. The guests didn't know yet.

Lilly looked around and noticed that an officer who had been tasked with keeping people inside was looking in the other direction. The Juniper Lake Manor staff was just as curious as the guests and were trying to see what was going on outside. She nudged Hassan. "I'm going out there," she whispered.

"Lilly, don't. There's nothing you can do to help. You don't want to get in trouble." He kept his voice low.

"Bill's out there. I won't get in trouble."

She kissed Hassan's cheek before he could protest again. He shook his head and closed his eyes as if in resignation. "Be careful," he said.

She gave him a discreet thumbs-up and glanced at the officer again. He was talking to one of the guests. She slipped through the swinging door into the manor's large kitchen, which was empty.

She left through the back kitchen door and hurried down to the lakeshore, avoiding the spotlights so the guests inside wouldn't see that she had left the manor. She *had* to know what was going on. After all, she had been the one who hired Maureen and orchestrated this disaster of a reception. Maureen lay on a long slab of rock just above the surface of the water.

"Medical examiner isn't far behind," one of the paramedics was saying as she approached. "We can take a preliminary look at her." He lifted Maureen's hand and held it at the wrist. He shook his head. "No pulse." He took out a stethoscope and listened to Maureen's heart, shook his head again, and checked his watch. "Can one of you guys help me pull the body up onto the grass?"

Several of the police officers reached out to help and soon Maureen's body was resting on the grass. Lilly couldn't help staring at the woman's vacant eyes. When Darla tapped her shoulder, Lilly jumped and let out a little shriek.

"Sorry about that," Darla said. "I didn't mean to scare you. Someone just told me the medical examiner is coming up the drive. Shall I bring her around the side of the manor so no one sees her van?"

"Definitely. We can't keep this a secret forever, but we can keep the lid on it for a little longer."

$\mathcal{D}$arla disappeared and returned several minutes later, leading the medical examiner around the side of the manor. Several uniformed police officers followed them, lugging more large lights and electrical cords.

The uniformed officers immediately conferred with the officers who had been at the wedding. Once they had told the new officers everything they had learned, they trudged back up to the manor. No one told Lilly and Darla to go inside, so they stayed outside.

The medical examiner got to work on the body as the police officers rigged up powerful lights near the water. Lights shone in every direction—in the water, into the trees, and up the length of the lawn to the back of the manor. It wouldn't be long before guests realized what was going on. Lilly and Darla stood off to the side.

Two Lupine officers approached them. "Who found the body?" one of them asked.

Darla spoke up. "I did. I've already spoken to one of the officers who was a guest at the wedding."

"Maybe so, but I'm afraid you're going to have to answer

several more questions for me." The woman led Darla away while the second officer, a young man, turned to Lilly. "So there's a wedding reception going on?" he asked.

Lilly nodded.

"And where are the bride and groom?"

"They're inside. The groom is my brother, Bill Merriweather."

"I know Bill. He finally got married, huh?"

"Yes. There were a number of officers here as guests. As soon as the plane buzzed us and crashed just a minute later, they took off to look for the plane. They're back now, though."

"All right. I'll talk to them soon. Do you know who was in charge here?"

"Darla is the wedding coordinator for Juniper Lake Manor. She's the one talking to the other officer over there. I'm the one who planned this particular wedding."

"Do you work here?"

"No. I own Juniper Junction Jewels. I just planned the wedding as a favor to my brother and his now-wife, who is my best friend."

"And did you hire the caterer?"

"Yes."

"How did you come to hire her?"

"Noley Appleton, the bride, is a chef. She gets involved with the culinary classes at the community college whenever she can, and she thought it would be nice to hire a culinary program graduate to cater the wedding. I found Maureen and hired her. Noley has been out of town for a while, so that's why I—"

"Why has she been out of town and for how long?"

"She has been traveling to promote her new cookbook. She left Juniper Junction in March and only got back a couple of days ago. She needed to rely on someone here to plan the wedding."

"Do you know where Bill is?"

"I can find him for you. He was out here earlier and I know he's already told someone what he knows."

"Okay. Tell me, did you have any problems with the caterer?"

Lilly hesitated for just a moment. "Well, yes, I suppose you could say that. She turned out to be very difficult to work with."

"How so?"

"She was fine until I signed the contract to hire her, but then she said she was short several employees, then she wasn't able to get one of the tapas I ordered, then she announced that everyone would be having fish because she couldn't get the beef for the meals, and finally she called to say that it was hard to work with Darla. I've heard that she caused some problems with the staff of Juniper Lake Manor, though I don't know the details."

"And how did you respond when she told you of the staffing shortage and the problems with the food?"

"I was mad. Who wouldn't be?"

"And who would be able to talk to me about the problems they had with her here at Juniper Lake Manor?"

Lilly pointed to where Darla was still speaking to the other officer. "Darla would know."

The officer scribbled down Lilly's contact information and promised to be in touch. He moved over to where the other officer was still questioning Darla; Lilly took that chance to go back into the manor.

Small groups of guests stood around the room talking. No one was dancing, though the band was playing one lively tune after another. *Might as well have a soundtrack to this nightmare*, Lilly thought. A sea of fish sat uneaten on plates at each table. Lilly shook her head. She found Hassan and they walked over to Noley and Bill, who were talking to a small group of guests.

"Bill, the officer who questioned me wants to talk to you."

"All right. I'll go out now. Excuse me." He kissed Noley's cheek and hurried out the back door.

Guests began to swarm around Lilly, Noley, and Hassan. Not surprisingly, they wanted to know what the heck was going on. Noley apologized profusely that the reception had turned into a catastrophe.

"Don't be silly," one guest assured her. "Are you kidding? We will never forget this wedding!" The other guests exclaimed and nodded in agreement.

"Bill and I never even had our first dance!" Noley wailed suddenly. She looked around for Bill, but Lilly reminded her that he had gone outside to talk to the police.

"And that gorgeous cake is just sitting there, waiting to be cut," she said. She squeezed her eyes shut and opened them, letting out a long sigh. "All right. I'm trying to stay calm amidst the worst wedding-gone-wrong in history. Lilly, what happens next? Should we just send people home with pieces of cake?"

"Can I talk to you for a minute, Nol?" Lilly asked.

Noley followed Lilly upstairs and into the bridal parlor. "No one can leave," Lilly said. "The police are going to want to question everyone here, I'm sure."

"Oh, my God. You're kidding. Remember when I said that this is the worst wedding in history? I was wrong. *Now* it's the worst wedding in history. Who invites people to a wedding only to have everyone questioned by police like criminals? Not a single guest is ever going to speak to me or Bill again."

"Noley, nothing that has happened tonight is your fault or Bill's fault or anyone else's fault."

"Something killed that caterer." Noley's eyes widened and she covered her mouth with her hands. "Oh, no. What if there's a murderer walking around Juniper Lake Manor?"

Lilly didn't want to let on that Noley had spooked her. "Let's get a grip, Nol. Since everyone is stuck here until the police have asked all their questions, let's make it fun. Let's dance, eat cake, throw the bouquet, the whole shebang."

Noley nodded. "All right. You're right. We need to get out there and pretend everything is as normal as possible."

"But they don't know about the dead caterer yet, so maybe don't mention that."

"Definitely not."

They returned to the reception space and Bill came up to them. He had been looking for Noley. He held her at arm's length and smiled. "We wanted a wedding no one would forget, right? I guess we should be careful what we wish for." She laughed and leaned into his chest. People began to gather around them and Lilly took the opportunity to slip away to ask the band to play the first dance.

When the band struck the first notes, Noley looked up at Bill and grinned. He took her hand and spun her around as the guests moved back to give them room. Without anyone saying a word, people seemed to know this was the first dance and they clapped and cheered as Noley and Bill moved around the room, gliding effortlessly in each other's arms. Lilly caught Bev's eye and Bev was smiling from ear to ear, obviously enjoying the moment. When the song was over and Bill and Noley kissed, the guests went wild with catcalls and cheering. *Now* it felt more like a wedding reception.

Unfortunately, the feeling of gaiety didn't last long. After dancing to a couple of songs, Bill joined several of his groomsmen at the bar. Tom sauntered up and asked the bartender for two glasses of wine.

"Where's your date, Tom?" Bill asked. Lilly clenched her teeth. She had forgotten about Tisha in the evening's madness. Bill smiled as Noley joined him and put an arm around his back. Lilly and Hassan were with her and Hassan asked the bartender for two mojitos.

"She's at the table over there." Tom pointed to Tisha. Bill blanched and Noley noticed.

"What's wrong?" she asked.

"Nothing. Nothing's wrong. Want to dance again?" Bill smiled down at Noley.

"I need a break," she said. She asked the bartender for a glass of soda water with lime, then turned to Bill once she had the drink in hand. "Let me drink this and then we can dance again."

Bill's attempt to get Noley away from the bar, noble though it was, had failed. Lilly followed his stony gaze. Tisha was walking toward the bar, her hips slinking in time to the music. She slid her arm around Tom's waist, but not before landing a light kiss on Bill's lips.

"Tisha." Bill gulped.

CHAPTER 23

"Hello there, stranger. Congratulations on your wedding," she purred. Noley was staring at her, open-mouthed, until Lilly nudged her. She clamped her lips shut and gave Bill a glare that he didn't notice.

"Uh, Tisha, I'd like you to meet my wife, Noley." Bill put his arm around Noley's shoulders. Tisha grinned and held out her hand. Noley took it and gave it a limp shake as she nodded her head toward Tisha. She didn't smile. She didn't say anything.

Finally Tom cleared his throat. "Ready, Tish?" He handed her a glass of wine.

Tisha gave Bill a smoldering look and turned toward Tom. "Yeah, hon. Let's dance."

They walked back to their table, Tisha's bottom swaying in her too-tight dress.

Lilly held her breath as Noley rounded on Bill. "Is that *the* Tisha? The old girlfriend your mom was talking about? I see she's exactly as Lilly described. Why didn't you tell me she would be here?" She was practically hissing.

"I ... I had no idea, Nol. I swear. I didn't know she and Tom were dating. And she didn't go through the receiving line after the ceremony, so this is the first I've seen her."

Noley was clenching her jaw so tightly Lilly thought she would break a molar. She reached out and put her hand on Noley's arm. "Nol, just forget about Tisha. Obviously she's as stupid as ever and she was only trying to get under your skin."

"Well, she succeeded."

"Noley, please don't be mad," Bill said. He took her hand. "You can't possibly think I feel a single thing for Tisha. I don't now and I never did."

"Please don't talk to me about feeling Tisha."

Lilly wanted to laugh, but she knew better. She gave Hassan a sidelong glance and nodded toward the dance floor. He took her hand and they moved away to give Bill and Noley time to deal with Tisha's presence.

"Wow. That was ugly," Hassan said.

"It sure was. What kind of woman goes to the wedding of her ex-boyfriend with a different guy?"

"You're going to Beau's wedding with me, aren't you?" Hassan's eyes twinkled.

"Of course. But that's different. Beau and I have a history of more than just dating. We have two children together and since he moved back to Juniper Junction we've been in regularish contact with each other."

Just then one of Maureen's staff came up to Lilly. "Are you in charge here?" he asked.

"No. That would be Darla Smithers, the venue manager."

"She's busy. I need some answers. Do you know where Maureen is?"

"Unfortunately, she had to leave unexpectedly. She won't be back."

"Any idea why she didn't tell her staff?"

"She didn't know."

"If you say so."

Apparently Maureen hired people not unlike herself—rude and brusque.

"What is your name?" she asked.

"Brad."

"Brad, I can't say much right now, but there's been an accident and Maureen was hurt. The police and ambulance are here now, down by the water. But she won't be coming back tonight."

She hated to deceive him, but she felt it wasn't her place to tell Brad all that had happened. And technically, everything she had said was true. She just hadn't told the *entire* truth.

"Oh. Is she going to be all right?"

Lilly opted to ignore the question, and luckily he didn't press her for an answer. "It's probably best if we keep this between ourselves for now, at least until the authorities come in and tell us what's going on."

"Okay." Brad nodded. "We'll go ahead and start clearing the plates. I'm surprised at how many people didn't eat."

Um, where have you been? It's a wonder anyone could eat anything. And besides, most people didn't order the fish.

The words that came out of Lilly's mouth were a little more diplomatic. "Yes, well, most people didn't order the fish and probably weren't that hungry, anyway, after everything that's happened."

"I suppose you're right."

"We'll have the cake as soon as the catering staff have the dinner plates cleared away," Lilly said.

Brad nodded and headed back toward the kitchen. Lilly went in search of Noley, and found her sitting with her parents. All three of them looked grim.

CHAPTER 24

"Noley, I talked to one of Maureen's employees. He's going to have the catering staff clear the plates so the cake can be served."

"Why was fish the only entrée? I know I ordered the beef."

"It's a long story."

"I have to use the ladies' room," Noley said. "I'll be back." Noley kissed her mother's cheek, then her father's cheek. "Don't blame Bill. This isn't his fault." She spoke in a quiet voice, but Lilly heard.

Lilly wanted to bolt immediately. She didn't want to get sucked into a conversation with Noley's parents about why one of Bill's old girlfriends was at the reception.

But it was too late.

"Tell me about this Tisha," Russell said, switching seats so he was right next to Lilly.

Lilly suppressed a groan. The truth was, she didn't know very much about Tisha. She had been relieved when Bill broke up with her and hadn't thought about the woman in years.

"I don't know how much I can tell you," Lilly said. "I haven't seen her in many years. I think I heard she got married at some point. She must be divorced."

"How long did Bill date this woman?"

"Russ, let's not bother Lilly with our questions. Bill is family now. We need to speak to him directly."

"You're right. Where is he?" Russell stood up and looked around, zeroing in on Bill almost immediately. "I'm going to talk to him."

Before Lilly could think of a way to keep Russell at the table, he stalked away. Melissa watched him go. "He doesn't want to see Noley get hurt," she said.

"Of course not. No one does—least of all Bill. He had no idea Tisha was here, and if he had known she was coming, I'm sure he would have advised Tom to bring someone else."

"I think I'll wait until Russell comes back to see what Bill has to say. There's no need for me to go up there and badger him, too." Melissa took a sip of wine and sighed, closing her eyes briefly. "This isn't the way I expected tonight to go."

Lilly reached out and put her hand on Melissa's arm. "This evening hasn't gone the way *anyone* thought it would, believe me. This is the kind of reception you read about or see on television. You don't think it's going to happen to you."

Melissa smiled. "You worked so hard to make this evening perfect. I don't think Russell or I have thanked you for everything you've done for Noley. This evening's events must be very hard on you, too."

Lilly sighed. "I did my best. Some things are just out of our control, I guess. Listen, Melissa, I hate to leave you, but I need to go check on Mom. Will you be all right by yourself for a few minutes?"

"Oh, yes. Russ will be back soon, I'm sure."

Lilly stood up and made her way to the table where Bev still sat with Nikki and Beau.

While Lilly talked with them, she saw the back door of the

manor open and Darla come inside. She looked wan and tired. She scanned the crowd, spotted Lilly, and headed straight for her.

"What's up?" Lilly asked her. "How are you doing?"

"I would never have thought it could be so draining just to answer questions. But I'm wiped out."

"It's the stress of it all."

Darla nodded and spoke in a low voice. "Can I talk to you privately?"

Lilly excused herself from the table. "What's up?"

"They're taking the body away now. Does anyone know about Maureen?"

"I told one of her employees that she was in an accident and wouldn't be returning tonight, but that's it. I think it will be pandemonium when the police come in asking to talk to people. I don't know why they haven't come in yet. I mean, there's an officer posted at the front door. Surely people have realized that."

"I heard them talking about it down by the water. They know that since it's a big occasion, they want to give the guests, and especially the bride and groom, at least a little time to enjoy themselves. But I think they'll be in soon to start questioning people." Darla shook her head.

"That's actually good to hear. Honestly, the sooner this evening is over, the better."

"You said it." Darla looked around. "How did the fish go over?"

"Like a lead balloon."

"I guess I don't have to worry about telling Maureen that she's not welcome back at Juniper Lake Manor," Darla said.

CHAPTER 25

As soon as the catering staff had cleared the tables, it was time for cake. Noley and Bill had agreed when they were first talking about the wedding that they would not feed each other the first piece of cake. Noley found the whole idea weird and Bill had no feelings about the tradition one way or another. Of course, Bev's comment at the time, "It's a filthy thing to do and you each learned how to feed yourselves decades ago," might have sealed the deal. But they did cut the cake together. Noley was still angry, but she let Bill place his hand over hers and they cut into the bottom tier of the cake. Afterward the cake was whisked away, sliced, and quickly served to each guest.

Most people were still eating dessert when the back door opened and four police officers came inside. Three of them assumed an authoritative stance—feet hip-width apart and hands on their belts—while the fourth nodded toward Darla and walked toward the band. He picked up the microphone.

"Ladies and gentlemen, there has been an incident down by the water and we're going to have to ask everyone to stay in the building until we've questioned all of you."

People's reactions varied from wide eyes to gasps to groans. A round of police questioning probably wasn't what most of them had in mind when they had RSVP'd to the wedding.

"What happened?" one woman asked.

"I'm not at liberty to discuss the details, but a body has been found."

At this news, there were more gasps and a couple of people cried out in alarm. Lilly looked quickly around the room and noticed Maureen's employee, Brad, standing in the kitchen doorway. He looked ashen.

"Please remain calm," the officer was saying. "The quicker we get to all of you, the quicker you can go home." He handed the microphone back to the bandleader and motioned for the other three officers to fan out. They were all armed with notebooks and pencils and each one began their questioning at a different table. The officer who had done all the talking started with the head table where Bill, Noley, and the rest of the wedding party were seated. Long before the seating arrangements had been finalized in the weeks before the wedding, Lilly had declined to sit with the wedding party, opting instead to sit with her mother and Hassan.

The wait was agonizing. If these things had happened a year ago, Bev would have pulled out a deck of cards to play poker to keep their minds off the police activity all around them. Instead, Nikki led her over to a cushy sofa against one wall and Bev laid her head back against it. She appeared to be asleep within a few minutes. Lilly looked around the room and noticed that most people were on their phones, very likely announcing on social media that they had gone to a wedding reception and a murder investigation broke out.

Juniper Lake Manor staff fanned out across the room and deposited Laurel's mini Bundt cakes on every table so each guest could take one as they departed after talking to police. The cakes were wrapped in cellophane bags and tied with green and ivory ribbons. They looked elegant. At least one thing had gone as planned.

Harry and Alice had been seated with some of the younger people at the reception, and when they had been questioned, Harry led Alice to Lilly's table. "I'm going to take Alice home now. Great party, Lilly."

Lilly couldn't help laughing. "Alice, you know I'm always available as a wedding planner. Schedule my services today if you, too, want a spectacular event like this one."

Alice laughed. "Lilly, you're too funny. Of course none of this was your fault, but it *is* kind of a downer." She slid her arm through Harry's and they left. One by one, as the police finished their questioning at each table, couples began to shuffle toward the head table to offer their thanks and good wishes to the bride and groom. Bill and Noley looked tired and unnerved. Lilly didn't know how they were managing to hold everything together after such a disastrous evening.

She wanted to know more about what the police had discovered, if anything, down by the water, but she didn't dare get up to go ask Darla any questions. She knew they would be free to talk to each other soon enough.

Finally the police officer who had questioned everyone at the head table came and sat down heavily at Lilly's table. "The new Mrs. Merriweather told me that one of you planned the wedding, so I wanted to conclude the questioning with you." He looked around expectantly.

"That's me. I planned the wedding." Lilly raised her hand just off the table.

The officer proceeded to ask questions about the process of planning the wedding, with particular focus on how Lilly chose Maureen to cater the wedding and how she reacted when Maureen failed to uphold her end of the contract.

"I was not happy about it, of course, but I just dealt with it. There wasn't much else I could do. I had a wedding full of guests to feed and there wasn't nearly enough time to hire someone else by the time Maureen told me she would be short-staffed and wouldn't be able to provide the food she had promised."

The officer asked still more questions about Lilly's business, her friendship with Noley, and how well she knew many of the guests and the wedding party.

"Obviously, most of them are friends and co-workers of Bill or Noley. I remember some of them from growing up, but a lot of them are new to me."

While Lilly was talking to him, Nikki led Bev back to the table. When the officer had finished talking to Lilly, he asked questions of Hassan, Bev, Nikki, and Beau. He had already questioned Tighe and Laurel as part of the wedding party. Lilly looked around, noticing for the first time that Laurel wasn't in the room.

CHAPTER 26

"Have you seen Laurel?" she asked Beau. He shook his head and scanned the room, too, but she wasn't there. Lilly hurried over to where Tighe was standing. "Have you seen your sister?"

He crooked his thumb in the direction of the kitchen. Lilly looked through the doorway and found Laurel, standing in bare feet talking to Drew. Lilly smiled and decided not to interrupt. Laurel deserved to have a fun evening, too, after all the work she had done on the mini cakes and helping with the wedding planning and decorations. And talking to the police ... and experiencing an out-of-control plane ... and being nearby as a possible murder was committed....

Gradually the manor emptied until the only ones left, besides the manor and catering staff, were Noley, Bill, Lilly, Hassan, Laurel, and Tighe. Nikki and Beau had driven Bev home after the police officer had questioned all three of them.

"Oh, my gosh, Tighe. I completely forgot you needed to get back to school. Why didn't you say something?"

"It's okay, Mom. It's not like I would have been able to leave. I'll head up first thing in the morning."

"I'm sorry, honey."

"Don't worry about it. I can study for it every minute from the time I get back to school until the test starts on Monday."

"Okay. I think it's time for us to head home. I'll find Laurel and pry her away from that boy and then we'll leave. Hassan, are you going straight to your house?"

"Yes. Do you guys want to come over for a little while?"

"I'd love to, but we probably shouldn't. It's been a long day. Want to join Laurel and me for dinner tomorrow?"

"Sure. I'll talk to you in the morning." Hassan kissed Lilly goodbye while Tighe cleared his throat and looked the other way.

"It's weird to see your mom kissing someone," he said after Hassan left.

Lilly laughed. "Is it? Sorry to offend you, my boy. I'll be right back. I'm going to get Laurel."

Lilly stuck her head into the room where Laurel and Drew had been earlier, but they weren't there. She spotted Darla talking to one of the bartenders, so she joined them.

"I'm looking for Laurel. The last I saw her, she was with Drew. Do you know where he went?"

"Yes. He's cleaning up the coffee bar. That's probably where you'll find her. Are you leaving?"

"Yes. Noley and Bill are going back to Noley's house tonight. Hassan just left and I'm taking the kids home. Then you'll have Juniper Lake Manor to yourself again. It's been quite an evening."

"It has. Listen, I'll touch base with you tomorrow, okay? We can settle the bill and clean up any loose ends then and I'll pack up your decorations tonight or early tomorrow morning and you can pick them up at your leisure. I also need to talk to the owner to see if we're going to adjust your balance at all because the evening was such a dismal failure."

"That's fine. Just let me know." She shook hands with Darla and thanked the bartender.

Laurel was indeed by the coffee bar with Drew. They were wiping down urns and picking up sugar packets and stirrers. Laurel pouted when Lilly told her it was time to go home.

"Already?" she whined.

"Yes, already. It's been one of the longest nights of my life."

"Can't we just stay a little longer?"

"No. We're leaving. Drew, it was nice to see you again."

"Nice to see you, ma'am."

"I'll be right there, Mom. I have to get my shoes." Laurel looked around on the ground, but there were no shoes there.

"I think you left them in the other room," Drew said. "I'll help you look."

Lilly followed them out of the room. She and Tighe stood by the front door while Laurel took forever to put on her shoes. When she finally joined them, she wore a hundred-watt smile.

"What are you so happy about?" Tighe asked.

"I'll give you one guess."

"You know who killed Maureen and this nightmare can come to an end," Lilly said.

"Of course I don't know who killed her, Mom. Drew asked me out!"

"Oh, that's nice. He seems like a nice boy."

"He's not a boy. He's a guy. And he's super nice. He's going to pick me up and take me to dinner tomorrow night."

They picked up Barney on their way home and dropped into bed as soon as they could get into pajamas.

CHAPTER 27

ighe was up before dawn the next day, packed and ready to go. He had made coffee before Lilly even went downstairs.

"You're up earlier than I expected," she said.

"My car won't start," he announced.

"Uh-oh. Do you want me to drive you?"

"Do you mind?"

"Not at all. Let me wake Laurel." She went upstairs and tapped on Laurel's door, explaining what had happened and that they were taking Tighe back to school. Then she hurried to get dressed. By the time she went back downstairs Laurel was in the kitchen. She had thrown on jeans and a sweatshirt and was rubbing her eyes and yawning. "I don't know why I have to go," she groused.

"So that you can drive if I'm too tired."

"What if *I'm* too tired?"

"You can rest while I drive. Then by the time I'm ready to rest you'll be fine. I'll take you out to lunch as a thank you."

"My eyes will be baggy for my date tonight."

"Your eyes will be beautiful, just like they always are. Let's go."

Laurel slept in the back seat with Barney splayed across her lap for most of the trip. Tighe maintained a tight-lipped nervousness as the miles rolled away, only occasionally breaking out of his funk to ask how much longer Lilly thought they had to drive.

"I'm really sorry about the way last night turned out," Lilly said. "Everything that could have gone wrong, did."

"I'm sure Uncle Bill and Noley feel the same way," Tighe said. "Are they leaving for Aruba today?"

"Their flight isn't until tonight. They were going to talk to the police today and make sure it's okay for them to leave the country. During a murder investigation, usually the police tell people to stay local. They might make an exception this time because it's a honeymoon and maybe even because Bill's a police officer."

"I hope they can go."

"Me, too."

Laurel stirred in the backseat. "We're not there yet? What time is it?"

"It's not even ten o'clock. You've got more than enough time before your date."

"All right. I just need plenty of time to get ready."

Tighe turned to look at her. "Laurel, do you hear me complaining? And I'm the one who has to do well on a huge final exam. Knock it off."

"Oh, yeah? When was the last time you had a date? You're so wrapped up in your studying that you can't even slow down to enjoy yourself."

"Mom, make her stop."

"Laurel, stop. There's no reason for you two to argue."

"He's acting like he's the most important person in the world."

"She's acting like a spoiled little girl."

"Kids, do not make me stop this car."

The threat still worked, even after all these years.

Once Tighe was safely back at school, ensconced in his room and surrounded by books, Lilly and Laurel left for home.

"We'll find a way to get you home after your exam," Lilly said, hugging Tighe goodbye. "Good luck on your test and make sure you're eating and sleeping before it. That's just as important as knowing the material, you know."

"I know, Mom. Don't worry. Now that I'm back and Sally Anne is coming over to help me, I'll be fine. See you Wednesday or Thursday."

"Let me know how the test goes."

"I will, I promise."

Lilly hugged him one more time and Laurel kissed his cheek without looking at him. They were still mad at each other.

CHAPTER 28

On the way back to Juniper Junction they stopped at a little roadside diner for lunch. Laurel must have looked at her phone a thousand times while they waited for their food.

"Why do you keep checking your phone?" Lilly finally asked in exasperation.

Laurel shrugged and put the phone face down on the table. "Just bored, I guess."

"Thanks."

"Mom, that's not what I meant."

"Are you hoping Drew will text?"

"Maybe."

Lilly grimaced. They hadn't even been on one date yet and already Laurel was becoming moody and uncommunicative. *Great. That date had better go well tonight or I'll have to move in with Noley and Bill. Or Laurel will.*

"How are the wedding plans coming along for Dad and Nikki's wedding?" Not Lilly's favorite topic of conversation, but she wanted to get Laurel to stop thinking about Drew for a few minutes.

"Okay, I guess. They're getting married in a church. Did you know Nikki has six sisters and they're all in the wedding? It's just me and all of them as bridesmaids. And Nikki has chosen lemon yellow for our dresses. I'm going to look terrible."

"You'll look beautiful, I'm sure."

"I wonder if Drew will be able to come to the wedding as my plus-one."

"Let's not get ahead of ourselves, Laur. See how the first date goes before you go inviting him to your father's wedding."

Laurel scowled. "Of course I won't invite him right away. I'm just thinking, that's all. Why is our food taking so long?"

"They're pretty busy. I'm sure it won't be too much longer."

"Can Noley and Uncle Bill still go on their honeymoon?" Laurel had slept through Lilly's earlier discussion of the honeymoon.

"They're waiting to get the okay from the police. But they're assuming it will be all right for them to go, so they'll leave for the airport in time to check in and board even if they haven't heard from the police."

"I would love to go to Aruba. Why don't we ever go on vacation to places like that?"

"Because I'm not made of money."

"Hassan could pay, couldn't he?"

"Well, Hassan makes more money than I do, certainly, but I would never ask him to pay for our family to go on vacation in Aruba."

"Seems like he'd offer."

This conversation was ridiculous and beginning to annoy Lilly.

"Oh, thank God. Here's our food." Laurel picked up her fork, ready to attack when the server placed her food on the table.

They ate quickly, without saying much. If Laurel could have ordered a to-go box for Lilly to take her food and finish it in the car, Lilly was pretty sure she would have. She fidgeted and sighed loudly, tapped her fingers on the table, and did every-thing but screech at Lilly to hurry eating.

Laurel went outside and waited by the car while Lilly paid the bill. Just for fun, Lilly went to the restroom, too.

CHAPTER 29

"*W*hen we get home I need to take a shower, do my hair, and figure out what I'm going to wear to dinner." Laurel ticked off her to-do list on her fingers.

"Where are you going for dinner?"

"I don't know. That's what makes dressing so hard."

"I would think something casual, but nice, would be good no matter where he takes you."

"Yeah, I guess."

Laurel closed her eyes and slept the rest of the way home. Lilly would love to have napped while Laurel drove, but she didn't want to deal with any attitude from Laurel if she made such an unreasonable request. So she willed her eyelids to stay open until they arrived at home. She called Noley as soon as she walked inside.

"Have you and Bill recovered from last night?" she asked.

"I think so. It wasn't the wedding either one of us had been dreaming about, but we're married and that's the important thing. I just feel so bad about the caterer."

"Speaking of her, have you heard anything from the police yet?"

"Yes. Nothing about Maureen, but they said it's okay for us to go to Aruba. They made us give them the address and phone number of the hotel there. We're packing now. I'm so excited!"

"I'm so glad you're able to go. I'll miss you guys. Send me a postcard."

"Of course I'll send you a postcard. I might even get you a souvenir." Noley giggled.

"Is Bill there? I know you're busy. I'll only talk to him for a minute."

"I'll get him."

A few moments later Bill picked up the phone. "Hi, Lil."

"Hi. How are you doing this morning?"

"Better than last night, that's for sure."

"You never did tell me what you found when you and your pals from work went after that downed plane."

"Just the plane. No sign of the pilot and the tail number had been sandblasted off. Someone wanted to keep their identity a secret."

"Any idea who it could have been?"

"Not a clue. We could see a vague path of broken branches where the pilot must have gotten away from the area where the plane crashed, but after a short distance there's a clearing in the woods and we lost the trail. I'm sure they'll get dogs up there today if they didn't do it last night. Hopefully they can find the person who did it so we know what exactly happened."

"Do you think someone buzzed the reception deliberately?"

"That's hard to say. It didn't look like the plane was out of control, but who knows? I'm not a pilot. I have no idea what it looks like when a pilot is trying to regain control of an airplane. And if it was deliberate, was it directed toward someone in the wedding party, or a guest, or someone who works for Juniper Lake Manor, or someone who works for the caterer? There are so many variables."

"Maybe I can sniff out some answers while you're in Aruba." Lilly was only half-joking.

"Don't you dare, Lil. Don't think it, don't say it. I'm up for a promotion to deputy lieutenant and if you go sticking your nose where it doesn't belong and sniffing out answers, there's no way they'll promote me."

"Okay, fine. You just got married. You shouldn't be so grumpy."

"I wasn't grumpy until you called. Listen. You'll have your hands full with Mom this week. She's already called me three times today asking when we'll be home from Arabia."

"Arabia?"

"Yes."

Lilly sighed. "All right. I'll keep my eye on Mom. She seemed pretty good yesterday and all last evening, considering the stress we were all under during the reception. I'm surprised she was able to stay lucid for the most part."

"Apparently she used up all the lucidity yesterday. Just keep an eye on her and we can talk when I get back. Obviously, call me if there's an emergency. But it costs a fortune to call over-seas, so don't call if it's not an emergency."

"You got it. Hopefully you won't hear a word from Juniper Junction while you're away. Just go and enjoy yourselves."

"We'll try. Gotta run, Lil. Love you. See you in two weeks."

Lilly hung up and curled up with Barney on the sofa in the living room. It was warm in the house, not too hot, but just right for drifting off with a snuggly dog.

CHAPTER 30

She woke up with a start to the sound of Laurel yelling her name. She sat up, confused and wondering what time it was.

"Mom! Hurry!"

Barney stretched and yawned, obviously not concerned by Laurel's cries for help. Lilly, on the other hand, fell onto her hands and knees trying to catapult off the couch without disturbing him. She recovered herself and raced up the stairs.

"What's wrong?" Her heart was beating double time.

"I can't get my hair right!" Laurel wailed.

"You woke me up for that?"

"This is important, Mom!"

"All right. Calm down. You need to keep things in perspective, Laur. It's hair."

"Do you even remember being my age? Remember your first date with Dad?"

"I'm not so old that I can't remember being young. On my first date with Dad, I was older then than you are now, and yes, I remember it very well. He picked me up to go to a movie and we got a flat tire. I waited while he walked to the nearest gas station to call his father to pick us up because he didn't have a jack in his car. We never saw the movie. We didn't get dinner, either, because everything was closed by the time his father picked us up by the side of the road. Oh, and it was in the middle of winter, so it was below freezing and I had the frost-bite to prove it."

"Okay, so you remember. I do not intend for this date to be anything like yours. Can you just help me with my hair?"

"Of course I'll help you, but you have to remember that this is a first date and you're not going to the Academy Awards."

Laurel scowled as Lilly took a curling iron to her hair. In a few minutes the problem was solved and Laurel's hair looked beautiful, as usual.

"Thank you. I'm sorry I was mean to you."

"Apology accepted. When is Drew getting here?"

"Any minute now. Do I look okay?" Laurel twirled around for Lilly, just as she used to do as a little girl. Lilly's breath caught in her throat as it had done when she saw Tighe in his tux. Her kids were growing up.

"You look great. I want you to have fun, be careful, and don't do anything stupid."

"I never do stupid things. And I'm always careful."

"I know."

Her phone beeped and she grasped it with both hands. "He's here. Are you sure I look okay?"

"Beautiful. Now get down there before he gets sick of waiting for you."

Laurel let out a tiny squeal and raced down the stairs. She waltzed out the front door as if she didn't have a care in the world and didn't look over her shoulder to see Lilly standing in the living room window, waving goodbye.

Hassan had promised to come over for dinner, so Lilly got

busy making a charcuterie board. She only felt like nibbling rather than eating a whole meal, so charcuterie was perfect. And she knew it was a favorite of Hassan's, too.

Dinner was ready when he knocked on the back door a little while later and came into the kitchen. He kissed her as Barney jumped around them in circles, wanting to join in the fun. Finally Hassan bent down and petted Barney, laughing. "Barney, you get to see her more often than I do."

They enjoyed a glass of wine outside before going inside for a delicious spread of sliced meats, cheese, and fruit. While they ate Lilly mused aloud about Maureen's death.

"I wonder who could have wanted her dead. Maybe the better question is who *didn't* want her dead. She was miserable. I wonder if she was a good boss."

"She seemed young to have her own catering business."

"I thought so, too, but as I understand it, she was a go-getter when she was in school. Her dream was to be a caterer and she went for it as soon as she graduated. And she made a success of herself, apparently. The reviews of her business online weren't too bad. Mostly they were about how good the food was."

"Maybe the reviews came from her mother. Or people who love fish."

Lilly chuckled. "Probably. If she hadn't died, I know Bill and Noley would have left her a scorching review."

"Speaking of Bill and Noley, I'm glad they got to go on their honeymoon. They deserve a vacation."

"I'm glad the police let them go. And since they did, I wonder if that means there are already suspects in either the plane buzzing or Maureen's death."

"It's going to be hard to find out when your source inside the police department is out of the country," Hassan said with a smile.

"He's up for a promotion, so he's asked me to stay as far

away from the whole business as I can. Can you believe it? Like I would intentionally get involved."

Hassan made a scoffing noise.

"What was that all about?" Lilly asked. She already knew the answer, of course.

"Oh, nothing. I hope you listen to your brother this time."

CHAPTER 31

"This time? What's that supposed to mean?" But Lilly was grinning. "I'm just curious, that's all. And I like to help my family and friends when they're in trouble."

"Well, no one seems to be in trouble this time—yet—so you don't have to do a thing. And I don't have to worry constantly about where you are or what you're up to, so it's good for my blood pressure, too."

"As long as we're on the topic of blood pressure, do you want to go over to Mom's with me after we're done eating? I haven't been over there today and I promised Bill I'd keep a close eye on her. Apparently she called him several times earlier and she's been pretty confused."

"Your poor mom. She probably worked so hard yesterday to keep her thoughts straight that she's exhausted from the effort. Sure, I'll go with you."

After dinner they cleaned up and left for Bev's house. Nikki was helping Bev slip into pajamas when they arrived, so they waited in the living room. When Bev came in from the bedroom, she was shuffling and arguing with Nikki over her shoulder, which looked painful. Her neck was often stiff, and she tended to lean to one side, so arguing like that didn't look comfortable.

"What's wrong, Mom?"

"Oh, that woman thinks I need this walker all the time and I don't."

"What woman?"

Bev sounded exasperated. "The woman who comes here every day." Lilly resisted the urge to panic, a feeling that was becoming all too common. *This is just part of the process*, she reminded herself.

"Do you mean Nikki?"

Bev didn't answer.

"Nikki's right, Mom. You should be using your walker. We got it so you wouldn't fall."

"I have never fallen."

Lilly bit her tongue to keep from arguing. "Well, would you use it as a favor to me?"

No answer.

"So, what did you do today?"

"Nothing."

"Did you go outside?"

Bev gave Lilly a withering stare.

"So you didn't go outside. Did you watch television or play cards?"

"We played cards."

Nikki came into the room. "Hi, Lilly, Hassan. I knew you were in here so I took a couple of extra minutes to tidy up some things in the bathroom."

"Thanks, Nikki. We were just asking Mom what she was up to today."

"I called Billy," Bev said.

Lilly didn't want to get into a discussion of where Bill went on his honeymoon because she feared it would only confuse her mom. "Can I get you something to drink?" she asked instead. She glanced up and noticed Nikki shaking her head.

"She's been having some trouble getting up at night. Haven't you, Bev?" Nikki turned to Lilly and lowered her voice while Hassan sat down with Bev and chatted with her about his own parents.

"Suzanne told me your mom has had several accidents in the past week or so because she can't get to the bathroom in time. It upsets her." Suzanne, the night nurse, was responsible for reporting any overnight incidents to Nikki each morning.

"No one told me. Does Bill know?" Lilly asked.

"There wasn't any reason to tell you about it specifically. Suzanne deals with it and your mom goes back to bed."

"So she doesn't drink anything before bed?"

"That's right. If she doesn't drink anything after dinner, she doesn't have an urgent need to use the bathroom during the night. That makes things easier and more comfortable for her."

"All right. Sorry I asked about getting her a drink. I had no idea. This is normal?"

"Not only is it normal, it's expected. She doesn't sleep well to begin with, but spending time in the middle of the night changing pajamas and bedsheets makes it even less likely that she'll get a good night's sleep, as you can imagine."

"Poor Mom."

"I'm afraid it's not going to get any better, Lilly."

CHAPTER 32

"*I* know. I hate watching it happen," Lilly said.

"So do I. But your mom is still lucid sometimes—she was terrific at Bill's wedding. She was exhausted when we finally got her home. She slept most of the way back to Juniper Junction."

"It was a stressful evening, that's for sure. She did great."

"The lucky thing was that she got a lot of down time at the table, just sitting with me and Beau. She's always worse when she's tired. That helps explain why she's so confused today. I'm sure Bill told you that she didn't understand where he was going for his honeymoon."

"Yeah." Lilly smiled. "She thought he was going to Arabia."

Nikki also smiled and nodded. "That's typical. I wasn't able to get her to rest this afternoon, so she's pretty out of it tonight. As soon as you and Hassan leave I'll help her get in bed and hopefully she'll sleep long and hard tonight."

"We'll leave now. There's no sense in keeping her up just to talk to us. I'll check in on her tomorrow."

Lilly and Hassan kissed Bev's cheek and left just a couple of minutes later. Lilly sighed as they descended the porch steps.

"What was Nikki saying?"

"Just that Mom's exhausted from the wedding and that's part of the reason she seems so spaced out tonight. And why she was confused all day. Did you notice that she didn't know who Nikki was when we got there?"

"Yeah. I'm sure it won't be long before she doesn't recognize me."

"Or the rest of us," Lilly added. "It's hard not to take it personally." They got into the car and Hassan headed back toward Lilly's house.

"The one time she didn't know who I was, it hurt. I thought it meant she didn't care enough about me to remember me," he said.

"That's why it's hard not to take it personally. Watch. She'll forget who I am and remember Bill every day for the rest of her life. It would be my luck."

Hassan laughed. "It would. But don't take it personally, remember?"

Lilly chuckled. "I'm eager to hear about Laurel's date. I wonder when she'll get home."

"Do you want me to head back to my house?"

"Of course not. I want you to stay. Don't you want to know how the date went?"

"Mostly, I just want to spend time with you. I haven't seen much of you lately because you've been so busy with the wedding preparations." Lilly took up his hand and kissed it.

"Then let's go spend time together."

Laurel was home less than an hour later. She walked inside flushed with excitement.

"How did it go?" Lilly asked. "It looks like it was a successful date."

"Drew is so great! He took me to the café off Main Street, then we went for a walk around the square. I showed him your store and some of the other good places to shop."

"What did he think?"

"He loved it."

"Do you think you two will go out again?"

"Definitely! He said he'll call me this week. Wouldn't it be great if I could work at Juniper Lake Manor when I graduate? He's practically the owner."

"Whoa, there, Laur. Let's slow the train down."

"I know. I'm just excited. He's so cute, isn't he?"

"He's definitely cute, yes. But let's not worry about going to work for his family just yet."

"Mom, you make too much of everything."

"I do, huh?"

"Hassan, you tell her. She's making too much of this."

He laughed and put both his hands up. "This is a mother-daughter thing and I am staying as far out of it as I possibly can."

"Well, I'm going to bed. Do you think Drew will call tomorrow? I hope so." Laurel dashed up the stairs and they heard her bedroom door close.

"She's obviously in love," Lilly said.

"Could be. He seemed like a nice kid."

"He did, you're right. I had forgotten that his family owns Juniper Lake Manor. I'm sure they've been visited by the police because of what happened at the wedding."

"I'm sure. They're probably the first people Darla called after —or maybe during—the plane incident. And then again when Maureen's body was found." He chuckled. "I wonder if they know their son had a date with the daughter of the wedding planner."

"If they don't know it already, I'm sure they'll find out. They'll put a stop to it fast."

"Why would they?"

"Because I'm a jinx, that's why. They won't want their son dating the daughter of a jinx."

Hassan pulled Lilly close. "Jinx or no jinx, you were the most beautiful person at that wedding and I was your lucky date." He nuzzled her ear as Laurel came downstairs again.

"Eww. Vanessa's parents don't do that in public." Vanessa was Laurel's best friend from high school.

"We don't, either. This is my living room, not a public place."

"But I can still see you."

"Then close your eyes," Lilly said with a laugh.

"I forgot to tell you that Drew's parents have hired a private investigator to figure out what happened at the wedding. They're afraid if the police don't solve the murder and the whole plane buzzing thing soon, their reputation will be ruined and people will stop going to Juniper Lake Manor for weddings and stuff."

"A private investigator? That's got to cost a fortune. Why not just wait until the police solve the crime with public resources? That's why we pay taxes."

Laurel shrugged. "They must feel like a private investigator will get the job done quicker. Anyway, you two can get back to whatever gross necking thing you were doing. I just forgot to tell you that."

She returned upstairs while Lilly and Hassan digested what they had just learned.

"A private investigator. They're really serious about getting to the bottom of whatever happened," Hassan said.

"I wonder if I could talk to the person they hired."

"Why would you do that? I thought you were going to stay out of it like Bill asked you to and so that I don't have to worry about you."

"I didn't say I was going to get involved. I would merely love to get the name of the person and talk to him. Or her. I'm curious, that's all. Do private investigators work with police?"

"I have no idea."

"It looks like I have some research to do."

"What kind of research?"

"I'm going to figure out a way to find out who they've hired."

"Lilly...." Hassan's voice held a warning tone.

"Don't worry. I'm just going to do a little digging. Nothing that will affect Bill or his chances for the promotion at work."

"He'd be furious if he knew what you're up to."

"In that case, how lucky that he's on his way to Aruba." She winked and Hassan shook his head. "You love me and you wouldn't have me any other way," she said to him.

"I love you, all right, but my nerves would get a break if you stayed out of this."

CHAPTER 34

Monday morning Lilly was in the jewelry shop early. She had emails to answer and mail to go through before the store opened. Harry showed up not long after she arrived.

"Any word about what happened at the wedding?" he asked as soon as he saw her.

"Nothing yet. And my contact inside the police force is in Aruba, so I'm short on information."

"I wonder if the police will put anything online or in the paper, you know, asking for the public's help."

"It's possible, if they're really stuck for leads. But it's also possible that they have a suspect and they're holding their cards close to the vest. We'll have to wait to hear anything."

"I would think that the caterer's death would be the priority, since it's a much more serious crime. Do you suppose it's related to the plane incident at all?"

"I have no idea. And though the caterer's death is the more serious crime, it's the plane buzzing that's actually more interesting to me because that's the one that was more likely directed at someone in the wedding party or at the reception."

"It's scary to think that someone at the reception could have been the target. Does anyone know what happened to the pilot?"

"When I talked to Bill yesterday before he left on his honeymoon, he said there was no sign of the pilot anywhere in the clearing where the plane crashed."

"That's so odd. So the pilot got away."

"There was some broken brush near the wreckage that probably indicated the pilot had escaped in that direction, but once the investigators got to the nearest clearing, they couldn't tell which way the person had gone. Bill said they'd take dogs there to pick up the pilot's scent, if possible."

"But they should at least be able to identify the owner of the plane, right? From identification numbers or something?"

"The tail numbers had been sandblasted off the plane. I'm sure there are other places on a plane that identify it, but I don't know that for sure. We'll have to wait to hear anything."

"Do you know anything about the caterer?"

"Not really, only that everyone there despised her despite having met her for the first time on Saturday. She was not a nice person or easy to work with."

"She was that bad?"

"She didn't have enough staff, plus she couldn't provide most of the food we ordered."

"Yeah. I ordered the beef and got fish."

"You and almost everyone else."

"I didn't pay much attention. Alice ordered the fish, so she got what she wanted."

"At least someone got what they wanted. You know, if Maureen had dealt with the problems more professionally, it probably wouldn't have bothered me so much. But she basically told me I would have to suck it up."

"Did she end up charging you the full price?"

"I haven't gotten the final bill yet." She explained when she saw Harry's look of confusion. "Our deal was that I would pay half the contract price up front, then the balance after the reception."

"Oh."

"Actually, I should head over to the caterer's office today. That way I might be able to talk to someone about the bill *and* find out a little more about Maureen."

Harry grinned. "I should have known you'd do more than just settle a bill."

"As I told Hassan when he implied something similar, I'm curious about the whole thing. I promised Bill I wouldn't interfere with the police investigation, but just being curious is not interfering. So not only would I *not* technically be interfering, but how would Bill even find out? I'll go over at lunchtime."

CHAPTER 35

As soon as it was Lilly's turn to go to lunch, she hurried out to her car and drove over to the block of offices where Maureen's Catering was located. The lights were on, so she opened the door and stepped inside.

She found herself standing in a tiny room with a small metal desk and standard-issue swivel chair. There was a phone, an old-model desktop computer, and a short, squat filing cabinet. A small brass bell sat on the desk, too, but before tapping the top of the bell, Lilly craned her neck to see what was in the room behind the little office. It was a kitchen, and it looked like it was clean and well-appointed, with tall stacks of catering supplies such as long aluminum pans, cheap-looking chafing dishes, and rows of takeout boxes.

She dinged the bell once and called out, "Hello?"

"Be right there!" came a muffled voice.

Lilly stood by the desk and waited. It wasn't long before someone came out of the kitchen. Lilly recognized him immediately—it was Brad, the employee Lilly had spoken to the night of the reception. She hadn't recalled him being so muscular, but she hadn't been paying all that much attention.

"Oh, hi. We met at the Saturday night event," Brad said.

"Yes, I remember. I'm Lilly Carlsen. I was in charge of planning the wedding reception, so I'm the one Maureen was dealing with. Brad, right?"

"Yes. How can I help you?"

"I came in to see about the balance for the reception on Saturday evening. As you may know, most things didn't go as planned, and I am assuming the balance of the contract will reflect that. What I mean is, Maureen wasn't able to provide most of the food we ordered, and she was also short-staffed that evening, both in violation of the contract she and I signed."

Brad gave Lilly a hard look.

"Really? You've come to ask for a discount? Maureen is *dead*."

"Yes, and I'm very sorry for your loss. But there is still an outstanding balance, and I don't think it's appropriate for me to pay the entire amount."

Brad straightened his shoulders and glared at Lilly. "Well, I'm afraid I can't do anything about that right now. I have to wait until the lawyer tells me it's okay to go ahead and settle the outstanding bills. We have to fulfill the remaining contracts and we can collect full amounts due, but we can't change contract terms without the lawyer's go-ahead."

"All right. I can leave you my number and maybe you can give me a call when you've heard from the lawyer."

"Sure."

Lilly was dangerously close to having to leave without getting any information about Maureen. She had to think of something to say, and quickly. Brad checked his watch, clearly waiting for her to leave.

"Again, I'm sorry for your loss," she finally said. "I didn't really know Maureen, but it seems like she was well-respected and well-liked by her friends." The bald-faced lie left a sour taste in her mouth. Also, she thought, is there anyone who *isn't* well-liked by their friends?

"She was great. This was her life's dream, you know, to open a catering business."

"How long has she had this business?"

"Several years. It's really been taking off lately. I've been with her from the beginning. We knew each other from culinary school."

"Oh, you went to the community college, too? My daughter is in the culinary department there now."

"I graduated near the top of my class," he said proudly.

"Congratulations. Catering must be a fun way to earn a living."

"Fun, but stressful."

"I'm sure." She waited a beat before asking another question. "Are there a lot of other events planned that you'll have to handle now that...." Her voice trailed off as she realized how heartless she sounded. But Brad didn't seem to notice.

"Yes, there are quite a few. It won't be easy to do this without her, especially because I've not only lost a boss, but a girlfriend, too."

Lilly tried to mask her surprise. "Maureen was your girlfriend? I had no idea. In that case, I'm doubly sorry for your loss."

"Well, I mean, we were sort of taking a break from our relationship, but we would have gotten back together. You know when you meet your soul mate, right?"

"Um, yes, of course. Wow. Maureen was your soul mate?"

"Oh, definitely. Mo was the jelly to my peanut butter, as we liked to say." His smile held a far-off wistfulness.

"That's a great analogy."

"Food is what brought us together."

"How lovely."

"But it's also the reason we were taking a break."

"Oh?" Lilly hoped he would keep talking.

"Yeah. Not food so much, but the business of it. She was my

boss and it made her uncomfortable for two reasons. First, she wanted us to be equals, but this is her business. And second, because it doesn't look good for a boss to be dating an employee. That's just good business."

"Yes, I suppose you're right. What's going to happen to the business now that … now that Maureen is gone?"

"She had a will, but I'm not sure what was in it. The lawyer hasn't told me. As for me, I'll probably start up my own catering business. It's what I've always wanted to do."

"Well, I should get going, Brad. I do wish you the best as you continue with the remainder of her business. You'll call me when you hear from the lawyer?"

"Yes."

CHAPTER 36

illy got into the car and drove back to work. Her mind replayed the visit and she tried to distill what she had learned about Maureen—first, that she and Brad had a romantic relationship at one point, second, that the relationship was on hold because Maureen was uncomfortable having her boyfriend working for her, and third, that the boyfriend didn't know what was going to happen to the business now that Maureen was gone.

When she got back to the office Harry was eager to find out what Lilly had learned.

"I learned that Maureen was dating one of her employees, for one thing, and that they recently broke up. Wait, no. I shouldn't say that. They're 'taking a break.'" She made quotation marks with her fingers.

"Well, at least they *were* taking a break. Is it rude of me to say that?"

"No. It's true, right? I also learned that the employee, Brad, doesn't know what's going to happen with Maureen's business. He has to talk to the lawyer."

"So you talked with the ex-boyfriend?"

"Yes. He was in Maureen's office. I don't know what exactly he was doing in there, but he did say he and the other employees were trying to honor Maureen's outstanding catering contracts."

"That can't be easy without the boss."

"No. But honestly, I would have preferred to deal with anyone but the boss. She was unfriendly and unprofessional. And I'm not the only one who felt that way—the staff from Juniper Lake Manor didn't like the way she treated them, either. Like they were her servants. They weren't there to help the caterer. They all had their own jobs to do."

"I did hear a couple of the Juniper Lake Manor staff complaining about her," Harry said.

"Really? Which ones? I wonder if the police are aware of that."

"Two young women. They weren't saying anything bad, just that Maureen was difficult to work with and they were glad they didn't work for her. Although, from what you've said, she was sort of treating them as her own employees that night."

"Well, if Bill were here, I would make sure he knew about the women. But there's no one for me to tell, so I guess I'll just file it away in my own head. It's so frustrating! I would love to be helping figure out what happened to Maureen."

Harry laughed. "I'll bet Bill wouldn't love you helping."

"He definitely would not. But he's not here, so he wouldn't even know." She smiled. "The police are going to have their hands full chasing down the person who killed Maureen, so maybe I'll just do a little poking around to see what I can find out about the pilot of the plane."

"Who are you going to ask?"

"I haven't really thought about it. There were a bunch of officers who went to the plane crash site with Bill. I know some of the people he works with, but not well. His friend Tom, one of the guys in the wedding party, is on the force, though he stayed behind and took charge of the Maureen thing. I suppose I could reach out to him for help. I have his contact info because I had to email the members of the wedding party from time to time. Maybe I'll give him a call tonight."

But that call had to wait, because something else came up.

After work Lilly stopped at Bev's house. Nikki was running from the kitchen to the bathroom when she arrived.

"Nikki, what's going on? What happened? Can I help?"

"Hold on a sec, Lilly." Nikki raced away. Lilly followed her.

Bev was lying motionless on the bathroom floor.

CHAPTER 37

"Mom! What happened? Is she okay, Nikki?"

Nikki had knelt down beside Bev's head and whipped something small and white out of her pocket. She waved it under Bev's nose and Bev started coughing and blinking her eyes rapidly.

"Smelling salts." Nikki spoke over her shoulder to Lilly, who had knelt down beside Bev, too.

"Did she faint? Mom, are you all right?"

"What happened?" Bev's mumbled words were hard to understand.

"You fainted, honey," Nikki told her.

"Where?"

"You're in the bathroom."

"What happened?"

"I was standing behind you while you were washing your hands and suddenly you were on the floor." Then Nikki turned to Lilly. "The walker was in front of me, so I couldn't catch her, only soften the fall."

"Thank God you were in here with her or it could have been a lot worse."

"Bev, let's get you back into the living room so I can check you out."

Nikki and Lilly each took one of Bev's arms and she allowed herself to be helped to her chair in the living room.

"Let me have a look at you, Bev," Nikki said. She reached for her medical bag, which she always kept under the end table next to the sofa. She pulled out a blood pressure cuff and a stethoscope. First she listened to Bev's heart, then she listened again while the blood pressure cuff was wrapped around Bev's arm, and then finally, she took Bev's pulse.

"Blood pressure is pretty low," she murmured to herself.

After that she pressed the bones of Bev's face very gently with her fingertips. Bev winced when Nikki touched the skin around her right eye.

"Does that hurt?" Nikki asked. She stopped pressing as Bev nodded slightly.

Nikki had been crouching next to Bev, and at that she straightened up and turned toward Lilly. "We should probably have her eye looked at. She may need X-rays."

"I'm not going anywhere." At least those words were clear.

"Bev, you have to. You don't have to go in an ambulance. Lilly or I can drive you. Is that okay, Lilly?"

"Yes, of course. I can drive you, Mom. But you need to do what Nikki tells you to do. If she thinks you need X-rays, you need X-rays."

"Where's Billy? I want him to take me."

Lilly had to fight the urge to sigh dramatically. "Bill is on his honeymoon, remember? He'll be home in a few days."

"What about Daniel?" Daniel, Lilly's father, had passed away many years ago. It wasn't uncommon for Bev to ask about Daniel as if he were still alive.

"He can't drive, Mom. He won't be able to take you." Lilly's initial reflex was always to remind her mother that her father was no longer alive, but some time ago she had learned that it was better to play along with her mother's confusion. She felt like she was deceiving Bev, but Nikki had assured her that it wasn't hurting Bev to think that Daniel was still alive.

Tears began to fall down Bev's face. "My eye hurts," she whimpered.

Lilly swallowed around the lump in her throat. "Nikki, is it okay if I take her? You can follow and meet us there." She couldn't explain it, but she wanted to be alone with her mom for a few minutes. They almost never had any time alone together anymore, and Lilly suddenly wanted to have her mom all to herself.

"Sure." Nikki smiled softly, as if she understood what Lilly was feeling. "Bev, is that okay? Lilly's going to drive you over to the hospital and I'll follow. I'll see you there. I'm going to call them and let them know we're coming."

Bev merely nodded, wincing again.

Nikki made the call on her cell phone while she and Lilly helped Bev into a jacket, led her out to the porch, and gingerly helped her down the stairs to the front walk. Her legs appeared to be in reasonably good shape. She was shuffling, but that was nothing new. Nikki helped Lilly situate Bev in the front seat. Once Bev was belted in and leaning against the headrest with a look of pain on her thin facial features, Nikki closed the door gently and Lilly drove away. Nikki wasn't far behind.

CHAPTER 38

"We'll get you fixed right up, Mom. How are you doing?"

"I hurt."

"I'm sure they'll be able to give you something for the pain when we get to the hospital. Just hang in there a few more minutes."

"Thank you for taking me, dear."

Tears sprang to Lilly's eyes and she brushed them away roughly. "You're welcome, Mom. I'm glad I got to your house when I did. Have you had dinner?"

"I don't remember."

"Well, if you're hungry we can get you something to eat at the hospital, too."

"I'm not hungry,"

"Okay." Lilly reached over and covered Bev's papery hand with her own. It felt cold.

"Want the heat on, Mom?"

"No, I'm fine."

"Okay." More than anything, Lilly wanted to help somehow, to make her mom comfortable. She couldn't think of anything that would help short of pain medication.

"Not much longer now." Lilly was driving as fast as she dared. As the silence in the car deepened, she found herself starting to panic over what might be going on inside Bev's body that they couldn't see. Was she bleeding internally? Was there a head injury? Was there soft tissue damage? She forced herself to take several slow, deep breaths in order to calm her racing heart. Bev was mumbling to herself.

"What did you say, Mom?"

Bev didn't answer and Lilly didn't press. She could see the lights of the hospital up ahead, and it was all she could do not to press the accelerator to the floor to get there faster. She swung into the valet parking circle in front of the emergency department and jerked her door open as she came to a stop.

Lilly ran around to the passenger side as Nikki pulled up in front of her.

"How's she doing?" Nikki asked.

"All right. I just started to panic over what could be wrong that we can't see."

"That's part of the reason I wanted her looked at here." Nikki opened the passenger door and Bev slumped sideways toward her, her seatbelt the only thing keeping her from falling out.

"Oh, my God. Has she fainted again?" Lilly asked. She couldn't keep the growing alarm out of her voice.

"Yes. Would you run inside and get someone out here who can help us? She needs a gurney."

Lilly whirled around and ran into the reception area of the emergency department. Apologizing, she brushed past the person waiting to be checked in and told the woman at the desk that her mother was outside and unconscious. The woman immediately called for someone who could help. Three agonizing minutes later, two orderlies whisked through the lobby of the emergency department wheeling a gurney between them. They were brisk and efficient, but calm and professional.

They helped settle, if only a little bit, the nerves that were jangling throughout Lilly's body. She stood right behind them, watching them with eagle eyes as they lifted Bev onto the stretcher and strapped her in for the short ride into the hospital.

Bev came to as they were locking the gurney wheels into place in a curtained room in the emergency department. One of the orderlies had pulled the curtains closed around them and the quiet *shushing* sound woke Bev. She immediately started crying.

"What's happening?" Lilly asked in alarm.

"It's okay. That's a perfectly normal response to waking up from unconsciousness," Nikki said. One of the orderlies nodded his agreement.

"I'll let the nurse know she's in here and awake," he said. He followed his partner into the busy emergency department.

CHAPTER 39

*L*illy went around to the other side of the bed where she could stand at her mother's head. She brushed her mom's forehead with her fingers. "How are you doing, Mom?"

"What happened?"

"You fainted again just as we pulled up to the hospital."

"My head hurts." Her words were slurred. She winced from the overhead light and closed her eyes. "What's going to happen?"

Nikki spoke up. "The orderly has gone to get a nurse. The ball will start rolling once the nurse comes in. It won't be long now until we get you some pain relief and someone to look at that eye of yours."

Bev nodded almost imperceptibly. "Lilly? Are you still here?"

"Yes, Mom. What can I do for you?"

"Nothing. Just stay here."

"I won't go anywhere, Mom. I promise." She swallowed hard and reached around to pull a chair closer to the bed. "Would it help if we turned the light off?"

Bev gave a slight nod. Nikki looked around for the light switch and flicked it. The ceiling light over the bed went out but the room was still fairly bright from the other lights outside the room and a smaller light behind the head of Bev's bed. "I can't do anything about the other lights, Bev," Nikki said. "Keep your eyes closed. Maybe I can find something dark to put over your forehead so you aren't bothered."

"No," Bev replied. "It hurts."

Nikki frowned and glanced toward the curtain as if willing a nurse to come in. Tears seeped from the corners of Bev's eyes, but she kept them closed and said nothing. Lilly could recall other emergency room trips where Bev had made a pill of herself, annoying everyone from the nurses to the doctors to the techs to her own family members. But this time was different. Lilly thought she might just prefer the annoying Bev to the helpless woman in front of her.

"Shouldn't someone Mom's age take precedence?" Lilly asked Nikki in a whisper.

"Sometimes. It depends on what other stuff's going on. I'm sure it won't be too long."

And true to Nikki's word, a harried-looking nurse came in a few minutes later. "How are we doing in here?" she asked. Like the orderlies, she moved with brisk efficiency, but exuded a calm that made Lilly feel a little bit better.

Nikki explained what had happened at the house, then went on to tell her that Bev had fainted again as they pulled up to the hospital doors. "Her blood pressure was low when I took the measurement at her house," Nikki said. She shared the numbers with the nurse.

"Let's check it again now," the nurse suggested. She disappeared into the hallway and returned a few seconds later pushing a small cart with a blood pressure monitor attached. She strapped the cuff onto Bev's arm and listened closely through her stethoscope as the machine did its work. She frowned. "Still low," she said.

"What does that mean?" Lilly asked.

"Could mean lots of things, but don't worry about it yet. She could simply have low blood pressure. A doctor will be in soon to take a look at her. She pressed her fingers around Bev's eyes and Bev mumbled.

"I can't hear you," the nurse said in a gentle voice. "Are you able to speak up a little?"

"That hurts," Bev said.

"Okay. I won't do it anymore. I'm just trying to give the doctor an idea of what to expect when she comes in." Bev whimpered in response.

After the nurse left it was only a few more minutes before the doctor came in. She introduced herself and asked a few questions about what had happened earlier in the evening. She wanted to know what Bev had eaten for dinner.

"I couldn't get her to eat anything," Nikki said. "She said she wasn't hungry."

The doctor nodded. "I'm going to get her hooked up to an IV with some calories in it, as well as a medication for the pain." She raised her voice a little. "How does that sound, Bev? Ready for some pain relief?"

Bev nodded ever so slightly and the doctor patted her leg. "I'm going to order some tests, including X-rays. That bone around the eye is concerning me, plus I want to make sure there's no bleeding anywhere inside." Nikki nodded. "In the meantime, we'll get that drip started." The doctor departed and shortly the nurse returned with an IV bag and a syringe.

"I'm going to get this set up and she can take it with her when she goes for her tests," she explained. She worked busily, adding the medicine to the tube connected to the IV bag and getting a needle inserted into Bev's hand. Bev didn't move a muscle when the needle slid under her skin. Lilly had to look away.

"There," the nurse said when she was finished. She took Bev's hand in hers. "We've already started the pain medicine, Bev. That should make you feel better soon. I'll be back."

CHAPTER 40

Over the next several hours hospital technicians came and went from Bev's room, taking her hither and yon throughout the hospital for different tests. During that time, Lilly worried about whether she should call Bill and let him know what was going on. She texted Hassan and Laurel to let them know where she was, but she didn't tell Tighe. She texted him to ask how his final exam had gone, and he replied that he was pleased and that he'd get the grade in a couple of days.

Lilly eventually decided that she would wait for the doctor to provide a diagnosis for Bev, and then she would decide whether to call or email Bill. She was loath to contact him and had promised herself she wouldn't, barring some unforeseen catastrophe.

Even if the diagnosis turned out to be somewhat serious, she might not contact him. There was nothing he could do from far away except worry, and she didn't want to be the reason he worried throughout his honeymoon. On the other hand, wouldn't he want to know? She knew she would want to know if their roles were reversed.

If the diagnosis was, God forbid, something life-threatening,

Lilly would not hesitate to call him. She hoped it wouldn't come to that.

Nikki had insisted on staying with Lilly and Bev until the doctor knew what was wrong. She had called Suzanne to let her know what was going on, so Suzanne was on standby, waiting to hear from Lilly before she went over to Bev's house.

It was after midnight when the doctor finally came in to talk to Lilly and Nikki. Bev was still having a test done and wouldn't be back for a little while.

"She's got some broken facial bones," the doctor said. "I think we can rectify the problem with a closed reduction." Lilly looked blankly at Nikki.

"That means no surgery," Nikki said. The doctor nodded and Lilly breathed a sigh of relief.

"What, exactly, does it entail?" she asked.

"Resetting the facial bones," the doctor said.

"Oh, that sounds awful. Isn't there another way?"

"I'm afraid not, not without surgery, and surgery would end up causing far more pain than the closed reduction." The doctor looked down at the folder she was holding. "We'll make sure she gets as much pain medication as she needs, so don't worry about that. I'm not a fan of letting a patient suffer when there's pain relief available."

"Okay." Lilly looked at Nikki. "Should I tell Bill?"

The doctor looked from Lilly to Nikki and back again, but didn't say anything.

"He's my brother. He's on his honeymoon or he would be here with us."

"I see. It's up to you whether you tell him or not. But this doesn't appear to be life-threatening. I'm still waiting for test results that may help explain why your mother fainted, but at this time I don't see anything remarkable in the test results I've looked at."

Lilly nodded, trying to absorb all the information she was being given.

"I'll be back shortly, once I have the results from her last test." The doctor left.

Lilly sighed. "Nikki, why don't you go home? I can stay here with Mom. You need some sleep."

"I promised your mom I would stay here. I don't mind. I have all day to sleep if necessary. Dawn is still hours away. You should be the one going home to sleep."

"I can't leave. Bill would never forgive me. *I* wouldn't forgive me."

"I understand. At least sit down and close your eyes for a little while. I'm going to go move my car."

"Okay. I'll have Harry take care of things at the store in the morning so I can sleep once I get home."

Bev was wheeled back into the room a short time later, and she was followed not long after that by the doctor.

"The test results don't show anything really out of whack," she said. "What likely happened is that her blood pressure fell as a result of not eating enough and she fainted. Then the low blood pressure, combined with the pain from her fall, caused the second fainting episode. So here's what we're going to do: we're going to work on her facial bones here in the hospital, then you're going to take her home and watch her carefully. Expect a lot of swelling and bruising, but she'll be okay."

Lilly didn't know whether to cry or hug the doctor. Relief flooded through her upon hearing that the fainting likely hadn't been caused by something serious, but that was quickly followed by the dread of knowing how much pain her mother was going to experience in the coming hours.

"I'm not going to call Bill." She made the decision on the spot. "If anything goes wrong, God forbid, I'll let him know. But for now I don't want him to worry."

"I think that's the right decision," Nikki said.

The doctor had left for just a minute, and when she came back she was with another doctor. "This is Doctor Wang. He's going to work on your mom's facial bones and then she can go home." She left and Doctor Wang shook hands with Lilly and Nikki. He explained what he was going to be doing, then instructed them to wait in the emergency department for him to return. He went in search of an assistant and Nikki and Lilly sat down to wait.

CHAPTER 41

*L*illy was surprised at how quickly the doctor completed the work on Bev's face. A technician wheeled Bev back into her room in the emergency department and the doctor followed along shortly thereafter. He explained that he had given her a rather strong sedative and assured Lilly that Bev didn't feel a thing while he worked. Her face looked almost normal, with the exception of a couple of deep purple bruises beginning to show around her eyes.

"You'll see the swelling very soon, and the bruising is going to get much deeper and more extensive. Don't worry about it, because it's normal. Here's a prescription for pain medicine. I recommend that you have this filled as soon as possible so it's ready when she is. The sedative should start wearing off very soon. Do you know where there's an all-night pharmacy?"

Lilly nodded. There was one in Lupine. The doctor continued his spiel about Bev's care over the next few days and wished them well. As soon as he left, a nurse came in.

"So what do we do now? Just wait for her to wake up?" Lilly asked.

The nurse nodded. "Yes. It shouldn't be long now. As soon as she can move around a little bit, we'll discharge her and you can get her home."

Lilly and Nikki sat by Bev's bed, waiting for signs that the sedative was wearing off. Pretty soon she let out a low groan, followed by some mumbled words and a few slight hand movements.

"She's coming around," Nikki said. "Let's give it a few more minutes and I'll go get the nurse."

While they watched, Bev opened her eyes and quickly closed them again. Lilly was able to make out Bev's words, "What's happening?"

"You're in the hospital, Mom. You've had quite an evening. As soon as you feel able, we're going to get you home. Nikki's here with me."

"Bill?"

"No, Bill's on a trip. But he'll be home soon and he'll come to see you just as soon as possible, I promise."

Bev sighed and flopped her hand on the bed. Lilly reached for it and held it in her own hand. Her mother gave an almost imperceptible squeeze.

Nikki excused herself to go in search of Bev's nurse and came back a few minutes later. "She'll be in soon. How are you feeling, honey?" She reached for Bev's other hand and squeezed it.

Bev grunted in response, but opened her eyes and looked around. She looked a little more alert.

It took the nurse a while to return, but by the time she came in, Bev was more alert and wriggling around on the bed, trying to make herself comfortable. The nurse made quick work of assessing Bev and pronouncing her ready for discharge. She bustled around the bed, asking Bev all kinds of questions about her age and her hometown. Lilly worried because Bev often didn't know that information on a good day, but she was able to remember some of the details. The nurse even got Bev to smile when she asked about Fred, Bev's Cocker Spaniel. Finally, she called for a wheelchair and made sure that Nikki or Lilly or another responsible adult would be with Bev at all times.

It seemed to Lilly like days had passed by the time she finally left the hospital in the wake of the orderly pushing Bev in a wheelchair.

There was a parking ticket stuck to her windshield.

"Crap. I forgot to move the car last night." She turned to Nikki. "Do you believe this?"

Nikki just chuckled. "Kind of the perfect ending to a miserable evening, huh?"

"Yeah, it does seem that way. Well, no matter. Let's get Mom home." The orderly was not allowed to help Bev into the car for liability reasons, so Lilly and Nikki managed to get her comfortable in the front seat. Finally, they were on their way home.

Lilly helped Nikki get Bev into the house, where they set her up in the living room. Nikki left Lilly with Bev for a few moments while she went into the bathroom and the bedroom and covered the mirrors with sheets. Lilly had suggested that so Bev wouldn't be too upset by seeing her reflection once the bruising and the swelling became worse.

After that, Nikki sat with Bev while she waited for Suzanne to show up. Lilly had phoned her before they left the hospital. Lilly hopped into her car and drove out to Lupine, filled Bev's prescription, and raced back to Juniper Junction. The sky was just pinkening when she pulled up in front of Bev's house. She dashed off a quick text to Harry, asking him to open the shop and take charge in case she wasn't able to get in all day, and then she went inside. Suzanne was already there. Nikki had left with a promise to return a few hours early for her shift the next day, and Suzanne had agreed to spend the day with Bev and stay overnight for her regular shift.

Lilly could have cried with relief when she learned of the

plan the two nurses had worked out between them. She would have been happy to stay at Bev's house, but felt it was best to have a nurse there with her. She had been worried that the nursing agency would have to send over a stranger to sub for Nikki during the day, and she didn't want Bev to have to deal with a new nurse on top of everything else she had been through lately.

All the moving around had heightened Bev's pain. Lilly handed the medicine to Suzanne, who quickly administered the first dose. Bev settled down about fifteen minutes later, so Lilly thanked Suzanne and headed for home. She needed sleep.

CHAPTER 42

*L*aurel met her at the door when she walked into the kitchen.

"How's Gran? Is she okay?"

"She'll be fine. Some broken bones in her face and she needs to make sure she's eating better, but nothing more serious than that, thank goodness. You can go see her later, but don't go right now. She's just had some pain medication and she was falling asleep when I left."

"You're not going into the shop, are you?"

"No. Harry's taking charge today. I'm going straight to bed."

"Okay, Mom. I've got class, but I'll let Barney out now before I leave. Do you think I can stop and see Gran on my way home later?"

"I think that would be nice. But listen, Laurel. She's going to look pretty scary when you see her. Don't be surprised, and don't let on if it upsets you. I'm trying to keep Gran from realizing how bad the bruising is."

"It's that bad?"

"It's pretty bad."

"Okay. I won't let on. Is she going to be okay?"

"She'll be okay. But dementia is ugly. We just need to be prepared for whatever might be coming."

"What do you mean by that?" Laurel wore a suspicious look.

"I mean, if she has to be moved to a place where she can be better cared for, we need to be prepared."

"But isn't that why you hired nurses to stay with her?"

"Yes, but the time may come when she needs to be in a place with faster access to more advanced care. Like a doctor on staff."

"I don't want to talk about it."

"I don't, either. Let's put that discussion off for another day."

"Okay." Laurel let Barney out and came back into the kitchen with a glum look on her face. "Do you think Gran could move in here?"

Lilly had started up the steps to her bedroom, but she stopped and turned around. "I wish she could, but I don't think that's possible, honey. We just can't give Gran the care she needs. Not even with nurses."

"Okay." Barney was done with his business and already scratching at the kitchen door. Laurel let him in and he bounded toward Lilly and right past her on up the stairs.

"Have a good day, Laur. Be careful."

"I will." Laurel closed the door quietly behind her and left.

Lilly fell into a deep sleep and woke up in the middle of the afternoon feeling refreshed and alert. Her first thought was of Bev, so she called Suzanne to get an update.

"She's in a lot of pain," Suzanne said in a low voice. "It's almost time for another dose of the pain meds."

"Okay. I'll stop by later on to see her. I need to go into the shop, but I'll be over as soon as I close up for the day."

Harry was polishing a display case when she came into the shop from the office. He spun around. "Boss! What are you doing here? I thought you were going to take the whole day off! How's your mom?"

"I took the whole weekend off. I couldn't very well just take another day to sleep. And my mom is going to be okay, thanks for asking. How'd things go here today?"

"Great. Oh, before I forget, the owner of Ivy's old place came in to see you."

"Mallory? What did she want?"

"She said she needed to talk to you about what happened at the wedding. I didn't ask any questions, so I don't know what she meant by that."

"I'll give her a call after we close up. Thanks, Harry."

Lilly took care of paperwork that had piled up on her desk while she was sleeping the day away, then she sent Harry home a little early and closed up shop. After she had locked the doors, she sat in her office and called Mallory.

"Hi, Mallory. Harry said you stopped by and wanted to talk to me about the wedding. What's up?"

"I just wanted to tell you that I know someone who went to the wedding and I heard all about it first-hand. I mean, to have a caterer die at a wedding reception. It must have been awful. Are you all right?"

"Yes, I'm fine. Thanks for asking. Who do you know who was at the wedding?"

"My sister, Tisha. She was there as a plus-one."

CHAPTER 43

"Wait. Tisha's your sister?" Lilly shook her head as if to dislodge cotton from inside her ears. Had she heard that right?

"Yeah. Didn't you know that?"

"No. I mean, I knew you lived with your sister, but I had no idea it was Tisha."

"So you knew Tisha before the wedding?" Mallory asked.

"Of course. She used to date Bill. You didn't know that?"

"Are you sure we're talking about the same Tisha?"

"Blonde, tall, wearing a form-fitting blue dress?" Lilly left out the words "unnaturally buxom" and "dumb as a post" in her description.

"Yeah, that's Tisha. I had no idea she used to go out with your brother."

"Wow. Small world."

"Well, anyway, she said she was scared out of her mind."

How would she even know? Lilly thought uncharitably. Aloud she said, "It was pretty scary. The plane buzzing was scary enough, but when the caterer died, it felt like a hole had opened under the whole event and we were being swallowed by it."

"Is that why you were out today? Dealing with the aftermath?"

"No. Unfortunately, I was out because my mom fell last night. I was up with her all night at the hospital, so I had to get some sleep today."

"Oh, I'm sorry to hear that. How's she doing?"

"Okay. She's home now and on stiff painkillers, so I'm grateful for that."

"Anything I can do to help?"

"It's sweet of you to ask, but there's really nothing. I'll stop over to see her after I leave the shop. Then I'm going to bed early."

"You must be exhausted. What a nightmare you've lived through these past few days."

"Honestly, if the wedding itself hadn't been so perfect and so beautiful, I would be in much worse shape. At the reception, there were so many things going on that my head was in a million places at once. I've barely had time to think since it all happened."

"Do they know what happened to the caterer?"

"I haven't heard her cause of death. But I know the police are investigating it as a case of foul play."

"Tisha said the police talked to her at the reception and they said they might need to talk to her again. What do you think? Will they be coming around to her house?"

"I have no idea. I can sometimes get a little hint about that sort of thing from my brother since he's a police officer, but he's in Aruba and I won't be talking to him unless something goes really wrong with Mom." Then Lilly had a thought. "But wait. Wasn't Tisha there as Tom's date? He's a police officer. She could ask him—he would probably be able to tell her."

"He's already told her he can't give her any information."

"Oh. Well, I wish I knew more, but unfortunately I don't. In fact, I've been wondering if they're planning to talk to me again, too."

"Will you let me know if they do? I'd like Tisha to be prepared. She gets nervous at the thought of unpleasant surprises."

But being the cause of one isn't a problem? Like showing up at my brother's wedding? Lilly thought with a flash of anger.

"So Tisha really didn't mention that she was going to Bill's wedding?"

"No. I mean, she told me she was going to a wedding, and I knew Tom was her date, but I didn't ask any questions other than that. We live under the same roof, at least for now, but we don't exactly have slumber parties or all-night gab sessions."

"It's nice of her to let you stay there until you find a house."

"It sure is," Mallory agreed. "Listen, I've got to run. I've got a load of stuff in the kiln and I need to take everything out."

After she hung up, Lilly left the store and drove straight to her mother's house. Suzanne gave her a tired smile when she walked in.

"How are you holding up, Suzanne? You must be exhausted."

"I'm fine. Just doing my part. Your mom has been weepy today, Lilly, and the swelling and bruising have gotten much worse. Laurel just left a little while ago and she could barely keep it together while she was here."

"Has Mom seen herself yet?"

"Not yet. I have stayed with her in the bathroom and in the bedroom, and she made no move to touch the sheets hanging over the mirrors. I don't think she's even noticed them."

"Good."

"I just want you to be prepared when you see her. She's lying down right now."

"Okay. I'm ready."

CHAPTER 44

*B*ut she wasn't ready.

She followed Suzanne into Bev's bedroom and after one look at her mother lying on the bed, Lilly gasped and turned away, walking into the living room and sitting down hard on the sofa. Suzanne didn't follow her.

She could hear her mom's low voice coming from the bedroom. She was hard to understand. It wasn't long before Suzanne came looking for her.

"I figured you could use a couple of minutes alone to compose yourself before going in again," Suzanne said. "You are going in again, right?"

"Yes. Definitely. I...." Lilly shook her head. "Even though you warned me, I was not prepared for that."

"Just remember that it's getting better with every passing hour and that the pain meds are working very well. Her pain level has been a little better."

"Is she pretty doped up?"

Suzanne nodded. "She'll be ready for more before too long. This particular medication isn't habit forming, so there's no reason for her to be in pain when she doesn't have to be."

"I agree completely. I just wish it had never happened."

"She knows you're here. I told her you had to use the bathroom."

"Thanks, Suzanne. I'll go in now."

Suzanne stayed in the living room while Lilly sat next to her mother's bed for the next hour, telling her about her day and how excited Tighe was going to be to visit. She promised he would be over to see her as soon as he got home from school. Bev managed a smile at that.

"I heard Laurel was here to see you, too, Mom. And I know Hassan will be coming over. You'll be sick of us in no time!" She laughed.

But Bev didn't laugh. In fact, tears trailed silently between the wrinkles in her cheeks.

"Don't cry, Mom. What's wrong? Do you hurt?"

Bev managed a loud swallow and sniffled, wincing from the pain in her face. Her words were clearer than they had been since the wedding. "I hurt. But that's not why I'm crying. I'm crying because I hate being like this."

A stab of grief shot straight through Lilly, lodging in her heart. "Oh, Mom. None of us like to see you like this."

Bev didn't reply, but sniffled again.

"I'll ask Suzanne for more pain meds. I'll be right back."

By the time Lilly went into the living room to talk to Suzanne, her own tears were falling. Suzanne looked up in alarm and leapt to her feet.

"What's wrong?"

"Mom is crying and that made me cry, that's all. She says she hurts. Can you give her more medicine?"

Suzanne looked at her watch. "I can in a half hour. I'll see if she wants me to read to her. Sometimes she likes that and it makes the time go fast."

"Okay. Do you want me to read to her?"

"Honestly, Lilly, normally that would be great. But I'm so

exhausted that I'm afraid I'll fall asleep if I don't do something to stay awake until she falls asleep tonight. Do you mind if I read to her, just so I can keep my eyes open?"

"Of course not. I'll go tell her you're going to read to her, and then I'm getting some sleep myself. Hopefully you and I and Mom and Nikki will all be on a more regular schedule by sometime tomorrow."

Lilly went in to say goodbye to Bev and explain the plan. "Suzanne is really tired, Mom, but she wants to read to you. That'll help her stay awake. I'll be back tomorrow, I promise."

"Okay. Goodnight, Lilly."

"Goodnight, Mom."

As soon as Lilly got home she called Hassan. She had waited all day to hear his deep voice.

"How's your mom doing? When can I go see her?" he asked as soon as he picked up the phone.

"How about tomorrow?"

"That sounds good. Want to have dinner first?"

"Sure."

"Okay. I'll pick you up and we can eat at the diner."

"Great."

"Have you had enough sleep?"

"Almost. I'm going to bed early and hopefully by tomorrow I'll feel like the old me. I mean, the old young me."

She could hear the smile in his voice. "The perfect you. Listen, wear something warm tomorrow night because I have plans for us after we leave your mom's house."

CHAPTER 45

"What plans?" Lilly asked.

"It's a surprise. Just make sure you wear a coat."

"Okay. I'm so tired I can hardly see straight. I'm going to check in on Laurel and then I'm going to bed."

"Have you had dinner?"

"I don't want dinner."

"You should keep a regular schedule even if you're exhausted. That will help your body return to its normal rhythms. Trust me. I've traveled enough across many time zones to know this. Make sure you eat something before you go to sleep."

"I will. Promise."

"I love you, Lilly."

"I love you, too."

Lilly hung up the phone. "Laurel!" she called. Laurel came bounding down the stairs. She appeared to be bursting at the seams.

"Guess what! You'll never guess. Drew called me and he

wants to go out again tomorrow night!" She let out a little squeal of excitement.

"Wow. That was fast. You said yes, I assume?" Lilly smiled.

"Of course! We're going to dinner and then maybe a movie or something."

"That sounds like fun. Make sure you're done with your schoolwork before you go out."

"I will. I'll spend the morning at school. Then I'll study here for a while before he picks me up. When is Tighe getting here?"

Lilly had completely forgotten that Tighe was coming home. Beau had agreed to pick him up since his truck needed repairs. She might have to reschedule her plans with Hassan.

"I haven't even asked him. I'll call him in the morning and see what his plans are."

Lilly fixed a sandwich from the slim pickings in the fridge, then went straight to bed. She was beginning to formulate a plan for the next day, and if she could manage it so she could talk to Drew for a few minutes, that might fit into her plan rather nicely.

The next morning Lilly texted Tighe before she went to work.

Still planning to come home today?

To her surprise, he texted back right away.

Yes

What time will you be here?

Mid afternoon

Will you be home for dinner?

Actually I wanted to talk to you about that

Uh-oh. What is that supposed to mean?
OK. What do you want to talk about?

I've been seeing this girl

That's nice. What's her name?

Sally Anne

The one who was helping you study?

Yeah she's really smart

So what do you want to talk about?

I was wondering if she could come home with me for a few days

Ooohhh no. That is not happening.
I don't think that's a good idea.

Why not?

I don't mind if she comes to visit at some point, but staying overnight is not an option.

Why not?

Do I have to spell it out? I'm too young to be a grandmother.

MOM SHE WON'T GET PREGNANT

YOU'RE DARNED RIGHT.

Can she stay at Noley's house?

No. I'm not interrupting her honeymoon to ask if a total stranger can stay at her house.

This is stupid. Sally Anne is really really nice

I don't doubt it. I'm sure she's very sweet. But no overnight stays.

Fine. When can she visit?

Where's she from?

Denver

She's welcome to spend the day anytime she wants.

Today?

So you'd come home this morning?

Yeah and she'd stay the rest of the day

Does she have a car or would we have to take her to Denver?

She has a car so she would bring me home and then drive herself home. I've already told Dad so he doesn't have to pick me up.

I love it when Beau knows the plan before I do.
All right. That's fine. So I'll see you later. What do you want for dinner?

I was thinking I would take her out somewhere.

So much for a welcome-home dinner with my son.

Okay. Then I'll keep my dinner plans with Hassan. When will I meet her?

I'll bring her to the store

Okay. If Laurel isn't home when you get there, no funny business.

MOM STOP

Love you.

Love u 2

*L*illy slumped against the kitchen counter. A girlfriend serious enough to come to Juniper Junction and meet the family. *Oh, dear. This is a whole new level of anxiety.*

She got ready for work and she and Laurel left at the same time. "Oh, Laur, Tighe's coming home this morning and he's bringing a friend."

"I know. Sally Anne. She's really cool."

"You've met her?"

"Not in person, but we follow each other on social media."

"So he told you he's bringing Sally Anne home?"

"Yeah."

I really am *the last to know anything around here.*

"How long is she going to stay?" Laurel asked.

"Not as long as he wants her to."

"Why not?"

"Because."

"Because why?"

"Are you four or nineteen? Anyway, I'd like you to be here when they get here."

Laurel gave her mother a suspicious look. "Why? Tighe's old enough to be by himself."

"I agree. It's the *not* being by himself that is the problem."

"Oh, Mom. That's ridiculous. Nothing's going to happen."

"It definitely won't if you're here. So be here by eleven, please."

"That's so embarrassing."

"You have no reason to be embarrassed. You're just doing what I'm telling you to do."

"Well, then, you should be embarrassed."

"I'm a mom. Embarrassing myself is my superpower."

Laurel let out a beleaguered sigh and slung her backpack over her shoulder. "All right. I'll be back by eleven."

Lilly went to work. As soon as she saw Harry she began to pepper him with questions. "Harry, how old were you when you met Alice?"

"Twenty-five. Why?"

"Because Tighe's bringing home a girlfriend and I'm terrified. How soon did you know Alice was The One?"

"Immediately."

"How long did you wait before introducing her to your family?"

"A while, but mostly because my parents live in Arizona."

"And you don't have much to do with Alice's family, right?"

"No, because they're weird. She'd be the first one to tell you that."

"Did you have any girlfriends when you were around twenty?"

"Plenty. I mean, I don't want to brag, but I went out with lots of girls."

Lilly had to stop herself, as she had while texting Tighe, from reminding Harry that the females of the species were called "women" by the time they were twenty. Not "girls."

"Okay. So you were just having fun, right?"

"I have to be honest, boss. This is making me a little uncomfortable."

"I'm sorry, Harry. I didn't mean to make you uncomfortable. It's just that I'm so nervous and you're the only man I know who's young enough to vividly remember being twenty."

"Don't worry about him, Lilly. He'll be fine. You've raised a good kid."

"Thanks, Harry. I wish I could stop worrying."

"But that's how it is with kids, isn't it? Once you have a child, you worry, no matter how old they are. That's what parents do."

"For someone without children, you seem to have it all figured out."

"My parents worry about me. That's how I know."

"Thanks, Harry. I'm sorry for making you uncomfortable."

"All in a day's work, boss." He grinned and Lilly knew she had been forgiven.

CHAPTER 47

The shop was busy that day, but a little before lunchtime Tighe came into the store wearing a wide smile. A pretty young woman with long brown hair and glasses was beside him. Lilly came out from behind the counter and gave him a big hug.

When she had finally let him go, he gestured toward Sally Anne. "Mom, this is Sally Anne." Lilly didn't know whether to hug her or shake hands, so she opted to go conservative and shake hands.

"It's so nice to meet you, Sally Anne."

"Thank you, Mrs. Carlsen. It's nice to meet you, too."

"I thought I would take her over to meet Dad."

"That would be nice. I'm sure he'd like that." Lilly suddenly felt shy. What was Sally Anne thinking about her? Was she mad that Lilly had nixed their plan for a longer stay in Juniper Junction? Her tongue appeared to be tied in knots.

Harry came over and Tighe introduced him to Sally Anne. Harry shook hands with her, too, and chatted amiably with both of them. Lilly was grateful to him for stepping in and doing the talking. He asked about Sally Anne's major, her minor, her thoughts about the college, and her hometown of Denver. Lilly listened to her responses, which were friendly and conveyed a great sense of humor.

I like her, she thought. *I'm still not ready to be a grandmother, but she's a nice young woman, thank God.*

"Well, I think we'll head out," Tighe said after several minutes. "We're going to go meet Dad and then have lunch."

Sally Anne nodded and held out her hand to Lilly again. Lilly took it and told Sally Anne how nice it had been to meet her. She meant it.

After Tighe and Sally Anne had left, Lilly grinned at Harry. "You saved me again, Harry. Thanks."

"No problem." His grin mirrored hers.

Thank goodness for Harry.

The afternoon passed quickly and after Lilly closed up the shop she went home to wait for Hassan.

When he arrived she slid into the passenger seat of his car. He leaned over, kissed her, and said, "I'm glad you remembered to wear a coat. It's getting chilly."

"Can't you tell me where we're going?"

"Not yet. You'll see."

After a quick dinner of club sandwiches and potato chips, they went to Bev's house.

"I'm telling you now, don't be shocked by what you see when we go in there," Lilly warned as they pulled up to the curb.

"I will probably be shocked, but I won't let on. Promise." He came around to the passenger side of the car and closed the door after Lilly got out. He took her hand and they went to the front door together.

Nikki greeted them with a smile. "I'm glad to see you both. Have you rested up, Lilly? I'm feeling much better. One more good night's sleep to recover from the emergency room visit and I should be as good as new."

"Me, too. How's Mom?" Lilly spoke in a low voice. She could

see Bev's profile—she was sitting in her chair in the living room. Her head listed to one side and she looked worn out. If she made a move to try to stand up, any of them could be by her side before she could go anywhere.

"She's been feeling a little better today. She even wanted to play cards this afternoon. I've been making sure she's eating several times a day, even if it's just a bite of fruit or a little piece of cheese. No more fainting spells, so that's good."

Lilly let out a long breath. She hadn't realized how much she was dreading Nikki's report, and she was relieved to hear that Bev seemed to be improving.

"And how does she look today? I can't see her face from here."

"About the same as yesterday." Nikki gave Lilly and Hassan a sad smile. "If it makes you feel any better, it looks far worse than it feels. I mean, she's in pain, but to look at her you'd wonder how she's still alive."

"That actually does make me feel a little better," Lilly said. She glanced at Hassan. "Ready to go in?"

He nodded and she led the way into the living room.

"Hi, Mom." She used the brightest voice she could muster.

Hassan dragged a chair over to Bev and sat down so he could look right at her. To his credit, he didn't flinch or even blink when he saw her face. He reached for her hand and held it in his.

"I'm glad to see you, Bev. I've been worried about you. How are you doing?"

Bev stared at him for several moments while Lilly held her breath. Finally Bev's face registered recognition.

CHAPTER 48

"I'm fine, Hassan. Thank you for coming to see me," she mumbled.

He gave her a broad smile and squeezed her hand. "It's my pleasure, Bev. What have you been up to today?"

"Well, we watched television. And played some cards."

"Did you win?" he asked with a wink.

She gave a mischievous grin. "Of course."

"I knew it. You're a tough one to beat."

He released her hand and smiled up at Lilly. "You want to sit here?"

Lilly could have given him the most passionate kiss in history right then and there. She was so moved by the way he treated her mother that she felt more love for him just then than she ever had, if that was possible. She hoped he could sense how she felt. She sat down in the chair he vacated and proceeded to tell Bev about her day.

"Tighe's coming to see you tomorrow, Mom," she said.

Nikki spoke up. "Oh, I forgot! He was here already. He brought his girlfriend to meet your mom."

"Sally Anne?" *As if he had another girlfriend to introduce.*

"I met her," Bev said suddenly. "Lovely girl." Lilly didn't correct her.

"I thought so, too," Lilly said.

"Hmm." Bev appeared to be done talking. She stared at the television again and ignored Lilly sitting right in front of her.

"Is it bedtime?" Nikki asked. Bev nodded.

"We'll head out, then. I'll see you tomorrow, Mom." Lilly leaned down and kissed Bev's forehead. Her cheek still looked too painful to touch.

Hassan followed suit a moment later and they left.

They sat in silence in Hassan's car for a moment. Finally Lilly spoke. "What did you think?"

"I'll admit I was a little shocked by how she looked. I don't think words can prepare someone for injuries like those. But I was encouraged that she knew who I was and was willing to talk to me for a couple of minutes. She's remarkable."

"The way you talk to her brings tears to my eyes. You're so gentle and so sweet. It was just beautiful to watch you two."

"That's how I always feel when you interact with her. I've known it from the first time I saw you two together. You can tell a lot about a person by watching how they treat their elders. Where I was born, it's one of the true measures of a person's character."

"I wonder how long it'll be before she doesn't know who I am."

Hassan took her hand in his and kissed it. "If and when that happens, you'll deal with it gracefully, like you always do. And we will get through it together. Now, enough sadness. Don't you want to know where we're going?"

"Yes!"

"We're heading up to the top of Zebulon Peak."

"What's up there?"

"The Eta Aquarids meteor shower. It's supposed to be fantastic tonight. A star-gazing club is hosting a watch event."

"How cool!" Lilly turned in her seat to look at him. "What a great idea for a date! How did you hear of it? I've never heard of it."

"I saw it online somewhere and thought it would be fun."

"I can't wait to see it."

CHAPTER 49

The drive up the peak was dark. It was the night of the new moon, which optimized viewing conditions. The road twisted and turned along hairpin curves, so Hassan drove slowly. They didn't talk much because he was so busy concentrating on the drive. When they finally arrived at the top of the peak, the vista opened up. There was a makeshift parking lot, already full of cars, in a clearing along one side of the road.

"I guess I wasn't the only one with this idea," Hassan remarked. He took Lilly's hand and they followed the signs, with the aid of his flashlight, toward the place where the astronomy club had set up telescopes for close-up views.

They found themselves in a large, hushed crowd. Everyone was looking skyward and occasionally pointing. Lilly tried to follow the paths of their fingers, but eventually found it easier to watch the sky herself to see what might be up there.

Hassan stood behind her and put one arm around the front of her shoulders. He would sometimes point if he saw something, but mostly they just watched. The first time Lilly saw a meteor, she had to stop herself from squealing with excitement.

"Look! There's one!" she whispered. She pointed and Hassan tightened his arm around her.

"I see it! That's amazing, isn't it?" He was speaking quietly—quietly enough that Lilly could hear a couple nearby giggling and kissing.

"Honestly," she said to Hassan in a whisper, "can't people just enjoy the view in the sky and keep their lips off each other for just a little while?"

He chuckled and kissed her ear. She grinned.

The giggling was getting annoying. Lilly glared at the people to her left. She couldn't see them and she was sure they couldn't see her, but it made her feel better to glare. Then she looked up at the sky again and scanned the heavens for more shooting stars.

After an hour and a half, they had seen at least two dozen meteors. Lilly sighed happily and leaned back against Hassan's chest.

"Are you getting tired?" he asked.

"Yes, but I wouldn't have missed this for anything."

"You want to head for home?"

"I hate to leave and miss more shooting stars, but I should probably get some sleep." She lowered her voice. "And that couple is driving me crazy."

He took her hand and they took a few steps across the uneven ground. She stumbled a bit, so he took out his flashlight and used it to light the way. "I hate to use this and disturb other people's viewing," he mumbled. "But how are we supposed to get out of here otherwise?"

As he spoke he, too, stumbled forward. The beam of the flashlight swung upward and cast an arc of light over the people who remained, still watching the sky. It flashed on the couple who had been standing next to Lilly and Hassan. They turned around to see what was causing the commotion and Lilly gasped.

Laurel and Drew.

"Are you all right?" Lilly asked Hassan.

He nodded. "I'm fine. Let's go over this way."

"Hold on. It turns out I'm not quite ready to go," she whispered.

Laurel and Drew had turned back the way they had been facing and Lilly could barely see Drew nibbling on Laurel's neck. She marched up to the young couple and tapped Laurel's shoulder.

Laurel jumped, startled, and turned around. "Mom!" she said a little too loudly. Several stargazers turned around to *shush* her. She lowered her voice. "What are you doing here?"

"Stargazing, just like you're supposed to be doing. But it didn't sound to me like much stargazing was going on."

"I'm sorry about that, Mrs. Carlsen," Drew said.

Lilly acknowledged his words with a nod. "Laurel, it's time to go home."

"I'm not ready."

"Yes, you are. We need to have a little talk."

"Mom, you're embarrassing me."

"You did a good job of that yourself. You're going home."

"Ugh. All right. At least let Drew drive me home. It's not fair if I have to go home with you and Hassan."

Lilly stood with her hands on her hips, thinking. She didn't want to make a scene here, but she didn't trust Laurel and Drew in Drew's car.

"Fine. He can drive you, but we're following you home. Come on, we're leaving."

Laurel let out a disgusted sniff and followed Lilly away from the small crowd. "Do you mind taking me home now, Drew?" she asked over her shoulder.

"Not at all. Again, I'm sorry about this, Mrs. Carlsen."

"Thank you. Now let's get going before we disturb anyone else."

Hassan kept the flashlight's beam on the ground and everyone followed him to the parking lot, Lilly bringing up the rear so she could keep an eye on the young lovebirds.

Drew slid behind the wheel of his car while Laurel climbed into the passenger seat. She scowled at Lilly. "You're following us?"

"Don't give me that look, Laurel. And yes, we're following you." She shifted her gaze to Drew. "Don't drive too fast."

"I won't, ma'am."

"And don't call me that."

Drew looked down at the steering wheel and said nothing.

CHAPTER 50

*L*illy and Hassan got into Hassan's car and pulled up behind Drew. "Are you being a little tough on her?" Hassan asked gently.

"No. Honestly, if I had ever behaved like that and my mother saw me, she would have knocked me right into the next week."

"She would, you're right," he said with a chuckle. "But don't forget, they're young. Lots of kids behave like that."

"I know," Lilly said with a sigh. "I just didn't expect Laurel to be one of them. It was disgusting."

Drew led the way back to Juniper Junction. Lilly had hoped that the drive would calm her down, but she was still fuming when Hassan pulled up in front of her house. Laurel was already waiting for her on the sidewalk.

She leaned over and kissed Hassan lightly on the lips. "Wish me luck."

"Good luck. And don't forget, she's just a kid."

"A kid with a lesson to learn."

"Let me know how it goes." Hassan pulled away from the curb. Drew had already left.

Laurel was glaring at Lilly. "That was so embarrassing, Mom."

"Don't start." She pointed at the front door. "Inside."

Laurel stomped up the steps. Lilly unlocked the door and Barney leapt around the vestibule to greet them. Lilly laughed in spite of herself. "Barney, we missed you, too."

Laurel knelt down on the floor to hug the dog.

"Sit." Lilly's instruction was to Laurel, not Barney.

Laurel sat on the sofa and gave her mother a baleful look.

"This will go much better if you don't look daggers at me like that," Lilly said. "I'm already in a bad mood and it's only going to get worse if you don't change your attitude."

Laurel managed to wipe the look off her face. She sighed and sat back. "All right. What do you want to tell me?"

Hassan's words echoed in Lilly's ears. She wanted to kick herself for listening to advice from a man with no children, but he had a point.

"Laurel, I get it. You're young, you've got a new boyfriend, you don't care who knows it. But really, to behave that way in a public place is just unacceptable. It was gross. I had to listen to those wet, sucking noises the whole time I was on the peak. It ruined my enjoyment of the meteor shower."

"*Ruined* it? Really?"

Lilly ignored the sass in Laurel's voice. "Yes, really. I would have enjoyed it so much more if I hadn't been subjected to the displays of lust playing out next to me." Laurel squirmed at Lilly's words.

"I'm sorry," she finally mumbled.

"Just don't do it again. It's fine to kiss Drew, but when you're in public you need to take it down a notch. Or two. Or three."

Laurel rolled her eyes. "Fine. Can I go upstairs?"

"Not just yet. So that I'm convinced you have learned your lesson, you can't see Drew for a week."

"That's not fair!" Laurel cried.

"Would you rather I come up with something better?"

"No."

"All right, then. One week. Then you may see him again."

"I saw Tighe and Sally Anne eating each other's faces. They were on Main Street."

"This is not about Tighe. It is about you." Lilly made a mental note to have a similar conversation with Tighe. Not that she was about to forget.

Laurel *harrumphed.* "Can I go upstairs now?"

"Yes. Goodnight."

Laurel didn't answer—Lilly hadn't expected her to—and stomped upstairs.

"No stomping or I'll make it two weeks," Lilly called after her. She shook her head as she heard the sound of Laurel exhaling every atom of air in her lungs.

She pulled out her phone and texted Hassan.

Went fine. No seeing Drew for one week. Thanks for the advice or it would have been much worse.

Hassan replied with a heart.

CHAPTER 51

The next morning during a lull in customers Lilly decided to call Tom and see if she could worm any information from him. She called the police station and asked to be patched through to him.

"Tom Toole," he said when he picked up his phone.

"Oh, hi, Tom. This is Lilly Carlsen, Bill's sister."

"Good morning. What can I do for you?"

"I was just calling everyone who was in the wedding party or at the reception to make sure they're okay," she lied. "It was such a horrifying experience."

"I'm fine. Police officers see things like that pretty often."

"I know. I'm glad you haven't suffered from PTSD or anything." She was winging it and it felt lame.

"Have you heard from Bill?"

"No, I haven't talked to him since he left for the airport."

"Oh. I was just wondering how Aruba is."

Lilly laughed. "I've got to assume Aruba is perfect."

"I'm sure you're right. Well, if there's nothing else...."

Lilly had to think fast. What came out of her mouth

surprised her as much as it probably surprised him. "So how long have you and Tisha been seeing each other?"

There was a beat of silence, probably for him to contemplate the rude and nosy nature of the question, before he responded. "Oh, off and on for a little while."

"She's so sweet."

"Yes, she is. A very nice girl." Lilly cringed. *Girl.*

"I was surprised to see her there. It's been years since I saw her last," she said.

"Yes. I know she used to date Bill, but I figured it was long over, so it would be no big deal if she went to the wedding as my date." He cleared his throat. "I guess I probably should have cleared it with Bill first."

"Don't worry about it," Lilly said breezily, as if she had been delighted to see Tisha at the wedding. "After all, he was there to marry Noley, right?" She laughed weakly.

"Exactly what I thought," Tom said. "Well, I do have to go, Lilly. Work's piling up."

"Oh, sorry for taking so much of your time. Thanks, Tom." She hung up. "Waste of time," she said aloud to no one. "He's not about to give me any information." *I should have been more forthright and just asked about the murder and plane investigations,* she thought. *Now what?*

A couple had come into the shop and Harry was waiting on them, so Lilly called Darla next.

"Hi, Darla. It's Lilly Carlsen."

"Oh, hi, Lilly. How are you? How are Bill and Noley?"

"I'm fine. Bill and Noley are in Aruba, so I'm assuming they're fine, too."

"I'm glad to hear it. What's new? Have you heard anything about the investigations?"

"No. In fact, that's why I called you. I was hoping you had heard something."

"I only hear things second-hand from the owners of Juniper

Lake Manor, the Hendersons. And I only hear from them when they come in here. Drew tries to keep me updated, of course, but I gather he doesn't talk to his parents about it much. I heard he and your daughter are dating, by the way. He's a nice kid."

"He seems very nice," Lilly said. "He's respectful to me and Laurel seems to be happy around him." She willed herself not to think about the face-sucking she had witnessed.

"He's quite a catch. I'm sure he'll be my boss one of these days. His parents own a number of other properties, too, but he likes this one the best."

Lilly was glad Darla had mentioned Drew's parents again, since she wanted to steer the conversation in their direction. "Oh? What other properties do they own?"

"Oh, gosh. I'm not even sure of all of them. They own several places between here and Denver, and then a couple of others in neighboring states. I think they have other venues in Wyoming and New Mexico."

"Wow. No wonder they don't get to Juniper Lake Manor very often. I imagine they're pretty busy keeping track of all those places."

"They are, but they live right up the road. I'm surprised they're not here more often. To be honest, I'm glad they don't come in all the time because I sort of have my own ways of doing things and they pretty much leave me alone."

"Have they mentioned anything about the private investigator they've hired?"

"Actually, now that you mention it, yes. Mister Henderson stopped by to leave me the PI's business card so that I could call her directly if I learn anything or so I know who she is if she calls here for any reason."

"Would you mind sharing the PI's name with me? I would like to talk to her, maybe see if she needs to ask me any questions. It's a little odd that she hasn't called me yet, don't you think?"

"I don't know. I don't have any idea which direction she's taking. She's working on both the murder of the caterer and the plane buzzing. I suspect she's investigating the murder first, but maybe she's doing the two things simultaneously. Let me grab her card...." There were some rustling noises and Darla came back on the phone. "Here it is. Celie Wolf." Darla spelled the PI's name, reminded Lilly to pronounce it like the arctic mammal —"sealy," she said—and read off Celie's phone number.

"This is great. I'll get in touch with her as soon as I get a chance," Lilly said. "Thanks, Darla. Would you keep me in the loop if you hear anything?"

"I sure will. And you do the same, okay? I'm dying to know what the police have learned."

CHAPTER 52

*L*illy decided to wait to call the private investigator until later that evening. She spent the rest of the day with customers, adding to her spring decorations, and cleaning the jewelry display cases.

"You've got a lot of energy today, Lilly," Harry remarked.

"I'm trying to get my thoughts in order," Lilly said with a laugh. "Cleaning and organizing helps."

"Why are your thoughts disordered?"

"I'm trying to figure out how everything went down at Bill and Noley's reception. I'm not coming up with much so far."

"Well, what do you have?"

"There's the conversation I had with Brad about Maureen. You and I have already discussed that. I also talked to Darla from Juniper Lake Manor and she gave me the name and number of the private investigator the owners of the place have hired to figure out what the heck happened that night. Apparently she's working on both the murder and the plane incident.

"And finally, I called Tom, who was in the wedding party and works for the Juniper Junction police department, to see what information I could get out of him. It was a big, fat nothing. Apparently he's a much tougher nut to crack than Bill."

"What can I do to help?"

"Well, I'm going to call the PI tonight. Could you do an internet search to see what information you can find about Maureen? I didn't even think to do it. Find out if she's been sued by any of her clients, disgruntled employees, ex-employees, anything you can find. That'll be a good start."

"Got it. I'll do that tonight."

"Thanks, Harry. Tomorrow we can put our heads together and exchange what we've learned."

"Sounds good. Say, how's your mom doing?"

Lilly sighed. "Better, but it's hard to look at her and imagine how much her face must hurt. She was up and around a bit yesterday." She grinned. "She even wanted to play cards with Nikki."

"Your mom is cool."

"Thanks. I'll tell her you said so."

Harry grinned. "Let me know if there's anything I can do to help you, boss. I'm always available to do whatever you need me to do."

"I appreciate that, Harry."

That evening after work Lilly stopped at Bev's house.

"How are you doing, Mom?"

"All right."

"What did you do today?"

"Nothing."

"You just sat in this chair all day?"

Bev nodded, but didn't say anything. A chill snaked its way up Lilly's spine. What if this was the way Bev was going to be from now on? Lilly didn't know how she was going to handle it.

Nikki jumped in. "We played cards this morning, remember, Bev? Old Maid." She glanced at Lilly. Old Maid. Lilly remembered when Bev's poker skills were fearsome.

Lilly nodded and dragged a chair over to where her mom sat in the living room. "Mom, I talked to someone today who said you're cool." She smiled.

Bev shifted her glance from something far away to look at Lilly. She seemed to comprehend what Lilly had said. "I'm cool."

Nikki laughed. "You're way cool, Bev."

Bev smiled just a little. Lilly's heart constricted at the sight.

"Were Laurel or Tighe here to see you today, Mom?"

Bev nodded. "Laurel. And I think Tighe."

"Tighe is still tired from studying for his exams. He was sleeping when I left for work this morning. And Laurel is busy studying for finals. I'm glad she came over."

Bev nodded again. Lilly looked helplessly at Nikki and shrugged. "Is there anything I can do for you, Mom?"

"No, thank you. I love you."

"I love you too, Mom."

CHAPTER 53

When Lilly got home Laurel had made roast chicken for dinner. Lilly slumped into a kitchen chair. "Thanks for making dinner, Laur. I'm exhausted. Is Tighe here?"

"Yeah. He's upstairs."

"I'll call him down for dinner."

"Don't bother," Laurel said. "He's not talking to me and I'm sure he won't eat anything I've made."

"Why are you two not speaking?"

"Because he was being a jerk and I told him that I told you about seeing him and Sally Anne kissing on Main Street."

"This is ridiculous. I'm calling him down here." Lilly went to the stairs. "Tighe!"

"Yeah?"

"Come on down for dinner."

"I'm not hungry," he yelled down.

"Come on down anyway."

A minute later Tighe shuffled into the kitchen. "I don't want dinner." He scowled at Laurel.

"You don't have to eat, but you have to sit and listen to me."

Lilly pointed to the kitchen table. "Set the table first. Then sit down." Tighe did as he was told.

Laurel placed food on two plates, and then set them on the table in her spot and in Lilly's spot. "Are you sure you don't want any?" she asked Tighe.

He scowled at her again, but didn't answer.

"Your sister asked you a question."

"I know."

"Then answer her."

"I'm not speaking to her."

Lilly let out a beleaguered sigh. "Sit down, both of you. And keep your mouths shut until I'm done talking."

Both kids glared at her with raised eyebrows. They were more alike than they realized.

"I realize both of you are in love, but there are certain things that are unacceptable to do in public, even between people in love."

Laurel sighed. "Mom—"

"I'm still talking, Laurel. Sucking the face off a loved one in public is unacceptable. Even if it's dark out. I don't care how young or old you are. You will not do it. Is that clear? Keep public displays of affection to a minimum and avoid grossing out the people around you. Tighe, it is not news to me that you and Sally Anne were doing that in public. I fully expected it. Laurel, same with you, except I was forced to witness it. Now, I want the two of you to start talking to each other again. Tighe, eat something."

Laurel and Tighe looked at each other. Tighe pushed away from the table and helped himself to a plate of food. He sat down again and they ate dinner together. It was silent, but not a stressful silence.

"This is good, Laur," he said.

"Thanks." She grinned at him.

Lilly exhaled with relief. That's the most a mother could hope for—that her children were friends.

After dinner she pulled up the number of the private investigator. She dialed it without giving too much thought to the questions she was going to ask.

"Wolf Investigations," a voice answered.

"Hi. I'd like to speak with Celie Wolf."

"Speaking."

"Hello, Ms. Wolf. My name is Lilly Carlsen. It was my brother's wedding that's been in the news. You know, the one where the caterer died and the plane buzzed the reception?"

"Yes. Thank you for calling. Your name is on my list of people to contact. That must have been quite a reception."

"An understatement if I ever heard one."

"Are you able to meet with me in person, say, for coffee sometime tomorrow?"

"Yes. I can ask my assistant to watch my shop for me while I talk to you."

They arranged to meet at a little coffee shop on Main Street the following day and Lilly hung up. This would give her some time to think about the information she wanted to learn, so before going to bed that night she wrote down the questions she wanted to ask the investigator:

Why was she hired to investigate the incidents, instead of leaving the cases to the police?

What had she learned so far?

Did she think the two incidents were related?

What did she know about Maureen?

Has she received word of a missing or stolen private plane?

Does she have any idea who the pilot might have been?

Does she know whether the pilot suffered injuries as a result of the crash?

If so, is the pilot expected to survive?

What are the Hendersons like?

The last question was purely to satisfy her own curiosity about the family of the young man her daughter was dating.

After coming up with her preliminary list, Lilly called Hassan to chat about their respective days, and then went to bed.

CHAPTER 54

She met Celie the next day around mid-morning. She was at the coffee shop at the appointed hour after leaving Harry in charge of the jewelry shop, saying she didn't have any idea how long this meeting would take.

Celie was already there, waiting for her at a table in the back of the shop, her back to the wall. She waved when she caught Lilly's eye.

Lilly approached her and held out her hand. "I'm Lilly," she said with a smile.

"I know. I recognize you from photos online."

That's creepy, thought Lilly.

She sat down across from Celie; the server was at her side almost immediately. "I'll take a decaf, cream, no sugar," she said. The server looked at Celie, who ordered the same thing.

While they waited for their beverages, they made small talk about the weather, the pros and cons of a May wedding in Colorado, and Lilly's shop. When the server had brought their coffees, she left and Celie moved her chair closer to the table. She leaned in to speak.

"So you planned the wedding with the help of the staff at Juniper Lake Manor."

"That's correct. The bride is my best friend and the groom is my brother."

"Yes, I know."

"Oh, of course. I forgot you're a PI."

Celie smiled. "Do you have any thoughts about who could have killed the caterer, Maureen Davies?"

"No. I was hoping you had some ideas. I talked to one of her employees, a Brad—"

"That would be Brad Salisbury."

"I assume so. He said they had been dating and that they were taking a break. It's possible that he could have killed her out of anger for breaking off their relationship."

Celie nodded and Lilly leaned forward to mirror Celie's position. "May I ask what you've been able to find out about Maureen?"

"I also spoke to Brad Salisbury, who confirmed it was Maureen who broke off the relationship. He had also seen Maureen with another man recently in an embrace that seemed more than platonic."

"Oh. I didn't ask him about that."

"I also found out that Brad Salisbury has a prior arrest for disturbing the peace. A domestic disturbance."

Lilly raised her eyebrows in surprise. "Did it involve Maureen?"

"No. A previous girlfriend."

Lilly pulled a face. "So Brad has a history with the police."

"It seems so."

"Interesting. Have you learned anything about the pilot?"

"Not yet. I'm concentrating on the caterer's murder first for two reasons: first, we have a confirmed dead body. And second, it's the more serious offense that took place on my clients' property."

"Of course. I didn't know if you had learned whether the two incidents were possibly related."

"Not that I've been able to determine. Tell me, do you know anyone with a pilot's license?"

Lilly was taken aback by the question. Was this woman suggesting that Lilly knew something about the plane buzzing?

Celie hastened to assure Lilly otherwise. "I'm not accusing you of anything, of course. I'm just trying to get an idea whether anyone at the wedding reception knows any pilots. It seems logical that the plane buzzing was directed at someone in the wedding party because it took place while the group was gathered for photos at the reception."

"I had that same thought. It seemed perfectly timed to coordinate with the photos."

"Exactly. So do you know anyone?"

Lilly sat back again and thought for a full minute. "I must know people with pilots' licenses. I mean, it's not such an unusual thing around here. But I can't think of anyone off the top of my head."

"Would you let me know if you think of anyone?"

"Sure. Would you be able to keep me in the loop on this thing? I'm perfectly willing to help you in any way I can."

Celie nodded, but didn't say anything.

"So what are the Hendersons like? I've never met them before."

"I assume you're asking me because their son is dating your daughter?"

This woman is good.

Lilly gave Celie a sheepish grin. "Since you guessed, yes."

Celie smiled. "They seem to be nice people. They hired me, as you can imagine, because they want to avoid as much negative publicity as possible. They're hoping I can figure out who did it before the police can and put a lid on the bad press flying around the ether."

"Do you think you can figure it out before the police do?"

Celie shrugged. "I don't know, but I'm determined to try. The police have greater manpower, so to speak, but I have the resources of the Henderson family behind me. I can learn a lot with my budget."

"That makes sense. Is there anything specific you'd like me to help you with?"

"If you could remember the name of anyone you may know with a pilot's license, that would help me. I could cross-check it with my list of all the pilots registered in Colorado."

"I'll try to remember. It's not a conversation I remember having with anyone, but there have got to be people I know with licenses."

"Also, any information you could give me about the wedding party members would be helpful. I have my own sources, of course, but if it's information that's very private or on the secretive side, it might take me a little longer to unearth it."

"If I come across anything, I'll let you know," Lilly said.

She left their meeting with the feeling that she had taken an unpaid job as the PI's assistant.

CHAPTER 55

When Lilly got back to the shop Harry wanted to know how the meeting had gone.

"Honestly, I don't know, Harry. I went in there thinking I could worm some information out of her, and I think I ended up getting information wormed out of me."

Harry let out a low whistle. "She must be good."

"She is. I did manage to find out that Brad, Maureen's assistant, has a prior arrest for a domestic problem—disturbing the peace, to be precise. That has me wondering if he was somehow behind the murder because Maureen had recently broken things off with him. And not only that, but he saw her hugging someone in a way that apparently didn't appear platonic."

"I thought they were just taking a break."

"The phrase 'taking a break' means different things to different people. Some people think it's just a phase and the relationship will pick up where it left off. Others think it's just a coward's way of saying 'we're done, but neither one of us wants to say it out loud.'"

Harry nodded, rubbing his chin. "So you're saying that Brad

might have been afraid he and Maureen wouldn't get back together, so he killed her? Like, if he can't have her, no one can?"

Lilly shrugged. "Anything is possible. I don't know the man, so I can't discount it."

"Do you know anyone who could tell you more about his arrest?"

"Well, there's Bill, but obviously that's not an option. There's also Tom, and he's proven to be very tight-lipped."

"Did you learn anything else?"

"She told me the Hendersons are nice people."

"Who are they?"

"The owners of Juniper Lake Manor, and the parents of the boy dating Laurel right now. They own tons of properties in three states, at least."

"They must be loaded."

"I have no doubt of it."

"Before I forget, I searched Maureen Davies online last night. Nothing much came up—some good reviews, some bad ones—I'm sure you saw her reviews—no lawsuits. Nothing remarkable. Even the bad reviews weren't that bad. People thought Maureen was hard to work with, but their experiences were nothing like yours."

A customer came in just then, followed by many more throughout the day. Lilly was grateful for Juniper Junction's reputation as a beautiful resort. It brought a lot of tourists to the area, no matter the season, and many of them wanted a piece of jewelry as a souvenir of their visit. It kept her busy when she would otherwise go crazy with overthinking things.

After work Lilly drove straight to Bev's house. Nikki was talking to Bev in a quiet, soothing voice when Lilly arrived, and Bev was responding in a garrulous tone. Nikki glanced up at Lilly with a harried look and turned her attention back to Bev, who was again listing to one side. Her head slumped forward a bit.

"Bev, let's get you ready for bed," Nikki said.

"No." That word came out with perfect clarity.

Lilly stood in the doorway, unsure of what to do. Should she offer to help? Should she keep her mouth shut and let Nikki do her job without interference? Should she call Hassan for help in case Nikki couldn't get Bev to move?

Nikki put her hand on Bev's arm. "Bev, Lilly came to see you."

Lilly hoped that was her cue to step forward and crouch down to eye-level with her mom. The bruises on Bev's face were a mottled yellow. Lilly suppressed a wince. "Hi, Mom. What's going on?"

"I'm mad." The phrase came out loud and clear.

"You're mad? Why?"

Bev clamped her lips shut. Lilly looked up at Nikki, who was standing and stretching her neck.

"She's upset because I've been trying to get her to eat and she's not hungry."

Lilly turned back to her mother. "Mom, you have to eat. Maybe just a little bite of something? Or a sip of a milkshake? Would you like me to run out and get you a milkshake?"

Bev didn't answer verbally, but managed to shake her head from side to side.

"All right. You don't have to eat. But if you faint because you haven't eaten enough, we're going to have to take you back to the hospital. They'll have to feed you with an IV and you might have to stay there for a day or two. That's why we try to get you to eat here at home."

Bev glared at her. Lilly nudged closer to Nikki. "I have an idea," she whispered.

CHAPTER 56

"Huh?" Bev asked in a loud voice.

"Nothing, Mom. I'm just chatting with Nikki." Nikki watched as Lilly pulled out her cell phone. She texted Tighe and Laurel in their family chat.

Too bad if Mom isn't supposed to drink in the evening, she thought.

Can you come on over to Gran's and bring milkshakes for you two and her?

She showed the text to Nikki, who nodded and grinned.

Both kids responded in a matter of seconds, saying they'd be right over.

What flavor? Laurel asked.

Chocolate for Gran.

Lilly, Nikki, and Bev sat in silence, watching the television. Lilly wasn't paying attention to it, and she suspected neither Nikki nor Bev was, either. To her relief, not ten minutes later, Tighe and Laurel knocked on the front door of Bev's house. Lilly hurried to open it.

"Thanks for getting here so fast," she said quietly. Both kids looked concerned.

"What's wrong?" Tighe asked.

"She's in a mood. And she's refusing to eat. I thought maybe if you two showed up with food, she might show some interest in eating. Sometimes you guys are the only ones who can get her to do something."

"I hope it works," Laurel said. She went into the living room, followed by Tighe and Lilly.

"Hi, Gran," the kids said in unison.

Bev looked toward them, not an easy feat with her head bent down, and smiled. Lilly and Nikki exchanged pleased glances.

"We brought you a chocolate shake," Tighe said. He held up Bev's shake. "Want some?" To Lilly's delight, Bev nodded. Nikki held out her hand to Tighe.

"Here. I can put that in a cup. It might be easier for her to drink it that way."

"No," Bev said.

"Do you want to drink it with the straw?" Nikki asked. She sounded surprised. Bev nodded.

Tighe handed her the milkshake and unwrapped the paper straw that had come with it. He stuck the straw into the lid of the shake. She lifted the shake with hands that trembled. She brought the shake to her lips and faltered as she tried to get the straw into her mouth.

Laurel and Tighe sat down on the floor on either side of her, the way they used to when they were younger. Both of them slurped on their shakes, pretending not to notice that Bev was having a hard time. Lilly was impressed. They weren't rushing to help her, but instead letting her do the work for herself. She had a feeling their instincts were better than her own. Her fingers were practically itching to reach out and help Bev.

After what seemed like an hour, but was in fact only about thirty seconds, Bev got the straw in her mouth. She took a sip of the milkshake and smacked her lips. "Good. Cold," she said. She smiled at the kids. "What kinds?" She tried nodding toward their drinks.

"I got strawberry," Laurel said.

"I got cookies and cream," Tighe said. "Want to try it?"

Bev shook her head and smiled again. After that everyone seemed more relaxed. Lilly and Nikki sat on the sofa and the kids chatted with their grandmother, telling her about the things they did all day. Tighe told her about the job he had gotten for the summer at a nearby state park.

After a little while, Bev began to nod forward. She looked exhausted. She had taken several sips of the milkshake, and struggling to get the straw into her mouth had probably not helped. Still, Lilly was glad she had stood back and allowed Bev to do it herself. "Is it time to get ready for bed, Mom?" she asked. Bev nodded slightly. "Okay, the kids and I will head out. I'm glad they got a chance to see you tonight."

Bev smiled and Lilly and the kids kissed her goodnight.

"Thanks, Lilly. Getting Tighe and Laurel to bring food over was a great idea. We'll have to remember that in the future if she refuses to eat."

"Now that Tighe is home for the summer and Laurel will only be taking one class, we can start leaning on them a little more to spend time with her. They love to come over here, of course, but sometimes they get busy with other things."

Lilly left with a promise to return the following evening.

CHAPTER 57

When she got home she read a book until she was ready for bed. The kids had gone upstairs right after getting home from Bev's, but now Tighe came down in search of Lilly. He sat down next to her on the sofa.

"Hey, Mom."

"Hi. Thanks again for going over to Gran's. Sometimes I have to get sneaky with her, and you and Laurel are always able to get her to do what Nikki and I can't."

"That's okay. Do you think she's going to be okay?"

Lilly sat back and exhaled heavily. "She's not getting any better. In fact, she seems to have declined more quickly than usual lately. We just keep on doing what we're doing and hope that she's able to stay in her house for as long as possible."

"You think she might have to go to a nursing home?" Tighe looked at his mother with a mixture of sadness and trepidation.

"I wouldn't be surprised. At some point she'll need more care than Nikki can provide in Gran's house, and certainly more than any of us could provide without professional help."

"I don't want to think about it."

"I don't either, believe me. But we can't ignore what's going on, either. Luckily, Uncle Bill and I are close and we talk all the time. We're typically on the same page when it comes to Gran's care. We're going to have to make a decision at some point, and if Gran keeps declining at the rate she has, that's going to be sooner rather than later."

Tighe leaned back, too. "I feel sorry for her."

"I do, too. But I don't know that she would want us to feel sorry for her. Just after she was diagnosed, she told me so. She said she knew there would be times when we would all want to cry, but she didn't want us to cry. I vividly remember her saying that every time we wanted to cry, we should think of something funny she did instead."

"Remember the time she told Uncle Bill that if he ever brought her white chocolate again, she would cut him out of her will?" Tighe laughed.

"I remember that! She's always hated white chocolate. Remember the time she hid in the back seat of the car because she didn't want her neighbor to see her at the bra shop? As if every woman her age in Juniper Junction weren't a customer there, too." Lilly was laughing, too.

Laurel came downstairs. "What's so funny?"

Lilly told her what she and Tighe had been discussing. Laurel started laughing. "Remember that time she entered the poker tournament under a man's name and wore a disguise? The men in charge figured it out so fast because she forgot to leave her purse in the car."

By now everyone was in stitches.

It seemed Bev's advice had been good.

The next day Lilly received a phone call from the lawyer for Maureen's catering business.

"Mrs. Carlsen, one of Maureen's employees asked me to call you because of some dispute over the bill for catering services at a wedding last weekend."

"Yes. It was my brother's wedding and I was in charge of

hiring the caterer. There were several things that didn't go as planned and Maureen was not able to honor her part of the contract."

"Things such as?"

"She wasn't able to adequately provide staffing for the wedding reception according to the terms of the contract. She also failed to provide most of the entrées that people ordered, as well as some of the tapas."

"Let me talk to the executor of the estate and explain the issue. I'll let that person decide what to do about the bill."

"Thank you. Do you mind telling me who the executor is?"

"Brad Salisbury."

Interesting.

"Oh. Did he know he was going to be the executor?"

"That is probably a question for Mister Salisbury."

"Thanks. I'll try to contact him."

CHAPTER 58

That afternoon she found Maureen's business card in her purse and phoned the number listed.

"Maureen's Catering, Brad speaking."

"Hi, Brad. This is Lilly Carlsen. I spoke to you about—"

"Oh, yeah. I remember you. You came in asking for a discount after your brother's wedding, right?"

"Yes. I just got off the phone with the estate's lawyer and he told me that since you're the executor, I need to talk to you about getting some money knocked off the bill."

"Yeah."

"So have you given any thought to my bill?"

"Actually, yes. I've had a look at the contract and it doesn't say anywhere that Maureen agreed to provide a certain number of employees for the wedding."

"That's correct. But it *does* state that sufficient staff would be provided in order to serve guests quickly and efficiently."

"And you're saying that didn't happen?"

"Yes."

"Wasn't there something about food, too?"

"Yes. She wasn't able to provide most of the food I ordered."

"But she provided a substitute, right?"

"Yes. But it was fish. People ordered beef. When you order beef and you get fish, are you happy about it?"

"I love fish."

"So do I, but not everyone does. And besides that, fish cannot cost the same as the beef."

"You'd be surprised."

"I'm sure I would."

"It sounds to me like you're balking at the bill after agreeing to the price, Mrs. Carlsen."

"You know that's not true. I'm balking at the bill because Maureen failed to fulfill the two key parts of the contract: the staffing and the food."

"I'm not going to authorize the estate to accept anything less than the price you and Maureen agreed to."

"Mister Salisbury, did you know you had been named executor of the estate?"

"I don't see how that's any of your business."

"Are you planning on continuing Maureen's catering business?"

"I haven't decided."

"You wouldn't want to start out with a one-star review," Lilly said.

"And you would do well not to threaten me, Mrs. Carlsen. I know all about people like you."

"And what do you mean by that?"

"People who agree to one thing and then renege on the deal." He disconnected the call.

Lilly was seeing red. Her fists, she noticed suddenly, were white balls of knuckle. She tried to relax by shaking her hands and rolling her head back and forth. "Fine," she said aloud to no one. "I'll pay the stupid bill. It isn't worth this kind of aggravation."

She stormed into the front of the shop, where Harry was cleaning a watch part for a customer.

"What's wrong, Lilly?" he asked.

"I'll tell you what's wrong. Brad Salisbury is a little toad. That's what's wrong."

"What did he do?"

"He is so rude. And he refuses to adjust the catering bill for the reception."

"Honestly, Lilly, with everything that was going on, I would be surprised if a single person even noticed the food or how many people were or weren't there to serve it."

"Do you think I'm overreacting?"

"Maybe just a teensy bit. That was a pretty stressful evening. I don't blame you for wanting something to go right. But, as Alice has told me a thousand times, something always goes wrong at wedding receptions. And, as she also tells me, you just have to get over it and move on."

"She's a keeper, you know." Lilly could feel her face getting hot, and very likely turning every shade of pink. "And she's right. I shouldn't be so petty. The executor has enough to deal with without me all but begging for a discount. I'm going to go ahead and pay the bill in full. I should call him back and apologize. And I will, but not today. I'm probably the last person he wants to talk to right now."

"Do you feel better?" asked Harry.

She gave him a rueful smile. "Yes. Thank you, Harry. This isn't the first time you've talked some sense into this stubborn, thick head of mine."

"All in a day's work, boss."

CHAPTER 59

*L*illy texted Hassan.

Dinner tonight? My house?

It only took him a moment to respond.

Sure! What time?

7, she replied. He sent her a happy face and a heart.

She stopped at the grocery store on her way home from work and picked up the ingredients she would need to whip up a meal of salmon, roasted carrots, and a springtime salad.

She got cooking as soon as she arrived at home. The carrots went into the oven, and while they roasted she tossed the salad and prepared the fish. When the carrots had just ten minutes left, she put the salmon on the stove, sprinkled it with lemon-pepper, and gave it a quick sauté. Hassan came in during the cooking frenzy and offered to help, but she asked him to pour them some wine instead. She grinned as she worked. "Having someone in the house who can cook better than I can has done wonders for my own cooking skills," she said. "How many times was Laurel watching Noley cook and I didn't even realize she was paying attention?"

"Kids watch and listen far more than we give them credit for, I think," Hassan said.

They clinked glasses and each took a sip. "How was your day?" Hassan asked.

"All right. I'm trying to make some headway in figuring out what happened at the wedding and I'm not getting very far. In fact, I've gotten practically nowhere."

"Who did you talk to today?"

"Brad Salisbury, Maureen's assistant, ex-boyfriend, and executor of her estate."

"Ex-boyfriend?"

"Yes. They were taking a break. Who knows if they would have gotten back together?"

"What do you know about him?"

"He looks to be in his mid- to late-twenties. He looks like a body builder. He graduated from the culinary program at the community college when Maureen did. That's where they met, apparently. According to him, he's been trying to honor the contracts Maureen made before she died."

"Would he have any reason to want her dead?"

"Only the obvious one that I can think of—he might have been afraid she was going to make their 'break' permanent and he wasn't going to let anyone else have her. He apparently saw her hugging someone and thought there was more to it than friendship. Or maybe he was afraid she would fire him from the catering service if they weren't dating. Keeping him on the payroll would certainly make things awkward, and maybe he was afraid he was about to lose his girlfriend *and* his job. He mentioned that Maureen's catering business was doing very well, though frankly, with service like she gave us, I don't know how."

"People have been murdered for lesser reasons," Hassan said.

"I also know he's been in trouble with the law before. A domestic issue."

"Did you talk to someone in the police department?"

"Well, yes. I talked to Tom, who was no help at all. I learned about Brad's trouble with the law from Celie Wolf, the private investigator hired by the Hendersons. They're the owners of Juniper Lake Manor and a whole slew of other places."

"Okay, let's think about suspects other than Brad Salisbury. Who else might have had a motive to kill Maureen?"

"Well, Harry looked online and it doesn't look like any clients had any reason to be too mad at her. People thought she was hard to work with, but that's it. As for the Juniper Lake Manor staff, it doesn't look likely. The wedding reception was the first time Darla had met her, so Maureen had never catered an event there before. I assume none of the staff had met Maureen before that night, either."

"You know what assuming does...."

CHAPTER 60

"You're right. I should double-check that information with Darla. Maybe someone on staff did know Maureen prior to Saturday." Lilly sat with her chin in her hand.

"And what about the guests?"

"I don't know about them, either. I've been sort of focused on Brad. But I should try to find out. It seems like the police would be working on that angle, right? And if they had a suspect in mind, wouldn't that be public information? A person of interest in a crime is public information, isn't it?"

"The person's identity?"

"No, I mean just the fact that there is a person of interest."

"I don't know, Lil." Hassan sounded skeptical.

"Well, maybe I need to reach out to Tom again and ask if there's a person of interest in the case."

"The only people who were at the reception were the guests, the wedding party, the catering staff, and the Juniper Lake Manor staff, right? No strangers?"

"As far as I know. I recognized most of the Juniper Lake Manor staff and Darla certainly didn't mention that there was anyone posing as a staff member. Maureen only brought three people with her, and one of them was Brad. I would recognize the other two if I saw them, but again, I'm sure the police have talked to them."

"I would think the police are still conducting interviews of the wedding guests and wedding party, wouldn't you?"

"It seems logical, unless they've finished talking to everyone and found nothing. They haven't followed up with you, have they?" Hassan shook his head. "They haven't called me back, either."

"That could be because they talked to the members of the wedding party in more depth the night of the wedding," he said.

"That's true. I should call Mallory and ask if they talked to Tisha again."

They sat down to eat. "I wish Juniper Lake Manor had security cameras in the back of the building. This could all be solved so easily," Lilly said with a sigh.

"Where would be the fun in that?" Hassan asked drily.

Lilly smiled. "You enjoy solving puzzles as much as I do."

Hassan had to get home after dinner to take an overseas phone call, so Lilly went to Bev's house. There was no change in Bev's condition. There was no change the following day, either. Since it was a Sunday, Lilly was able to spend most of the day there, and Nikki got a much-deserved break. It made Lilly nervous to have no nurse around, but she enjoyed spending quiet time with her mom.

The next day, though, things weren't as quiet.

CHAPTER 61

*L*illy was at work early when Nikki called. "Your mom doesn't seem to be doing too well this morning. I just wanted to let you know that I'm going to call the doctor to see if they can fit her in today."

"What's the matter?"

"She's just not herself. It's hard to explain. She's listing more than usual, she's refusing to eat anything, and she's complaining of a headache."

"Maybe she has a headache from not eating. I was able to get her to eat a couple of bites of a sandwich yesterday. Did she eat anything after I left her house last night?"

"Suzanne said she didn't have anything. I can usually count on her to eat at least a little bit of breakfast, but she's refusing it today. I'm just a little concerned. I'll let you know if the doctor can squeeze her in."

"Thanks, Nikki."

Lilly had managed to keep her mind and her hands busy for a little while once the store opened, but that was ruined by a visit from Mallory midway through the morning.

Mallory was flushed and out of breath when she came in.

"Hi. I have a favor to ask. I have to close the shop today because Tisha's pretty sick. She needs me to come home. Would one of you be able to run over to the shop after the mail is delivered? I'm expecting a check and I don't want to miss it."

"Sure. I hope Tisha's okay. What's causing her to feel so sick?"

Mallory's face flushed. "She's not physically sick. It's more of a mental sickness. She suffers from depression and she's in pretty bad shape today."

"Oh, I'm so sorry to hear it," Lilly said. She gestured toward Harry. "Let us know if there's anything else we can do to help." Harry nodded enthusiastically.

"Thanks, I will." Mallory tossed a set of keys to Lilly and left the shop quickly.

Lilly's phone rang just a minute later. "What now?"

It was Laurel. "Mom, Drew texted me. He wants to go to the movies tonight. Can I *please* go with him?"

"If I'm not mistaken, it hasn't been a week since you were grounded from seeing him. You and Drew both know that."

"Please?"

"I'm sorry, Laur, but I've got to stick to my guns on this one."

"That's not fair."

"Life isn't fair."

Laurel hung up. Lilly looked at the phone in disbelief. She flexed her thumbs. *Okay, missy, we'll do it your way.*

I'm adding 3 days to your sentence for hanging up on me. Do it one more time and I'll make it a month.

She received a mad face emoji in return. She sighed. "Harry, think very carefully before you and Alice decide to have children."

He grinned. "Problems at home?"

"Almost always."

"We'll keep it in mind."

CHAPTER 62

That afternoon Lilly received a surprise visitor at the shop. She looked up from a document she was reading when the bell above the door jingled. Drew walked in.

"Hi, Mrs. Carlsen."

"Hi, Drew. What brings you in here?" She didn't even bother to hide her surprise.

"Laurel texted me to say that she's been grounded for longer from seeing me."

"That's right."

"I just wanted to apologize and explain that it's all my fault."

"How do you figure?"

"Well, I was the one kissing her at the astronomer club thing the other night. If I hadn't been there, she wouldn't have gotten in trouble."

"Well, that may be true, but kissing requires two people. I appreciate what you're doing, but it's every bit as much her fault as it is yours."

"Is there anything I can do to get you to reconsider?"

"I'm afraid not, Drew. She needs to learn that she can't behave that way in public. She also needs to learn," Lilly added pointedly, "that I will not back down when I ground her. It's a tough lesson, I know, but it's one she's not likely to forget."

"The thing is, my parents would like to meet her."

"I'm sure they'll understand if you explain to them why I'm not letting her meet them right now."

Drew didn't say anything. Lilly raised her eyebrows to indicate that it was his turn to talk.

"They would really like to meet her. They're heading out of town next week and I don't know how long they'll be away."

"I'm sorry, Drew. It's just going to have to wait." *I'll be darned if I'm going to let total strangers dictate when my daughter is grounded.*

He grimaced. "Okay. At least I get an A for effort, huh?"

Lilly nodded. As long as she had Drew right in front of her, she might as well ask him the questions that had been brewing in her mind.

"Drew, could I ask you a couple of questions about the night of my brother's wedding?"

He gave her a wary look. "I guess so."

"Do you know if anyone who works at Juniper Lake Manor had met the caterer, Maureen, before that evening?"

He was silent for a moment. "I don't think so. At least, not that anyone has mentioned to me."

"Did it appear that the Juniper Lake Manor staff and the catering staff were getting along? Was Maureen causing any problems?"

He shrugged. "I didn't notice anyone not getting along. I mean, the JLM staff weren't happy to get bossed around by the caterer, but everyone was just going along and doing their jobs."

"So Maureen was bossing people around?"

"Definitely. Darla was not happy about it. She told me she was going to make sure that Maureen was kept permanently off the list of caterers we use at Juniper Lake Manor."

"Do you know if she shared that information with Maureen?"

"I don't know, but I doubt it. Darla's very professional, so if she was going to say anything to Maureen about it at all, it would have been after the reception, not during it."

"Do you know if the police have talked to the rest of the Juniper Lake Manor staff? Have they talked to you?"

"They haven't talked to me yet. I know they've talked to at least a few other staff members because those guys told me about it, but I haven't spoken to all of them."

Lilly had a sudden hunch. There could be no doubt that the plane buzzing incident would create bad publicity for Juniper Lake Manor. What if a disgruntled and off-duty staff member buzzed the reception just to cause havoc for the venue or its owners?

"Do any of the staff members have a pilot's license?"

"There are a couple. Why do you ask?"

"No reason. Were they working the night of the reception?"

"Yes. Most receptions are all-hands-on-deck. Just to make sure things run smoothly, you know. Only the really tiny ones are not fully staffed."

Lilly nodded. So much for that idea.

Her phone rang again. She looked at the caller ID and saw that it was Nikki.

"I'm sorry, Drew. I have to take this. Please apologize to your parents for me. Maybe Laurel can meet them when they're back from their trip." She hit the talk button on her phone and Drew waved goodbye.

CHAPTER 63

"Hi, Nikki. What's going on?"

"I just talked to your mom's doctor. He'll see her this afternoon. He says it sounds like the rate of her illness is accelerating, but he wants to see her to make sure it's not something else."

Lilly sighed. She had been afraid of this. "Does he want me to be at the appointment?"

"He said that would be wise, yes."

"All right. What time should I be there?"

"One."

"Okay. I'll meet you and Mom at the doctor's office. Thanks, Nikki. See you then."

She hung up. "Harry, do you mind if I leave you alone here for a little while this afternoon? My mom has a doctor's appointment and the doctor wants me to be there. I would have told you sooner, but I didn't know myself until just now."

"No problem. Is she okay?"

"She's getting worse at a rate we hadn't expected. She puts on a brave face when the kids visit, but she's refusing to eat and she hardly speaks at all."

Harry looked at Lilly with dismay. "I'm really sorry to hear that, Lilly."

"That's the problem with this kind of disease. It only gets worse, not better. There's no cure and not much in terms of effective treatments, either."

Harry looked down. "I'm really sorry," he repeated.

"Thanks, Harry." Lilly tried to get back to reading the document she had been perusing when Drew came in, but her concentration was gone. She had a feeling it wouldn't return for a while.

She arrived ten minutes early for the appointment that afternoon. Nikki and Bev were already in the waiting room.

"Hi, Mom." Lilly sidled onto the padded bench where Bev sat. Nikki was on her other side. Bev smiled in a way that looked more like a grimace. Lilly chose to believe it was an attempt at a smile. The three of them sat in silence while they waited for Bev's name to be called.

When the doctor was finally ready for them, Lilly and Nikki helped Bev stand and walk into the office. When she was seated comfortably, the doctor stood so Lilly and Nikki could both sit, too.

"I'm going to take a look at Bev. I don't know how she feels about anyone else in the exam room with her, but one or both of you can stay if you wish and if she wishes it. If you both wait in the waiting room, I'll have one of my nurses come in and assist with the exam. What do you think?"

Lilly squeezed her mom's hand. "Mom, do you want me or Nikki to be in here with you during the exam?"

Bev shook her head ever so slightly.

"Okay. You want us to wait in the waiting room? The doctor will have an assistant to help while he looks you over."

Bev nodded.

Lilly glanced at the doctor to make sure he was noting Bev's inability to respond verbally. He nodded gently at her and she turned back to Bev. "Nikki and I will be in the waiting room, Mom. We'll be in when the doctor is done with his exam." Bev looked at her blankly and Lilly followed Nikki out into the waiting room.

The exam didn't take long. When the nurse called Lilly and Nikki back to the exam room, Lilly moved as if her feet were made of lead. She had a twisty gut feeling that she knew what the doctor was going to say.

And she was right.

CHAPTER 64

Bev's dementia was getting worse, and doing so rapidly. The doctor used the words "moderately severe decline," and indicated that she was showing signs of more significant physical and mental strain. Bev sat listlessly, leaning a bit to one side, while the doctor explained to Lilly what was happening. Bev was going to need more physical, hands-on care in the coming weeks and months. The doctor also told her what to expect as Bev's condition worsened. Lilly wanted to take notes, but she knew this visit was just the first in a long series of visits, so she just listened and tried to take in everything the doctor was saying. She also knew that Nikki had been through this process before with other patients, so she and Bill could lean on her for information and support as time moved forward.

The thought of Bill was paralyzing. She longed to tell him about this visit, but she hated to ruin what was left of his honeymoon with ugly details about Bev's health and prognosis. She would wait to talk to him, and if he was angry with her, then so be it. At least he would have wonderful honeymoon memories, unmarred by worries about things at home.

Nikki drove Bev back home and Lilly followed in her car. Bev seemed to have rallied on the ride home, because when Lilly reached down to help her out of the car, she touched Lilly's hand lightly. "I'll do it."

Lilly smiled to see some spunk from her mom and stepped aside. Nikki kept her hand behind Bev's back as they negotiated the front steps, and Lilly was very pleased to see that Bev made it up by herself, though it took almost two full minutes to go up three steps.

Nikki turned around and gave her a thumbs-up and a smile. Lilly stood at the base of the steps and bid her mom goodbye.

"I'll see you later, Mom. Maybe I can bring the kids over tonight."

Bev turned around and gave a small wave. Lilly could see the light in her eyes from where she stood. *My mom*, thought Lilly, *never ceases to surprise me.*

When she went back to work, she told Harry the bad news and the good news: Bev was getting worse, but she seemed to be okay at the moment. "I'll take every positive thing I can get," she said.

Harry smiled. "I'm glad she's having a good afternoon. Do you think she understood everything the doctor said?"

The question took Lilly by surprise. She hadn't even thought to ask if Bev could comprehend all that the doctor was saying. Part of her hoped she could, because that would mean that she wasn't too far gone. But another part of her hoped she couldn't, because she didn't want her mom to know all the things that were going to happen to her.

"I don't know, Harry. That's something I'll have to ask her nurse." Lilly made a mental note to text Nikki as soon as possible to ask that very question.

"Oh!" Harry exclaimed suddenly. Lilly jumped. "Sorry, boss. I didn't mean to startle you. We forgot to get Mallory's mail. That is, unless you picked it up already."

"No, I didn't. I'm glad you reminded me."

"I can go get it now if you want."

"Don't worry about it, Harry. You've done enough for me for one day. I'll pick it up as soon as we close up shop tonight."

"You sure?"

"Absolutely. If that check came for her, I'll let her know."

When they had locked the shop door that evening and put all the jewelry in the vault, Harry left and Lilly walked up the block to the pottery shop. She smiled to herself. It was a beautiful evening and since the days were getting longer, there was still some bright blue sky overhead.

She squinted when she saw someone standing in front of Mallory's shop. As she got closer, she could see that it was Tom Toole. He wasn't dressed in his uniform, so she presumed he was off-duty.

"Hi, Tom," she said, walking up to him.

"Oh, hi, Lilly." He inclined his head toward the shop door. "I was hoping to be able to talk to Mallory. Do you know where she is?"

"She had to go home earlier in the day. I'm just checking on things for her before I head home myself." She wondered if he knew about Tisha's problem. If he knew, it seemed he would also know that Mallory was taking care of her.

"I've been calling the house and there's been no answer."

"I think Tisha wasn't feeling well. Maybe they've got the ringer off."

"Could be. What's wrong with Tisha, do you know?"

"Um—"

He hastened to add, "We don't date seriously, just once in a while. I'm not part of her inner circle."

"Oh. I'm not precisely sure what's wrong with Tisha, only that she's sick." If Tom wasn't one of Tisha's "inner circle," as he put it, she didn't want to reveal any further information.

"All right, thanks. I'll just keep calling, I guess."

"Good to see you, Tom."

"You, too, Lilly."

Tom sauntered off and Lilly fished in her handbag for the key Mallory had given her earlier. She unlocked the front door of the shop and flicked the light switch on the wall. She quickly locked the door behind her lest anyone walking past think the shop was open, and made her way to the back, where Mallory's office was located.

She didn't like being in the shop alone, even with lights on inside and daylight outside. She put her handbag on Mallory's desk and reached down for the mail on the floor just inside the back door. Like most shops along Main Street, Mallory's shop had a slot in the back office door for mail delivery. Lilly leafed through it quickly, not even glancing at the return addresses, trying to figure out which envelope might hold a check. She found one that looked the part, so she pulled out her phone and texted Mallory.

I think I found the check you're waiting for. Want me to drop it off to you? I'll need your address.

Mallory responded within a few seconds.

That's great. Thanks.

She added her address to the bottom of the text and Lilly replied that she would be there shortly.

It hadn't been Lilly's intention to snoop through Mallory's mail when she accidentally dropped the entire stack of it on the floor. She scooped up the envelopes and was rearranging them so they all faced the same way when she noticed that one of the envelopes was from the Federal Aviation Administration's "Flight Standards District Office" in Denver.

What the what?? Lilly thought. She flipped the envelope over to see if there was any further information on the back. *Why is the FAA writing to Mallory?*

Does she have a pilot's license?

She took her phone out again. Her fingers fumbled in their haste to dial Harry's number, but finally she succeeded in getting hold of him.

"Hi, Lilly. Is something wrong?"

"No, Harry. Everything is fine. I just wondered if you could do something for me tonight."

"Sure. What is it?"

"Can you go online and see if you can find out if Mallory is a pilot?"

There was silence on the other end. Lilly knew the import of her question had been clear to Harry.

"Yeah. I can do that. Give me a minute, will you?"

"I don't need to know right this second. In fact, I'm still in Mallory's shop and I'd like to leave. Take your time and just text me when you figure it out. I think I found the check she's waiting for, so I'm going to drop it off at her house."

"Is that safe?"

"I think so. Anyway, I won't be there long. I need to run over to Mom's house to check on her."

"Okay. I'll get on it."

"Thanks, Harry." She hung up and stacked the mail neatly on Mallory's desk. Then she hurried through the front of the shop to the door, locked it behind her, and returned to her own car behind Juniper Junction Jewels. Fifteen minutes from the time she left the pottery shop, she was delivering the envelope into Mallory's hand.

"Thanks so much, Lilly. I need to get this deposited as soon as possible, so now I'll be able to do it on my way to work tomorrow morning."

"How's Tisha?" Lilly asked.

Mallory sighed. "I don't know if you know anything about depression, Lilly, but this just happens sometimes. She'll snap out of it at some point, but until then it's very upsetting for both her and me."

Lilly nodded. She didn't know much about depression, but it sounded awful.

"I wish I could do something to help," Lilly said.

"Me, too. But unfortunately, there's nothing to do right now. She's on medication and we just have to work through this."

"Oh, before I forget, Tom Toole was out front of your shop when I got there to pick up the mail. He said he's been trying to call here and text Tisha, but there's been no answer."

Mallory frowned. "She told me to shut the ringer off the house phone and she turned off her cell phone. She doesn't want to talk to anyone."

"I figured that was the reason. I just thought I'd let you know that he was asking about her."

"Okay, thanks. I'll tell her. Maybe it'll perk her up to know that a good-looking guy was asking about her."

Lilly smiled. "Well, I hope Tisha feels better very soon. Let me know if there's anything I can do for you."

"I will. Thanks, Lilly."

Lilly walked back to her car, wondering how she could have worked a question about a pilot's license into the conversation. She determined on the way to her mother's house that there was no way she could have asked Mallory about it without being awkward or broadcasting her nosiness.

CHAPTER 66

*B*ev was still in relatively good spirits when Lilly arrived at her house. She couldn't remember where Bill was, or that he had been married just over a week ago, but Lilly was still cheered by her mom's smile and her eyes, which looked brighter than usual.

"I called the kids on my way here, Mom. I haven't been home yet. They're planning to come over after dinner. I can't stay long, but I wanted to stop and see how you're feeling."

"Good."

"I'm glad to hear it. What did you do this afternoon?"

Bev looked at Nikki, who answered Lilly's question. "We played cards for a bit, didn't we, Bev? And we watched an old movie."

Bev smiled. She had always loved old movies. At this point, Lilly didn't know if Bev could follow the plot, but it didn't really matter. What mattered was that her mother was doing something she enjoyed. And she had no idea how her mother could remember the rules of card games, but she was grateful for it.

When it was time for her to leave, she took Nikki aside for just a moment. She spoke in a low voice.

"Nikki, do you think Mom understood what the doctor was saying today?"

Nikki gave her a knowing and sympathetic look. "She may have understood some of it, but it's not likely that she'll remember what he said. I think that's a good thing. A little truth can be helpful, but too much of it is overwhelming."

"I agree. I know it's overwhelming for me. Thanks, Nikki. I'll talk to you tomorrow."

By the time Lilly arrived at home the kids had dinner ready —Monte Cristo sandwiches—and Harry had texted that there was no record of a Mallory Abbott with a pilot's license. She sat down heavily.

"What's wrong, Mom?" Tighe asked.

"I followed a hunch and got nowhere."

"What does that even mean?" asked Laurel.

"It means I thought I had an idea about who could have been piloting that plane last Saturday night, but I was wrong."

"Shouldn't you be leaving that to the police?" Tighe fixed her with an intent gaze.

"Don't worry about me."

"You didn't answer the question," Tighe said.

"You have sort of a knack for getting into trouble," Laurel said.

"Oh, pshaw. I'm not going to get into any trouble. Bill's not even here to keep tabs on me."

"That's what I'm afraid of," Tighe said.

Lilly changed the subject. "I think you'll find Gran in a good frame of mind tonight."

"Should we take her a milkshake?"

"I think we should just plan to do that from now on, at least for as long as we can. There will probably come a time when she can't swallow anymore, so let's spoil her while she still can."

Tighe and Laurel were silent. Lilly recalled Nikki's remark about too much truth and wondered if she had just given the kids too much truth. But the words were out of her mouth, so it was too late to worry about their impact. Besides, any online search of Bev's disease would tell them the same information and much, much more.

"You two get going and I'll do the dishes. Thanks for dinner. It was delicious."

The kids pushed away from the table, still not saying anything, and went upstairs. They came back down a couple of minutes later and left after Lilly gave them money to pay for the milkshakes.

As soon as the kids left she did the dishes and called Hassan.

CHAPTER 67

"Want to come over?" he asked.

"I would love to, but I'm exhausted. I still haven't caught up from being awake all night when we took Mom to the hospital. I'm going to bed as soon as the kids get home."

"Learn anything new today?"

"I had to go pick up Mallory Abbott's mail from the pottery shop and there was a letter from the FAA. I'm wondering if she's a pilot. Harry checked and there's no one by that name with a pilot's license, but she may have a license under another name. I saw that letter and all of a sudden I thought of a possible reason she might have buzzed the reception."

"What's the reason?"

"What if she has a thing for Tom? She mentioned how good-looking she thinks he is. Maybe she was mad that he took her sister as his plus-one instead of her. Maybe he spurned her and she was getting back at him."

Hassan made a *hmm* noise. "That sounds like a lot of maybes. Do we know if Mallory even knew Tom before he picked up Tisha the day of the wedding?"

"No. I'm just making a wild guess."

"Wild guesses are fine as long as you stay safe. Don't be going on any wild goose chases and not telling anyone where you are."

"I won't."

The kids were in better moods when they returned from Bev's house.

"She seemed interested in everything we had to say," Laurel said with a smile. Tighe nodded in agreement. "And she drank a little of the milkshake we took over."

"That's great. I think she had a pretty good day, all things considered," Lilly said.

"Mom, can Sally Anne come up this Saturday?" Tighe asked. Laurel immediately shifted her gaze to Lilly and fixed her with a stare that Lilly could feel boring into her brain.

"Um, well, let's wait until next week, Tighe."

"Why?"

"Well, since you and Sally Anne were a little—ahem—affectionate in public last time you saw her, and since Laurel has to be grounded from seeing Drew for a week, you have to face the same consequence for the same behavior." She tried not to look out of the corner of her eye at the smug look Laurel was sporting. Tighe glared at his sister.

"Okay. Fine." Tighe huffed, but he didn't stalk off upstairs, which, as far as Lilly was concerned, would have been the in-person equivalent of hanging up on her. She glanced at Laurel, who appeared to be just a bit disappointed over Tighe's reaction.

"I'm off to bed, kids. Can someone let Barney out in a little while? I'm still trying to catch up on my sleep from the other night."

"Okay. Goodnight, Mom." Tighe looked up from his phone, where he was texting, and Laurel kissed her cheek.

"G'night, Mom."
Lilly couldn't wait to get to sleep.

CHAPTER 68

Early the next morning, Lilly's phone rang. She checked the time—seven o'clock. She glanced at the caller ID. It was Celie Wolf, the private investigator.

"Hello?"

"Good morning, Lilly. It's Celie. The PI. I hope I'm not calling too early."

"Not for a work day, no. What can I do for you?"

"I think I've found the pilot who was at the controls of the plane when it buzzed the reception."

Lilly gasped. "Who is it?"

"A man by the name of Jeremy Folsom."

"That name doesn't ring a bell."

"Well, that answers my question. I was calling to see if you know anyone by that name. He's not from around here and he took the job because he owed money to the person who hired him. I'll start looking for local connections."

"How did you figure out it was him?"

"Easy. I figured if someone is willing to remove the tail number from a plane, which is a huge no-no, that person might also be willing to engage in other legally questionable activity. I searched for Colorado pilots with misdemeanor and/or felony convictions and came up with a very short list. Mostly misdemeanor stuff. I cross-checked the names and Folsom was the only one whose whereabouts were unaccounted for the day of the wedding. You'd be amazed at what you can find on social media.

"Anyway, no planes have been reported missing in Colorado, so I made the assumption that he owns the plane and doesn't keep it at a civil airfield. I did some checking and sure enough, he owns a plane and keeps it on a large tract of land he owns in the southwestern part of the state. I'm not a hundred percent sure it's him, mind you, but I'm reasonably confident."

"Wow. You've been busy. Do the police know about him?"

"I called them and alerted them to my information right before I called you."

"Have you talked to him?"

"Yes. I called him up and pretended to be a reporter. I told him I was doing a story on pilots of small aircraft and he was only too happy to talk. I turned the talk to the exorbitant price of flying and he let it slip that just last Saturday he flew a trip for someone he owed money too. Wiped out the debt by doing so, apparently. Unfortunately, he realized he had probably said too much and he clammed right up."

"*That's* interesting."

"I'm still trying to piece everything together," Celie said. "If you come across the name Jeremy Folsom, would you let me know? It's like the guy has dropped off the face of the earth."

"I'll certainly let you know if I hear anything."

"Thank you. Right now I need to turn my attention back to the murder of Maureen Davies."

"Do you think the two incidents are related?"

"I don't know yet. I'm leaning toward no, because the buzzing seems to have been directed at someone in the wedding party, whereas the murder obviously was not."

"I agree."

"Well, thanks, Lilly. Keep your ear to the ground, if you can."

"I will. Talk to you later."

After Lilly hung up she immediately called Hassan.

"Good morning, love," he answered.

She melted. "Good morning. What are you doing for lunch today?"

"Hopefully meeting you. What did you have in mind?"

"How about joining me at the store?"

"Sounds great. I'll see you around noon."

When Lilly got in to work Harry was already there. "I'm afraid I didn't find much when I dug around for information about Mallory last night."

"I appreciate you doing that, Harry. Nothing good, huh?"

"Not really. All I learned was that she was married, briefly, to a guy by the name of Folsom."

CHAPTER 69

$\mathcal{L}$illy had been walking toward the front of the store and she stopped in her tracks. "Jeremy Folsom?"

Harry stared at her. "How did you know?"

She told him about the early-morning phone call from the private investigator. His eyes grew wide as she spoke.

"So you're saying that the guy who buzzed the reception is Mallory's ex-husband? Why would he do that?"

"I have no idea. I'm having a hard time wrapping my head around the whole thing." Suddenly it didn't matter whether Mallory had a pilot's license or not. If it was her ex-husband at the controls of the plane, she clearly wasn't at fault.

"Mallory must have gone back to her maiden name after the divorce. Are you going to ask her about it?"

"I don't know yet. I need to think about it."

"Wow. The plot thickens, eh, boss?"

Lilly nodded, suddenly feeling weary and confused.

Hassan came in for lunch just after twelve o'clock. He held up two paper bags.

"What's for lunch?" Lilly asked. She leaned in for her kiss from Hassan.

"Mediterranean vegetable salad. I made it for dinner last night."

"Ooh, that sounds delicious."

Harry minded the shop while Lilly and Hassan ate in the office. Hassan wanted to know all about Lilly's phone call with the private investigator. Lilly told him what she had learned.

"Mallory Abbott and I have become friends, but obviously I don't know her that well. I had no idea she had been married or divorced. And until recently, I had no idea she was Tisha's sister. Since they don't share a last name, I never made the connection."

"So Mallory Abbott and Jeremy Folsom used to be married. It's a small world. Do you suppose she knows that he may be the one behind the incident at Juniper Lake Manor?"

"I don't know. This is mind-boggling."

"Why don't we have dinner tonight at The Water Wheel? I think you could use a break and we haven't been there in a while. Want me to call for reservations?"

Lilly looked down at her salad and smiled. *What did I do to deserve this guy?* She looked up again. "That would be so nice. Thank you."

"I'll call as soon as I leave here. I'll ask for a later seating so you can go see your mom. In fact, I can go with you if you want and we'll leave right from there."

"That would be great."

He left right after lunch, kissing her properly before they went into the front of the shop. He texted only a few minutes later. Dinner at 7. I'll pick you up at 6:30 and we can go see your mom first.

She smiled and sent back a thumbs-up and a heart.

When they arrived at Bev's house that night, though, Bev didn't know Hassan. In fact, she appeared scared that he was in the house—she kept asking Nikki to make him leave and making whimpering sounds.

Hassan took Lilly aside where Bev couldn't see them. "I can't stay in here, Lil. Just my being here is upsetting her."

Lilly swallowed hard and blinked rapidly, trying to keep the tears from falling. As many times as she had assured Hassan that it wasn't personal and that Bev would inevitably forget who he was, it hurt. She bid her mother a hasty goodbye and left, but not before getting a big hug from Nikki.

"Don't let this get you down," Nikki whispered. She gave Hassan a sympathetic smile. "It's hard not to take it personally, I know."

CHAPTER 70

*O*nce they were in Hassan's car, Lilly couldn't stop crying. Hassan called The Water Wheel to cancel their reservation, then drove her home, and sat down with her in the living room as she continued to sob.

"Mom?" Tighe and Laurel came clattering down the stairs and into the living room. "What's wrong?" Tighe sat on one side of her and since Hassan was on the other side, Laurel sat on the floor at her feet.

Lilly tried answering, but couldn't get enough breath to speak.

"Your gran didn't know who I was tonight," Hassan explained. "Your mom just took it hard."

Lilly was exhausted. Exhausted from worrying about her mother, exhausted from trying to figure out who killed Maureen, and exhausted from wondering who was behind the plane that sent everyone scrambling for cover at Bill's wedding. She finally sat back as the tears began to ebb.

"I'm sorry. This was sort of the straw that broke the camel's back."

"Mom, it's like you've been telling us for a while," Tighe said.

"We all knew this was going to happen. And she forgot Hassan once before, remember? Then she figured out who he was and everything was fine again. Maybe that'll happen this time."

"Maybe." But something inside Lilly knew it wasn't going to happen a second time.

"And we've known all along that I would probably be the first person she would forget. She's known me the shortest amount of time, plus everyone else spends more time with her than I do." Hassan smoothed a strand of Lilly's hair away from her face.

"I know. But it still stinks." Lilly leaned her head back against the sofa and let out a long breath. "I just have a lot going on right now. I think I need a break."

"Would you like to go somewhere?" Hassan asked. "I think I still owe you a trip of your choice." He grinned.

"I would love to go somewhere, but I can't go anywhere right now. It's not fair to Harry to leave him in the lurch at work, plus I need to stay near Mom. Look at all the things that have happened in just a few days that Bill doesn't even know about. If I go away now, I'll be wondering the whole time what's going on at Mom's house and I wouldn't enjoy myself. Not to mention everything that happened at Bill and Noley's wedding."

"Well, maybe now isn't the best time. But you *do* need to take some time for yourself," Hassan said. Tighe and Laurel voiced their agreement.

"I will. Just not right now." Barney came up to the small group and laid his head on Lilly's knees. She rubbed his ears. "I'm not going anywhere, Barn. Don't worry."

Tighe stood up. "If you're okay, Mom, I'm going upstairs. Call me if you need anything after Hassan leaves, Mom. G'night."

"I'm fine. Thank you. Goodnight."

"Me, too," Laurel said. "Mom, can I get you anything before I go upstairs?"

"No thanks, honey. I'm just glad you're both here."

Laurel smiled, kissed her mom's cheek, and went upstairs. Tighe fist-bumped Hassan and followed his sister.

"What great kids," he said.

"Thanks." Lilly smiled. "You'd make a great dad, you know that?"

"How about a stepdad?" He grinned.

"You'd make a great stepdad, too." She leaned over and kissed him. "Thanks for bringing me home. I'm sorry we missed dinner, but there was no way I could go out tonight."

"No problem. Maybe we can go out later this week."

He left just a little while later, after Lilly had promised to take a hot bath and go to bed. The bath felt sinfully good, and she dropped into bed and slept deeply afterward.

CHAPTER 71

The next day she had just opened the store when Mallory walked into the shop. Hers didn't open for another hour.

"Good morning. How's Tisha doing?" Lilly asked.

"All right, I guess. At least she's out of bed this morning. I went into the shop early to get some things done that I didn't accomplish yesterday."

This was Lilly's chance to ask Mallory about the letter from the FAA and her marriage to Jeremy Folsom. She wondered how to segue gracefully. *Come on, Lilly, think! Say something!*

"What brings you in here this morning?" Lilly asked. *That was brilliant, you dummy.*

"I just wanted to thank you again for picking up that check. My business is so new that I'm still living from one check to the next."

"Oh, I hear you. It was like that for me when I first opened this shop." Lilly said. "But it gets better."

"I'm sure it will. My ex-husband had his own business, and I remember it was really touch-and-go when he first started it. But things got better, as they usually do, and eventually he was making enough to support us. I was working, too, of course. I was managing a dress shop in a little town in the southwestern corner of the state. A little place called Rocky Springs." She paused and giggled. "It's lucky I had my own savings account that he didn't know about because he would have cleaned me out when we divorced. He always owed money to someone. Don't tell anyone I told you."

Lilly smiled. "It's our secret."

"Anyway, I'm off to the shop. Have a good day, Lilly. Thanks again."

"Happy to help. I'm glad Tisha's doing a little better."

Mallory waved and was gone.

He would have cleaned her out when they divorced. He always owed money to someone. Mallory's words. Maybe the private investigator was on to something. Maybe he did owe someone money and he pulled that stunt at Bill and Noley's wedding in order to settle a debt without actually having to pay.

It made sense.

That evening Lilly stopped at Bev's on her way home from work. She wanted to make up for leaving early the night before. When she walked into Bev's house she was pleased to see Bev and Nikki playing a hand of Old Maid.

"Can I join the next hand?" she asked.

"Sure. Maybe you can deflect your mother's razor-sharp Old Maid skills." Nikki laughed as Bev raised her eyebrows at her and Lilly.

Lilly waited for Nikki to deal her in on the next game. Bev smiled behind her cards. It was a dead giveaway and Lilly knew she and Nikki were going to lose this round.

They did. As they both laid their cards down on the table in front of them, Bev wondered aloud why they weren't playing for "real money."

Lilly laughed. "You want to play for real money, Mom?"

"Yes."

"All right. I'll bet fifteen cents. Nikki, do you have change?" Nikki nodded. "Good. Are you in for fifteen cents?" Nikki nodded again, grinning. "Okay, Mom. You're on."

Nikki dealt the cards again and they played another hand. Bev won thirty cents. By the time that round was over, she was showing signs of being tired. Her eyelids were starting to droop and she was having trouble holding her cards.

"Mom, I think it's time for me to head home. You get a good night's sleep and I'll see you tomorrow. Maybe I'll bring Hassan." She watched her mother closely to see if there was any hint of recognition. There was nothing.

When Lilly got home Laurel and Tighe were in the kitchen, getting dinner ready.

"We'll go over to Gran's as soon as we eat," Laurel told her. "You got home later than we expected."

"It's okay, guys. I went to see Gran because I was a mess when I was there last night. She's exhausted, so you should probably wait until tomorrow to see her."

Both kids wore disappointed looks, but Lilly didn't think it would be a good for Bev to have any more visitors for one evening. "We can do something together," she suggested.

"Like what?" Tighe asked.

Lilly shrugged. "I don't know. Want to see a movie?" She checked her watch. "If we hurry and eat, there's still time to get to one that starts around eight. Anyone?"

"Okay, I'll go," Tighe said.

"Great. Laur, you want to go?"

"I guess."

"Okay, good. Let's see what's playing, scarf down dinner, and I'll do the dishes when we get home."

Tighe and Laurel pulled up the movie schedule on their phones and argued for a minute or two about which movie they should see.

"Nothing sappy," Tighe said.

"Nothing in outer space," Laurel said.

Lilly looked over Laurel's shoulder at the phone screen. "How about superheroes? They're not sappy, and they work right here on Earth."

"Sounds good to me," Tighe said. Laurel agreed.

CHAPTER 72

They sped to the cinema to get good seats before the previews started. The kids shared a big bucket of popcorn. They offered some to Lilly periodically, but she declined. Buttered movie theater popcorn made her throw up.

After the movie, which was excellent, Lilly and the kids were leaving when two voices behind them made Lilly glance subtly over her shoulder.

"Tisha, you know I can't tell you that. It's police business and I can't reveal information about an ongoing investigation."

"But I'm your *girlfriend*," came the whiny reply. "You can't even tell little me?"

Sure enough, Tom and Tisha were right behind Lilly. They didn't seem to realize she was there or that she had heard them. *Tisha must be feeling better.* A desperate need to know what they were discussing swept over Lilly. Were they talking about the wedding?

"Girlfriend or not, there's nothing I can tell you," Tom was saying. "Honestly, there's nothing new about the case, anyway. Whoever killed that caterer didn't make any mistakes. But we'll find him—or her—don't worry. And the pilot that buzzed the reception is nowhere to be found."

They *were* talking about Bill and Noley's wedding. Lilly slowed her steps so she could hear the rest of the conversation.

"Tommy, you're so smart. You'll figure it out." Lilly couldn't help rolling her eyes. *Spare me,* she thought.

"Come on, Mom. What's taking you so long?" Laurel asked.

Lilly shook her head slightly as Laurel turned around to look at her. Laurel gave a questioning look. Then she shrugged and kept pace with Tighe several steps ahead.

"Tisha, you and I need to talk."

"What for?"

"It's cool to hang out, but I don't know about telling the whole world you're my girlfriend. I mean, we're not exclusive or anything."

Lilly could practically feel that slap on her own face.

"You're so funny, Tommy."

"I'm not trying to be funny, Tisha. I mean it. You have to stop telling everyone that I'm your boyfriend."

Lilly slowed even further as she could hear Tisha stamp her foot. She had a feeling Tisha had stopped walking.

"Are you breaking up with me, Tom Toole? Right here at the movies?"

"No, Tisha." Tom sighed. Lilly bent down to tie her shoe so her eavesdropping wouldn't be so obvious. "I just think we shouldn't rush into anything. You know, see other people."

"My baby clock isn't slowing down, Tom."

Lilly fought the urge to laugh out loud.

"Oh, my God. Not here, Tisha. Not now. Please."

Lilly pretended to be rummaging for something in her purse while she let the two of them pass her and continue out the doors of the theater. She shook her head and chuckled. It sounded like Tom might get an earful on the way home from the movies.

Tighe and Laurel were waiting for Lilly on the sidewalk, looking at the coming attractions. *Good. Tom probably didn't see them.*

"What took you so long?" Laurel asked.

"I was trying to eavesdrop on the couple behind me."

"Why?"

"They were at Uncle Bill's wedding. And the man is a police officer. I thought he might let something slip about the investigation."

"Did he?" Tighe asked.

"Nope. They got into an argument."

"About what?" Laurel wanted to know.

"Her baby clock."

CHAPTER 73

"So when are Uncle Bill and Noley getting back from Aruba?" Laurel asked on the way home.

"In a few days. I haven't heard from either of them, so I can only assume they're having a great time."

"I want to go to Aruba on my honeymoon," Laurel said.

"With Drew?" Tighe asked in a mocking voice.

"Shut up." Laurel whacked him on the back of the head from her spot in the back seat.

"Have you heard from Drew?" Lilly asked.

"Sure. He texts me all the time."

"The longer the police take to find out who was behind the incidents at Bill and Noley's wedding, the crazier his parents must be getting for answers."

"They are. Drew told me his mom and dad have both been impossible to deal with."

"That stinks for Drew. But when parents are stressed, it affects the whole family."

"We know that, believe me." Tighe rolled his eyes as Lilly turned to glance at him. She smiled in return.

"Good. That will come in handy when you have children of your own. You can thank me later."

"Kids with Sally Anne?" Laurel asked in a mocking voice to match her brother's.

He turned around to glare at her in the back seat. "Shut up."

"Both of you, stop it. No one is getting married and no one is having children any time soon, so there's no need to tease each other about it."

When they got home Lilly did the dinner dishes while both kids escaped upstairs to their rooms. Lilly took Barney out and was just getting into bed when her phone rang. She looked at the caller ID—Celie Wolf.

"Hello?"

"Lilly, it's Celie."

"Hi, Celie. What's up?"

"I need your help."

"Help with what?"

"I think I know who killed the caterer. I need someone to go with me to set a trap and I was hoping you'd be willing."

"What kind of trap?" Lilly didn't bother to hide the skepticism in her voice. "And who do you think killed Maureen?"

"First of all, I am quite sure her employee, Brad, is behind her death. And as for the trap, I need to go over to the catering office and have a secretly taped conversation with him."

"That sounds like something out of a sitcom, if you don't mind my saying."

"I do mind, actually. And it's a tactic that has worked for me in the past. Given Brad's propensity for domestic violence, I think he's a good candidate for such a strategy to work. He's volatile and likely to fly off the handle when confronted. If I can get a taped confession, that'll be the best outcome, obviously."

"What makes you think Brad is the killer?"

"Means, motive, and opportunity. First, if the medical examiner is to be believed and I see no reason to contradict the findings, Maureen was pushed into the water, hit her head on a rock, and drowned. Brad had the means to do that. He has hands like hams and shoulders to match, so we know he's strong. Second, he had motive. Maureen had just ended their relationship because she felt it would look bad for them to be dating as boss and employee. We also know he wanted a catering business of his own and was working for her because he didn't have the funds to start up a business of his own. We also know he saw Maureen hugging another man. So, classic murder motive. And third, he had the opportunity. After the incident with the plane, no one was paying attention to the caterer bringing the table indoors."

"Do we know for sure that he was outside with Maureen at the time of the incident?"

"The evidence is circumstantial, but my gut tells me yes. There's no one who recalls seeing him inside the manor at the time of the murder. So he had to have been outside." She paused for dramatic effect. "He's our man, Lilly."

It made perfect sense when she explained it that way. And she had been alone with Brad in the catering office not long after Maureen's death. Lilly shivered when she thought of how close she had been to him.

"Okay, what do you want me to do?"

"I've got the listening equipment in the car. I can pick you up and you can man the equipment while I go talk to him."

At least she wasn't asking Lilly to do the talking. That's why Celie was making the big bucks. "I suppose I can do that."

"Good. When are you available?"

"In the evenings after six thirty or so."

"That won't do. He's usually there in the daytime during the week."

Lilly sighed. "All right. I suppose I can ask my assistant to watch the shop for me while I help you." She hated to keep asking Harry to watch the store by himself.

"Tomorrow, then?"

"I suppose. Where will I meet you?"

"I'll pick you up in front of your jewelry store at one o'clock in the afternoon." Celie's voice was brisk and businesslike.

"Okay, I'll be ready."

Celie thanked her and hung up. Lilly sighed and reached out to pet Barney's head. "Barn, I don't know what I'm getting into."

CHAPTER 74

The next day Lilly asked Harry to mind the store for a short time while she helped Celie nab a killer.

"Boss, shouldn't the police be doing that?"

"I believe so, yes. But Celie wants to do the legwork so all the police have to do is go in and arrest the man who killed Maureen. It would be a big feather in her cap. It's not easy being a business owner, so I can understand where she's coming from. Every little accolade helps, and catching a killer would look great on her marketing materials."

"Is that a good reason to do this the vigilante way?"

"*I* wouldn't do it that way, if that's what you're asking. But she asked for my help, and truthfully, I want answers for Bill and Noley. If we involve the police, it's going to take much longer. They'll have to investigate before making an arrest and that would take valuable time."

"Just be careful, okay?"

Lilly smiled. "I will, Harry, I promise."

Celie pulled up in front of the store at the appointed hour and Lilly slid into the passenger seat.

"Ready?" Celie asked.

"I guess so."

"I'll pull over before we get to the catering office and teach you how to use the audio equipment."

Lilly turned around to glance into the backseat. "Where is it?"

"In the trunk."

Lilly watched Juniper Junction fly by as she and Celie drove to the outskirts of town where the office was located. About a mile from their destination, Celie pulled over and popped the trunk.

"Come on, I'll show you how to use the equipment."

Lilly got out of the car and joined Celie as she leaned into the trunk. Lilly looked down and, to her dismay, found a box with a mind-boggling array of buttons, dials, and toggle switches on top.

"Tell me this isn't the equipment I'm supposed to operate." Lilly turned to Celie and cocked her head.

"Of course it is."

"Are you aware that I do not have a PhD in engineering?"

"This is easy to learn. See this switch here? It's the main power switch." Celie pointed to a large red switch in the upper left corner of the terrifying machine.

"Okay."

"And this here is the secondary power switch." Celie pointed to a yellow switch next to the red one.

Lilly looked skeptically at the contraption. "Why does it have two power switches?"

"Why does anything have two power switches? In case of a battery failure."

Lilly grimaced. That seemed reasonable.

Celie proceeded to explain, in excruciating detail, how to work each quadrant of the machine.

"Celie, I don't think I'm the right person for this job."

Celie let out a frustrated sigh. "Lilly, I'm not asking you to reprogram a defense satellite. I'm asking you to tape a conversation."

"I know. Wouldn't it be easier to just turn on your cell phone recorder and record Brad that way?"

"Of course it would be easier. But what if my phone doesn't catch an important phrase? What if I move the wrong way and the recording stops? With this state-of-the-art listening device, we're guaranteed good audio with minimal chance of being detected."

"But, I'm telling you, I cannot operate this thing."

Another sigh. "All right, then, you go in to talk to Brad and I'll operate it."

This was a far worse prospect, as far as Lilly was concerned.

"I didn't sign up for that, Celie."

"We've come this far and I'm not leaving without a confession, Lilly." Celie put her hands on her hips and gave Lilly a hard stare.

Lilly was silent for several moments while she weighed the pros and cons. On the one hand, she could end this whole episode once and for all if she just went in and finagled a confession out of Brad. On the other hand, he could kill her.

But really, what were the chances of that? If things started to go south, Celie could get in fast enough to save her.

CHAPTER 75

*L*illy took a deep breath. "All right. I'll go talk to him on one condition. If you hear anything that sounds like a threat or a violent move or anything bad, you come and get me out of there."

"I will, I promise. Thank you. This is really important to me. If I can solve one huge case like this, I can get an in with one of the heavy hitting PI firms in Denver. That's my dream."

"Well, it's my dream to find out who ruined my brother's wedding and why, and to stay alive doing it."

"Then let's get this show on the road."

Both women got back in the car and Celie drove to the building where the catering office was located. She parked around the corner so Brad wouldn't see them.

"Do you know what to say?" Celie asked.

"Yes. I'm going to get him to confess to killing Maureen."

"Yes, I know, but do you know exactly how to approach it?" Celie sounded frustrated again.

"I find that it's better for me to ad lib than to rehearse," Lilly said. "I forget stuff when there's a script I'm supposed to remember."

"Don't mess this up, Lilly."

Lilly didn't think the PI had meant her statement to sound as threatening as it had. She couldn't help scowling, though. "Don't worry. Like I said, I want to find out what happened just as much as you do."

Celie nodded and Lilly got out of the car. Under Celie's instruction and watchful eye, Lilly inserted a miniscule earpiece that Brad hopefully wouldn't be able to see. Her heart thumped faster when Celie advised her to cover her ears with her hair so the chances of Brad seeing the earpiece were minimized.

What am I getting myself into? she wondered.

Finally Celie stepped back and gave Lilly a thumbs-up. Lilly took a deep breath and walked to the entrance of the catering office. With a quick backward glance, she knocked on the door and pushed it open.

She was startled to see Brad sitting at the tiny desk right in front of the door.

"Good afternoon, Mrs. Carlsen. What brings you in here?" he asked. He was not smiling, and his voice had a slight hardness to it.

"I came in because I wanted to apologize for causing so much trouble with my request for a price reduction for my brother's wedding." Lilly clenched her teeth as she smiled at the young man. It was almost painful to say those words when she so strongly believed that what Bill and Noley really deserved was a full refund.

"Thank you for coming around to the right way of handling the issue." Brad stood up and Lilly had to stop herself from backing away from him. She hoped he couldn't hear her heart beating in her chest.

"Well, I had an epiphany, you know? I realized that the important thing was that everyone enjoyed the food that was there. I mean, that's the only thing there was to enjoy, right? The rest of the evening was a total nightmare." She let out a meager chuckle.

Brad smiled sadly. "It was a nightmare, you're right."

"You must miss Maureen terribly." Lilly could feel a flutter of excitement in her chest. This conversation was going exactly the way she had hoped.

"I do. I miss her a lot."

"Do you know if the police have made any headway in the investigation?"

Brad shook his head. "I haven't heard anything. I suppose the longer we go without hearing any word, the less likely they are to catch the person who did it."

"It hasn't really been that long—only a week and a half. I have confidence in them. I think they'll get their man, so to speak."

"What makes you think it's a man?" Brad gave her a sharp look.

"That's just an expression. I mean, they'll get the bad guy. I mean, they'll catch the person who killed Maureen." Lilly was becoming flustered.

"I hope you're right."

"Do you have any suspicions?" Lilly leaned in closer, as if she were sharing a secret with him.

He shrugged. "It could've been anyone, but frankly, my money is on the manager of Juniper Lake Manor. I think her name is Carla."

"Oh, you mean Darla? I hadn't thought of her as the murdering type."

"Is there such a thing as the murdering type? Listen. Here's what I think: I think every person, pushed far enough, has the ability to kill another human being."

Wow. That got dark in a hurry.

CHAPTER 76

"You really believe that?" Lilly asked.

"Yup. I've had anger issues in the past, so I know. I know I've been angry enough to kill. But now that I'm in therapy, I can deal with those feelings of anger without resorting to violence. But a lot of people don't seek the treatment I did. They just let their anger fester and take over their lives. Let me give you an example. Not long ago I saw Mo hugging some guy. I was furious. Before I got treatment, I would have gone ballistic and socked the guy. But I didn't. Instead, I asked Mo about it. Turned out the guy was some friend of hers from high school. And he's gay. So there was no reason for me to be upset."

Well, that explains the embrace with another man. Hmm. Not what I expected to hear.

Lilly turned her attention back to the matter at hand. "But Darla doesn't seem like an angry person at all, do you think?"

"Angry people can hide it very well. I know I used to."

Lilly debated whether to reveal that she knew about his history of domestic violence, but then decided against it. No reason to make him think she was researching his background for any reason.

"Did Maureen ever make you angry?" *Perfect, Lilly. Exactly what a TV detective would say.*

Brad cocked his head and stared at Lilly. "Just what are you getting at?"

Lilly shrugged as nonchalantly as she could. "Just asking. I mean, you were in a relationship. You must have made each other angry at some point."

"I don't think it's any of your business whether Mo and I ever got angry with each other. I know what you're doing, Mrs. Carlsen. You're trying to get me to admit that I killed her. But you're barking up the wrong tree. I didn't kill her. I loved her."

"But you and she broke up. That must have made you upset." *You just can't leave well enough alone, can you?* Lilly held her breath while she waited to see what he would do.

But he remained calm. Had she actually been hoping he would fly off the handle and attack her? No, not really. But she *had* been hoping for some type of reaction. *His anger management therapist must be very good.*

"Of course it made me upset. It made her upset, too. We were perfect together. We were going to get back together when I found another job."

"You were looking for another job?"

He nodded. "I would like to open my own catering business, but taking over Maureen's would be too painful and I don't have the money yet to start my own. So I have to keep working for someone else. In fact, I was on the phone talking to a potential employer when Maureen was killed." He swallowed hard and looked down, then back up at Lilly. Were those tears in his eyes? "If I had been there with her, she would still be alive today."

"Wait. You weren't with her when she died?"

"No. I was indoors, in one of the service rooms. I needed to be where it was quiet to take the call."

"I thought you were with Maureen when she died."

"No."

"Did you tell the police that?"

"Of course. Why do you think I'm not under suspicion? I would have been the first person they accused if I hadn't been able to prove that I was on the phone when Mo died. And the person I was talking to backed me up."

Lilly nodded. This changed everything. She hoped Celie was listening hard. Lilly was mad. It seemed like this was something Celie should have known before attempting this wild goose chase. So much for her "gut feeling."

Brad's eyes narrowed. "You really thought I killed her, didn't you? You came in here to get me to say something incriminating." His tone was raw, accusing. Lilly took a step backward.

"I didn't know if you killed her or not, Brad, but it was worth a try. You can't blame me for trying." Brad had stood up and was pointing to the door with a hand that trembled.

"It's lucky for you that I go to anger management therapy or my hands would be right around your neck right now. Get out! And don't come back."

Lilly needed no further encouragement. She spun around and reached for the door, then half-walked, half-ran to the car where Celie was waiting. She yanked the passenger door open and threw herself into the car, locking the door immediately.

CHAPTER 77

When she had caught her breath, she glared at Celie. "He wasn't with Maureen when she died."

"I know. I heard him."

"I thought you said he was there."

"Well, obviously I was wrong." Celie sighed. "Back to the beginning, I guess. I'm sorry for wasting your time, Lilly." Celie looked genuinely remorseful. Lilly had wanted to light into her for being unprepared for Brad's revelation, but she kept her mouth shut. She suspected Celie felt bad enough already.

They drove back to the jewelry shop in silence. When Celie pulled up out front, Lilly turned to her. "What's next?"

"I've got some other leads I can follow." She didn't volunteer any information and Lilly didn't care to ask. If she was going to figure out who ruined Bill and Noley's wedding, she was going to have to do it herself and not depend on Celie, whose information was not as reliable as she had hoped.

She slid out of the car, waved to Celie, and went inside. Harry gave her an expectant look.

"How did it go?"

"Oh, it went. Brad behaved very well, considering he knew I

was trying to get him to confess to murder, and we learned that he wasn't even with Maureen when she died."

Harry ran his hand through his hair. "Well, that takes care of him. That narrows it down a bit, I suppose."

"A bit. It's time to look elsewhere. We need to know who was outside with Maureen at the time of her death. I wonder if Darla has security camera footage that would show who was in the reception space at the time. I know there were no cameras outdoors and no cameras in the smaller rooms, but I think I recall seeing them on the rafters in the reception space. That way we could rule out a lot of people."

"Why don't you give her a call?"

"I will. I'll take over here, Harry, if you want to run out and get some lunch. You've been wonderful about taking care of the shop so much."

After Harry left for a well-deserved lunch break, Lilly waited on a customer. After that woman had left the shop and Lilly was alone, she took out her cell phone and dialed Darla's number.

"Hey, Lilly. How's everything going?"

"Okay, thanks. Listen, Darla, I've got a question for you. Is there any security camera footage of people inside the reception space at the time Maureen was killed?"

"Unfortunately, no. The security cameras haven't been working for a couple of weeks. The security company is waiting for a part to come in before they can fix it."

"Ugh. Well, thanks anyway. I wish we had some answers."

"I haven't heard anything. The owners are going nuts because people are cancelling events right and left since your brother's wedding. The sooner the police find out who was behind the murder, the sooner we can get back to normal around here. Hopefully. Neither the Hendersons nor I want to have to lay anyone off, but without any events, I'm afraid that's coming soon."

"I'm also wondering about the plane that buzzed the reception. Are the owners concerned about that?"

"Definitely. But the murder is the more serious concern, obviously, so they're laser-focused on that."

"Well, thanks for the information, Darla. If you hear anything, can you let me know?"

"You bet. Stay in touch, Lilly."

Lilly sighed. So that line of inquiry was closed.

CHAPTER 78

When Lilly got home that night she found that Laurel had made spaghetti and meatballs for dinner. The scent was mouth-watering. Tighe sliced Italian bread as Lilly put her handbag away and poured herself a glass of wine.

When the three of them sat down for dinner, Lilly realized how hungry she was. "Laurel, every time I think your food can't get any better, it does. This is delicious."

"Thanks, Mom. It's really easy."

"Well, it doesn't taste like it was easy. It tastes like you cooked it all day long."

Laurel grinned and looked down at her phone. Lilly was going to say something, but decided against it because Laurel had been so sweet to make dinner.

Laurel looked at her phone several more times while they were all chatting. Lilly let it slide, but when Laurel looked down at her phone for the sixth or seventh time, Lilly had to put a stop to it.

"Laurel, what can possibly be so important that you can't stop looking at your phone? Is it Drew?"

Laurel put her phone face down and shook her head. "Sorry. I won't look again."

There was something about the tone of her voice that alerted Lilly. "What's wrong?"

"Nothing."

"Laurel, you're a terrible liar. What's the matter?"

Laurel looked like she was having an internal debate over whether to say what was on her mind. Finally she just blurted it out. "Vanessa just found out that she's pregnant."

If Lilly had been drinking her wine, she would have spit it out all over the table. She stared at Laurel, her mouth agape. Laurel's best friend, pregnant.

"Vanessa's pregnant? Is she sure?"

"Of course she's sure." Laurel's voice was tinged with annoyance. "Don't you think she's taken a test?"

"No need to get testy, Laurel. I just can't believe it, that's all."

"I can't, either. Neither can Vanessa."

"How far along?"

"Um, do I need to be here for this?" Tighe asked.

"You might want to think about staying. You don't want people to be having this conversation about Sally Anne."

Tighe reddened, but stayed where he was. "No one is going to say that about Sally Anne, Mom."

"Anyway, back to Vanessa. Does she know how far along she is?" she asked again.

"She doesn't know. She hasn't been to the doctor yet. But the test was definitely positive."

"Is she home from school for the summer yet?"

Laurel nodded.

"Do her parents know?"

"No way. She's not going to tell them until she has to."

Lilly gave Laurel a skeptical look. "Has she thought that through? If you were pregnant, God forbid, I would want to know right away."

"They'll die when they find out. She doesn't even want to think about it right now."

"And what about the baby's father? Does he know? Is he in the picture?"

Laurel nodded. "She and her boyfriend have only been together since January. But he knows about the baby."

"And how did he react?"

"He's being very supportive of Vanessa. He's cool."

"But how does he feel about the baby?"

Laurel shrugged. "I don't know. All Vanessa said was that he didn't run away in fear. They've talked every day on the phone since she came home from school. I think he's planning to visit her soon. That's being supportive, right?"

"I don't know how supportive he can be when he doesn't live nearby and he's not experiencing the physical part of being pregnant. How is Vanessa feeling?"

"Sick. She throws up a lot."

"What's his name?"

"The baby? How should I know?"

"Not the baby. The boyfriend."

"Cyrus."

"And where does he live?"

"Albuquerque."

"So not right down the road."

"No. It's a pretty far drive."

Lilly sat back in her chair and frowned. "This is why I keep telling you to take it slow."

"Mom, don't make this about me. Please."

"Or me," Tighe piped up.

"I'm not making it about either one of you. I'm just glad it's *not* either one of you. It's a very tough issue for a young person, especially a woman, and especially if she's trying to get a college education."

"I can't imagine what her parents are going to say," Laurel said.

"I wonder if they'll consider helping to raise the baby," Lilly mused.

"Not a chance," Laurel scoffed.

"Well, Vanessa knows she can come here whenever she wants to or needs to."

"That's what I told her. I was sure you'd help her."

"I'll do whatever I can. I'm afraid that won't be much. Most of this is going to be something only Vanessa can deal with."

"And hopefully Cyrus," Laurel added.

"Yes. And hopefully Cyrus."

CHAPTER 79

*L*illy spoke to Hassan that night before going to bed. She told him about Vanessa's unplanned pregnancy and about her trip to see if Brad could be tricked into confessing to something he obviously didn't do. Hassan spoke in a grave voice when he heard of the field trip.

"Lilly, you're smarter than that."

"Before you get mad, wait a minute. Celie was listening to the whole thing, so the second it started to get ugly, if it had gotten ugly, she would have come in to get me out of there."

"How do you know? You barely know the woman. All you really know is that she's after a big fish so she can put it on her resumé. What if Brad had gotten violent and she had just kept the tape rolling so she could get every word?"

Lilly had to admit that thought hadn't crossed her mind. "Well...." Her voice trailed off.

"That's what I thought. The next time you go off half-baked, would you at least call me first?"

"You would just try to talk me out of it."

"Probably, yes. But I wouldn't be successful, we both know that. And at least I could offer you some protection."

"Okay. I am feeling a little silly right now."

"Don't feel silly. I cherish you, love, and you know your family and friends do, too. We don't want to see anything happen to you."

Lilly could feel a comforting warmth spreading through her. "I know. Okay. I promise I'll let you know the next time I'm heading off half-baked, as you say."

She could hear the smile in his voice. "That's all I ask."

The next day Laurel texted Lilly at work.

Can Vanessa come over for dinner? I'll cook.

Lilly texted back in the affirmative, then asked Laurel to take her brother and go see Gran. Laurel texted back with a thumbs-up.

Lilly couldn't pinpoint why, but she was anxious about the kids visiting her mom. She paced the floor of the jewelry shop when there were no customers, checked her watch a thousand times, and jumped whenever her phone pinged with a text or a notification.

"Are you all right, Lilly?" Harry asked more than once.

"I'm okay," she answered each time. "Sorry if I'm making you nervous."

Finally Tighe called her. "Hi, Mom."

"Hi, honey. How's Gran? I've been worried about her."

"She seemed pretty out-of-it today. She's leaning far to one side and she didn't say much. She smiled when she saw me and Laurel, though."

"Thanks for going over."

"Are you going to tell Uncle Bill about Gran before he comes home?"

"No." Lilly didn't even have to think about it. She wouldn't tell Bill anything unless it became absolutely necessary. She wasn't going to ruin what was left of his honeymoon.

"I bet you can't wait for him to get home."

Lilly smiled ruefully. "You're right—I can't. But he deserves this break away from home and all the worries he has."

"I guess you're right. Did you know Vanessa is coming for dinner?"

"Yes. Laurel asked me."

"Do I have to be there?"

"Why don't you want to be there?"

"Because it'll be all girl talk, and I wouldn't be surprised to see tears. I just don't want to be around."

Lilly grinned. "All right. You might have a point. Why don't you and Mike do something?" Mike was Tighe's best friend from high school.

"I'll call him. Thanks, Mom."

"See you tonight, honey. Be safe."

"I will."

CHAPTER 80

*L*illy stopped to see her mom before going home for dinner with Laurel and Vanessa. She jogged up the steps to her mom's house and knocked before pushing the door open.

"Mom? Nikki?" she called.

She heard a muffled voice in response. "In here!"

Her heart skipped a beat. "Nikki? Is that you?" She dropped her handbag and raced in the direction of the voice.

In the doorway of her mother's room downstairs, she stopped short for just an instant. Taking in the scene in one quick glance, she saw Nikki kneeling on the floor with her mother next to her.

"Nikki! What happened?"

Nikki grunted. "Can you give me a hand, Lilly? She slipped and I'm trying to get her up."

Lilly was on the floor in an instant, doing as Nikki directed to get her mother up. Bev was more or less alert through the entire ordeal, trying to help them help her. She tried to put her arms and legs where Nikki told her to, but Nikki and Lilly were largely fighting inertia. Lilly hadn't realized just how uncoordinated Bev had become until tonight. It took several minutes to get Bev seated on the bed, and the three women sat together, taking deep breaths and holding Bev's hands.

"I'm glad you got here when you did," Nikki said. Bev nodded.

"I am, too. What happened? Should we take her to the emergency room?"

Bev was already shaking her head slightly from side to side. Nikki patted her hand and smiled.

"She slid to the floor while I was trying to help her get changed into her nightgown. Surprisingly, she went down very softly—almost like liquid—and I think she's fine." She looked at Bev. "What do you think, Bev? Do you hurt anywhere?"

Bev shook her head again, this time with a little more vigor.

Nikki smiled. "All right, honey. I don't think we need to take you anywhere. Want to give the nightie another try?"

Bev smiled and nodded. Lilly smiled, too, when she saw that her mom was all right. "Do you need my help?" she asked.

Bev nodded, so Nikki and Lilly dressed Bev together and then the three of them went into the living room. Nikki had apparently sliced half a banana for Bev earlier, and it sat on the table next to her favorite chair, uneaten. Nikki fed Bev a couple of pieces before Bev refused any more.

Lilly helped Nikki maneuver Bev into the bedroom again, and her heart constricted when she thought of the changes coming to Bev and to the rest of the family. It wouldn't be long, she felt sure, before she and Bill discussed other care arrangements for their mom.

Driving home, Lilly tried to push the negative thoughts and worries away from her. She wanted to be upbeat for dinner with Vanessa. The poor young woman was going through enough—she shouldn't have to deal with Lilly's melancholy, too.

When she got home Vanessa was already there. She looked up from the kitchen counter, where she was helping Laurel roll out pie crust, and broke into a broad smile when she saw Lilly.

"Mrs. Carlsen!" Vanessa cried.

$\mathcal{L}$illy opened her arms and approached Vanessa. They bear-hugged each other for several seconds, during which time Lilly could feel Vanessa's shoulders and back relax. She held Vanessa out at arms' length.

"How are you feeling?"

"Okay, I guess. I've been throwing up a lot, but by evening it seems to mostly go away."

"Good. I hope you came hungry. Laurel has become a fabulous cook." Laurel grinned and Vanessa turned toward her and smiled.

"I know. She's been telling me all about her classes. They sound like so much fun." Her face turned serious and she took a deep breath. "I don't know how long I'll be able to keep going to classes in the fall."

"Why not? Pregnant women can do almost everything non-pregnant women can do," Lilly said. She noticed a loaf of bread on the counter and picked up a knife to slice it.

"Oh, I know that. It's just that when my parents find out about the baby, I'm sure they're going to stop paying for me to go to college." Vanessa looked down at her abdomen as if expecting to start showing at any minute.

Lilly didn't know what to say to that. "Did you see the doctor today?"

"Yes. He says I'm about ten weeks."

"And you're going to wait to tell your parents until you're showing?"

Vanessa nodded. "Do you think I should tell them before that?"

"I can only tell you how I would feel about it if Laurel were pregnant. I would want to know early on. But I'm not your parents, and they may feel differently than I do."

Vanessa laughed, but it came out like more of a scoff. "I'll say. They're going to kill me when they find out."

"They might surprise you, Vanessa."

"Maybe, but I doubt it. I know them pretty well."

"That's true. That's why you're the only one who can make the decision about telling them. What about the baby's father?"

"Cyrus?" Vanessa smiled. "I told him right away. He's a good person. He's doing the right thing."

"What do you mean?"

"I mean, he has called me every day, he's coming to visit, he's told me we'll get married once he's out of school."

"Do you want to marry him?"

Vanessa shrugged. "I mean, I should, right? I could definitely see us getting married. But this isn't exactly how I thought it would happen."

Lilly had to tread very carefully with her next question.

"So you're going to keep the baby?"

Laurel gasped and Vanessa stared at her open-mouthed. "Do you mean get an abortion?"

"No. I meant keeping the baby as opposed to giving it up for adoption."

"I'm going to keep the baby for sure."

"It sounds like you've given it some thought."

"I haven't, actually. I just know I wouldn't want to give the baby up for adoption."

"Well, you know you have a place to come if things get hairy at home. Don't forget that."

"I won't, Mrs. Carlsen. Thank you."

CHAPTER 82

They sat down to a delicious dinner of chicken pot pie.

"I'm going to have to learn how to cook, I guess," Vanessa said.

"I'll teach you," Laurel offered. "It's easy."

Vanessa put her fork down and started to cry. It came out of nowhere. Laurel shoved her chair back and ran around the table to where Vanessa sat. She put her arms around Vanessa's shoulders. "What's wrong? What happened?"

Lilly, having experienced similar hormonal swings while she was pregnant with both her kids, put her hand over Vanessa's. "Does this happen a lot?" she asked knowingly.

"Yes." Vanessa gulped and tried to smile.

"It's hormones." Lilly looked up at Laurel, who looked relieved that it wasn't something more serious.

"You start crying, just like that?" Laurel snapped her fingers.

Vanessa nodded. "I can't help it. Here I am and I'm pregnant and you're both so nice to me. It's just overwhelming, that's all."

"Does it happen when you're at home?" Laurel asked.

Vanessa nodded again. "When it happens, I just make up

some excuse and go to my room. I don't want my parents to figure out that I'm pregnant because I can't stop crying."

"Well, I know just how you feel," Lilly said. "I cried constantly when I was pregnant with both kids."

Laurel laughed. "Is that hereditary?"

"It's hormonal, my dear. It happens to lots of people."

"Yikes." Laurel got up from the table. "Dessert, anyone? I made a chocolate cream pie earlier."

"Ooh, that sounds delicious," Vanessa said.

Laurel brought the pie to the table and set it down just as her phone rang. She checked it and glanced at Lilly. "It's Drew. He knew Vanessa was coming over for dinner, so it must be important. Do you mind if I take it?"

"Not if Vanessa doesn't mind."

Vanessa waved her hand dismissively and Laurel answered the phone. She turned around, Lilly supposed, to have a semblance of privacy. She fought the urge to roll her eyeballs. She could only hear Laurel's side of the conversation.

"Hi."

"Really?"

"Oh, no."

"Wow."

"Hold on. I'll ask." When Lilly heard this, she could feel her facial muscles tense.

"Mom, Drew wants to come over. His parents are off the rails and he needs somewhere to go. Can he come here? Please?"

Lilly motioned for Laurel to mute the phone so Drew wouldn't hear their conversation. "Doesn't he have any other friends?"

"Of course he does. But he wants to see me. Please, Mom?"

"Laurel, Vanessa is here. She's your guest."

Laurel turned to Vanessa, a pleading look on her face. "Vanessa, you don't mind if Drew comes over, do you?"

"I don't mind."

"Laurel, what do you expect her to say?"

"It's okay, Mrs. Carlsen. Really. It will be nice to focus on someone else's problems for a while." Vanessa laughed nervously.

Lilly knew it was Bad Parenting to let Laurel see Drew before her grounding was over, but it sounded like Drew really needed a place to go. Oh, well. She could be a good parent some other time.

"Okay, then. He can come over. But he has to leave when I'm ready for bed. No arguments."

"Okay. Thanks, Mom." She turned her back again and spoke into the phone. "Okay, you can come over. You have to leave when my mom goes to bed, though."

She hung up and sat down at the table again. "He'll be here in a little while."

Talk turned to innocuous subjects after Laurel's phone call. It seemed to Lilly that Vanessa was tired of discussing herself and wanted to keep her mind on other things. She and Laurel caught up on some gossip about friends from high school while Lilly washed the dishes. Then the two young women dried the dishes and finished cleaning up the kitchen.

About a half hour later, there was a knock at the front door. Laurel hurried to answer it while Barney raced ahead of her in a barking frenzy of excitement.

She ushered Drew into the living room and introduced him to Vanessa. He shook hands with her, then turned to Lilly.

"Thanks for letting me come over, Mrs. Carlsen. I know Laurel's not supposed to be seeing me for the rest of the week, but I just felt like I needed a calm place to go. This seemed like the right place."

"You're welcome, Drew."

They all sat down and looked at each other for a few seconds before Drew cleared his throat. "It smells good in here."

Laurel beamed. "Thanks. I made chicken pot pie for dinner."

"Have you had dinner, Drew?" Lilly asked.

"Yes, thanks."

"How about dessert?" Laurel asked. "I made a chocolate cream pie."

"Now I would have a piece of that." He grinned. Laurel hopped up and bustled into the kitchen, returning a minute later with a huge piece of pie. While Laurel was gone, Lilly and Vanessa and Drew looked around the room as if just discovering how fascinating it really was.

Drew's eyes widened when he saw the pie. "Laurel, you didn't have to give me the whole thing." He laughed and it broke the silence in the living room. Lilly and Vanessa laughed, too, and the kids all started chatting. Lilly was content to listen to the conversation, impressed with Drew's manners. Vanessa seemed more relaxed, too, talking about things other than herself. Laurel didn't stop smiling, having her best friend and her boyfriend in the same room for the first time. Lilly was happy for her.

CHAPTER 83

When her phone rang, Lilly went into the kitchen to talk. It was Celie Wolf.

"Hi, Celie. What's up?"

"I'm just calling because I feel bad about what happened with Brad."

"Don't worry about it. It's no big deal."

"Well, plus I have a question for you."

"What is it?"

"What do you know about Tom Toole?"

"Not much. I know he's a police officer, he was in my brother's wedding party, and he brought one of Bill's old girlfriends as his date."

"What's his rank in the police department?"

"I have no idea. I never asked Bill. What do you know about him?"

"Not much ... yet. I just like to know who I'm dealing with when I talk to people involved with this wedding reception debacle. He's handling the case files for both the murder and the aviation incident."

"I believe so, yes."

"What's the name of his date for the wedding?"

"Tisha Franklin."

"I think I talked to her. Didn't know much."

"That describes Tisha pretty well."

Celie laughed. "Do you know if they're serious? Tom and Tisha, I mean?"

"Actually, I do know a little something about that. I did overhear a conversation between them," Lilly said.

"Really? What did they say?"

"Tom was trying to tell Tisha that they should see other people and she was having none of it."

"And where was this?"

"At the movie theater."

"When?"

"Just a couple of nights ago."

Lilly turned when she heard a noise behind her. Vanessa was standing in the kitchen, looking a sickly pale green. "Celie, I'm sorry. I've got to run." She touched the phone to end the call. "Vanessa, are you all right? Here, sit down." Lilly took Vanessa's elbow and led her to the kitchen table.

Vanessa swallowed and gently pulled her arm away from Lilly. "I'm okay. I've got to go home. You should get in there." She motioned toward the living room with her head.

Lilly's eyes narrowed. "Why? What's wrong?"

"I'm going to throw up, Mrs. Carlsen. I need to leave *now*." Vanessa fled to the door, flung it open, and left. Lilly could hear her clattering down the back steps and hurried after her. She would never forgive herself if Vanessa fell going down the stairs and something happened to the baby. But Vanessa seemed fine. She was hurrying away from the house without a backward glance.

Lilly returned to the living room, where Barney had now set up a frantic barking. Laurel and Drew were sitting on opposite ends of the sofa. Drew was looking down at his hands, clasped in his lap, and Laurel was looking forward. Nothing appeared seriously amiss, but Barney was reacting to something, perhaps a certain level of tension in the room. Lilly could almost sense it herself.

"What's wrong with Barney?" she asked.

"I don't know." Laurel shrugged and her voice came out hollow. It sounded far away.

Lilly glanced at Drew, whose eyes had slid to the side to look at Laurel.

"What's happening here? Did you two argue? I mean, I know it's none of my business, but the atmosphere in here has certainly cooled since I took the phone call in the kitchen."

"Mom—"

"It's nothing." Drew interrupted her.

"It doesn't look like nothing to me," Lilly said.

"I think it's time for me to head home and deal with my parents."

"Drew, I...." Laurel sighed and flopped her hands in her lap. "You have to tell my mom. She'll know what to do."

Lilly's senses were immediately on high alert. Something was definitely not right.

"What's going on?" she asked. Barney continued barking. "Barney, be quiet." Barney kept up the racket. "Barney, want to go outside?" Lilly asked.

Barney stayed where he was, refusing to stop barking.

Drew looked up at the ceiling and blinked. Then his gaze shifted to Laurel again. "Can't you keep that dog quiet?"

"He's upset, Drew. What am I supposed to do?"

"I don't know."

"Okay, you two. Someone had better tell me what's going on in here right this minute. Does this have something to do with Vanessa?"

"No." Laurel shook her head in a tight left-to-right motion.

"She was pretty upset when she left just now."

Laurel was blinking back tears. "Mom, I—"

Drew cut her off by standing up suddenly. "Laurel, please don't say anything."

Barney stayed next to Lilly, but his body was trembling with barely restrained energy. Lilly knew he was standing in front of her to protect her. She put her hand on his head to try to calm him, then placed her hands on her hips. "Drew, I need to know what's going on here. Right now. If you're not going to tell me, then you can leave."

Drew's breath was coming in short, fast breaths.

"Mom, he killed the caterer."

CHAPTER 84

The words were the last ones Lilly had expected to hear. She whipped her head toward Laurel. "What? What are you talking about?"

"Tell her, Drew." Laurel shrank back into the sofa as if she expected Drew to attack her.

"I'm not saying a word."

Laurel jumped up from the sofa suddenly and screamed at Drew. "Tell her! You have to tell her!"

Barney could no longer control himself. He leapt toward Drew, who put his hands up to protect his face. "Get the dog off me!" he yelled.

Lilly's mind was reeling. She didn't understand a word of what was being said. "Barney!" she shouted. "No! Come!"

Barney returned to her side, but continued barking.

"Just make the dog be quiet. Please. I'll tell you everything." Drew's hands had come down from his face and he was pleading now.

"I'll be right back." Lilly took Barney by the collar and ushered him through the kitchen and out the back door. He howled to be let back inside when she closed the door. As much as Lilly wanted him in the house for protection and so he would calm down, his presence seemed to be preventing Drew from saying whatever he needed to say.

Did he really kill Maureen? How was that even possible?

She returned to the living room, where Drew was slowly walking closer to Laurel.

"Laurel," he said, "please believe me. I didn't mean to hurt Maureen. It was an accident." He seemed not to notice that Lilly had come into the room.

Lilly inhaled sharply. He had just admitted to murder, right there in her living room. His head jerked toward her when he heard her.

"You really killed Maureen?" Lilly asked in a quiet voice.

Drew held up his hands as if Lilly were rushing forward to beat him. "Please believe me. It was an accident." He turned to face Laurel again. "Why did you have to say anything?"

Lilly frowned. This would turn into an indictment of Laurel over Lilly's dead body ... though hopefully it wouldn't get that far.

Lilly quickly stepped between them, regretting the decision to send Barney outside.

"She said something for two reasons, Drew. First, because it's the right thing to do and I raised her to do the right thing. Second, because eventually someone would figure it out and the longer it takes, the worse it is for you."

"What do you mean by that?" he asked.

"I mean that you need to turn yourself in. The sooner, the better."

Drew stared at Lilly like she had just burst into flames.

"Are you kidding me?" he shouted. "There's no way!"

"Drew, it's the only solution for you at this point." She looked at Laurel. "Does Vanessa know this? Is that why she looked terrible when she left?"

Laurel's eyes were wide. "I think so, yes."

"So that makes at least four of us who know you killed Maureen: you, Laurel, Vanessa, and me. Does anyone else know?"

"I think my parents suspect."

"So why did they hire a private investigator?"

"They hired her before they started thinking I did it."

"So why do they keep her on?"

Drew shrugged. "So she pins it on someone else, I guess. Plus, they're not a hundred percent sure I did it. At least, I don't think so." He glanced in the direction of the front door while Lilly's estimation of his parents dropped precipitously.

"How did it happen?" Lilly asked.

"Why do you care?"

"Because it ruined my brother's wedding, not to mention someone died. I want to know how it happened."

He didn't answer for a long moment, but then he spoke.

CHAPTER 85

"Maureen and I were outside taking down a table. She had motioned for me to come out and help her. I was mad because she can't boss me around like that. I practically *own* that place, or at least I will."

Not anymore, thought Lilly.

"She started telling me all these things I needed to take inside before the table could be disassembled. It wasn't even our job. The caterer has to sign a contract with the venue stating the responsibilities of the caterer and the responsibilities of the Juniper Lake Manor staff. She totally ignored that."

"Did you point that out?"

"Of course I did. But she wasn't listening. She kept saying how hard it was to work with Darla and her staff. She said she was going to make sure that other caterers in the area black-balled Juniper Lake Manor. She said I was being uncooperative and self-centered."

"Okay, so she said something stupid. Is that why you killed her?"

"Stop saying that! I didn't do it on purpose."

Lilly clamped her lips shut in a thin line. She noticed Laurel watching her out of the corner of her eye.

"I told her that my father would sue her for defamation. She got right in my face and said that he wouldn't dare. She actually *shook her finger* right in my face.

"So I put my hands on her shoulders to push her away from me. I mean, she was in my personal space."

Lilly looked at him blankly. He killed someone for getting in his personal space?

"I shoved her harder than I meant to. She stumbled and tripped over one of the rocks that line the shore at that part of the lake. I think she hit her head. Then she fell into the water and didn't move."

"And you didn't run for help?"

"I was going to."

"And?"

"And I didn't because I think she was already dead! I mean, obviously!" Drew was shouting now. He continued. "If she wasn't dead, she would have told everyone I did it. It would have been he said, she said, and who would people believe? The kid or the adult? The adult, obviously. Plus, there are no cameras out there, so no one could prove I did it."

Lilly couldn't believe what she was hearing. This had to be the most spoiled, entitled, privileged young man on the whole planet. She recalled how pleasant he had been earlier that evening, when he and Laurel were cleaning up. He had just *killed* someone. How could he not have been sick with remorse and dread?

"I mean, she wasn't even nice to you, right?" Drew directed the question at Lilly. "Darla told me that you complained that Maureen was a pain."

"She was a pain, that's true, but that's no reason to kill someone."

Drew blew out a long breath between his perfect teeth. "You just don't get it."

He sat down on the sofa with his head in his hands, but stood up just a moment later. "And now you both know. Laurel, I really liked you."

Lilly caught his use of the past tense and felt her body stiffen. "Drew, you need to leave now."

"I'm not going anywhere just yet. We need to come to an agreement."

"What are you talking about?"

"What else? I need you both to agree not to say anything to anyone about this. You're sworn to secrecy."

Are you nine? Lilly thought.

"What do you mean, we're sworn to secrecy?" she demanded. "Of course we're not sworn to secrecy. You *killed* someone, Drew."

"How many times do I have to tell you *it was an accident?*" He was shouting at the top of his voice now. Lilly could hear Barney going wild outside. Drew took three rapid steps toward Lilly and grabbed her arm, twisting it behind her back.

CHAPTER 86

"Don't touch her!" Laurel shrieked.

"Laurel, stay out of this. It's between me and your mother."

With a primal scream, Laurel threw herself at Drew. Her fingers, like talons, scratched at his arms and neck.

"Laurel, I told you to stay out of this!" he roared. With one mighty shake, he tossed her to the floor. She scrambled up as he backed up toward the kitchen, still holding Lilly's arm behind him.

"Stop it!" Laurel screeched. Lilly looked at her in horror as a trail of blood snaked down the side of her face.

"Laurel, you're bleeding. Let me handle this." Lilly spoke in as calm a voice as she could manage. She hoped Drew couldn't feel her fear.

"Oh, my God. I'm so sorry, Laurel. I didn't mean to hurt you."

Lilly, hearing the tone of his voice soften just a little, tried to wrench her arm out of his grasp. He snapped his head toward her and gripped all the harder.

"Mom, are you okay?" Laurel was crying, the blood and tears mixing and running onto her clothes.

"I'm okay, Laurel. Don't worry about me. Call the police."

Laurel reached into her pocket and took out her phone, but Drew didn't seem to think that was a good idea. "Don't you dare call the cops." He held out his hand. "Laurel, give me the phone. Don't make me hurt your mother even more. I'll do it. You know I will."

Laurel let out a choked sob and handed her phone to him. Lilly managed not to react at all, though she wished Laurel had had time to dial 9-1-1 before handing him their lifeline.

Drew threw Lilly into the counter by the sink. A searing pain ripped through her hip and her leg buckled, but she managed to stay upright. She put out her hands to stop Drew from coming near her again.

Laurel was sobbing and screaming. Drew was cursing at the top of his lungs. He grabbed Lilly around her chest and held her from behind. Lilly was trying to get Laurel to calm down, repeating, "It's okay, Laur," over and over. Laurel wouldn't look at her, so focused was she on Drew's face. Lilly kept glancing toward the back door, trying to communicate with Laurel. If Laurel could open the door, Barney would come in and maybe his presence could distract Drew long enough for Lilly to grab something to use as a weapon.

But Laurel wasn't looking. Hatred for Drew burned from her eyes as she ran toward him, hoping to accomplish God-only-knew what.

Laurel had let out a keening scream when the back door flung open and Barney careened across the floor and into the melee.

Lilly almost collapsed with relief when Tighe sped into the room behind the dog.

"What's happening? Mom?"

"Tighe! Help!" Laurel let out a sob in relief at seeing her brother.

Tighe, who towered over Drew, ran forward, jerked Drew's arm away from Lilly's chest, and punched him in the face hard enough to make him fall to his knees. Then he grabbed Drew's arm, lifted him up straight, and punched him again. Blood flowed from Drew's nose and his eyes rolled back in his head. Tighe let go of him and he slumped to the ground.

"Tighe! Stop!" Lilly was screaming now, too. "Laurel, call the police." Drew had let Laurel's phone clatter across the floor when he fell and Laurel scrambled for it. She tried dialing 9-1-1, but her fingers trembled so violently that it took her four tries.

She told the dispatcher to send someone quick while Tighe was trying to make sure Lilly was all right.

"I'm fine," she said breathlessly. "I just didn't want you to get in trouble by hurting him anymore."

"He's lucky I didn't kill him." Tighe was grim, his face flushed and angry. "What happened?"

"He admitted to killing Maureen."

Tighe's eyes widened. "*He* killed the caterer?"

Lilly nodded, finally able to slow her breathing and speak without gasping for air. "He says it was an accident. He thought Laurel and I would keep it a secret."

"Mom, you should have promised to keep it secret," Laurel said.

Tighe looked at her and noticed the blood for the first time. "Laurel, you're bleeding! What happened?"

Laurel shrugged. "I must have hit my head in the living room when I fell."

Tighe looked from his mother to his sister and back again, bewilderment growing. "I never should have gone anywhere tonight."

"How could you have known Drew would try to kill us both?" Laurel asked. She stood up and finally quiet tears started to flow. Her shoulders shook as she covered her face with her hands. Tighe hugged her close.

"Let it out, honey." Lilly came and Tighe opened the circle wider to let her in. He released them a moment later to look at Drew, who still lay motionless on the floor.

CHAPTER 87

"What do we do now?" Laurel asked.

"Maybe I should tie him up," Tighe said.

"I don't think that's necessary," Lilly said. "The police should be here any minute and he doesn't look like he's going anywhere. If he does wake up, I think merely your presence should keep him from trying anything."

Barney had watched the scene unfold from the time Tighe knocked Drew out, and now that he could sense the drama had passed, he padded over to Lilly and waited for her to rub his head. She smiled at him. "You knew about Drew, didn't you, boy? You knew something wasn't right. Why didn't I pay more attention?"

Laurel sank down onto her knees and hugged Barney, who slobbered the clean side of her face with wet kisses. She laughed.

It was a good sound.

It wasn't long before two police cars parked in the driveway. Barney heard them first and alerted the entire house—and the rest of Juniper Junction—to their presence.

While Tighe stayed in the kitchen to make sure Drew stayed

put, Lilly met the officers at the front door. She was not surprised to see Tom standing there. He looked at her grimly. "Everything okay here?"

She smiled ruefully. "I think so."

"May we come in?" he asked.

"Certainly. Thanks for coming." Lilly stood back to let Tom and another officer into the living room.

"What happened?" Tom asked.

"Drew Henderson, who works at Juniper Lake Manor, confessed to killing the caterer at Bill's wedding. He attacked me and my daughter. When my son came home—you probably remember both kids from the wedding—and saw what was going on, he punched Drew. Drew is lying on the kitchen floor right now."

Tom looked incredulous. "Drew Henderson confessed?"

Lilly nodded. "I'll show you where he is." She led Tom and the other officer into the kitchen, where Tighe stood over Drew's body, which was beginning to move and squirm a little bit. A moan escaped the young man's lips.

Tom looked over his shoulder and instructed the other officer to start taking statements. The officer took out a note-book and pen from a small pocket and asked Lilly to talk to him first. She led him back into the living room to tell him what happened while Tighe and Laurel stayed in the kitchen.

When Lilly had answered a number of preliminary questions, it was Laurel's turn, then Tighe's, to talk to the officer. He instructed all three of them to come down to the police station the following day to make formal statements. Then he spoke quietly to Tom, who was talking on his radio.

The paramedics arrived and took Drew away after taking a look at Laurel's wound, which was superficial but had bled quite a lot. They bandaged the cut and pronounced her lucky. The officer who had questioned Lilly and the kids left with the ambulance and Tom remained. Lilly offered him a cup of coffee, which he accepted. They all sat in the living room talking while Tom drank his coffee slowly.

"We had an idea it might be Drew," he said. "No one recalled seeing him indoors at the time of the murder, so we thought he might have been outside with the caterer. But his parents have a lawyer for him and we had to schedule Drew's interrogation through the lawyer." He shook his head. "The appointment was supposed to be tomorrow."

"Do you think his parents knew?" Lilly asked.

"I don't know, but we're going to find out and they may be facing charges, too."

"What charges will Drew face?" Laurel asked. Her eyes were red and puffy, her cheeks were hollow. It looked like she hadn't slept in a week.

"I'm not totally sure, but my guess? Reckless homicide, at the very least."

"How about assault and battery?" Lilly suggested. "And making terroristic threats?"

"All those are strong contenders, Mrs. Carlsen," Tom answered. "The one thing I'm sure of is that he's in a lot of trouble." Tom stood up and Lilly reached out for his coffee cup. He handed it to her, thanked her and the kids and promised to be in touch. "Are you coming down to the station to file formal statements tomorrow?"

"Yes," they said in unison.

Tom put his hand on the doorknob, then turned around. "How's Bill doing? Having fun in Aruba?"

"I haven't even heard from him. He's probably forgotten we all exist."

Tom chuckled and then shook his head. "I couldn't blame him if he did."

CHAPTER 88

After Lilly had closed and locked the door behind Tom she went to the kitchen, where she found Tighe and Laurel already cleaning up the mess that had been made during the fracas with Drew. There was blood on the floor, but not much. Most of it seemed to have soaked into Drew's shirt, from what Lilly had seen.

"Why did he let Vanessa leave?" Lilly asked Laurel. "Why didn't he make her stay here with the rest of us?"

"He didn't outright admit to killing Maureen while Vanessa was still here, but I think she was figuring it out. I should have figured it out myself, but my brain just wouldn't let me believe it. Anyway, she made a little noise like she was going to be sick and I think he was afraid she was going to throw up in front of him. He told her he thought she should go home and she left fast."

Lilly wished for a fleeting second that Vanessa had said something to her before leaving, but maybe she was afraid she was going to be sick right then and there. Plus, Vanessa was a very young woman, and a pregnant one at that. She had other things on her mind when she fled from the house.

When the kitchen was scrubbed clean, everyone trooped upstairs to bed. Lilly couldn't wait to be asleep. First, though, she called Hassan to tell him what had happened.

He couldn't believe it.

"Laurel's boyfriend? He's the one who killed the caterer?"

"Yes. And he's certainly not her boyfriend anymore. I was starting to think he was a pretty nice kid with a solid head on his shoulders. I mean, am I a terrible judge of character or what?"

"You can't blame yourself. No one could have known."

"Except possibly his parents. I wonder if the private investigator suspected."

"I doubt it. Her career would be on the line."

"You're right. Wait 'til I call her tomorrow and tell her what happened."

Hassan chuckled. "And you did it all for free."

"And to think I went in and practically accused Brad of killing her. I shouldn't have listened to Celie."

"She sounds like a very persuasive person. She's probably used to getting people to talk and do other things she needs done."

"And I'm just a jeweler."

"You're also an awesome mom, a great daughter, and the best girlfriend a guy could ever ask for."

"Keep it up and you might never get rid of me."

When Lilly got up the next morning her first call was to Celie.

"Hello? Celie Wolf speaking."

"Hi, Celie. It's Lilly Carlsen."

"Good morning, Lilly. I'm glad you called. I had an idea and I wanted to run it by you."

"Wait. Before you do that, have you heard about Drew?"

"No. Drew Henderson?"

"The very same. Last night at my house he admitted to killing Maureen. He left in police custody in an ambulance."

There was silence on the other end of the line.

CHAPTER 89

"Celie? You still there?"

"I'm here. I can't believe it. Drew? He seems like such a nice kid. What happened? Is he okay?"

"I'm sure he's going to be fine. But you should probably ask his parents about the circumstances. I don't want you to get in trouble for knowing what happened before you even talk to them."

"You're probably right. It should come from them. You know, every time I asked to speak to Drew, they put me off—telling me he was out, telling me he was taking extra classes over the summer and couldn't talk because he was so busy studying, that sort of thing. I also know they hired a lawyer to run interference between Drew and the police, but I assumed they just did that because they have the money to do it. Now I wonder if they knew all along."

Lilly declined to comment on that. "Well, I've got to go to work. I just wanted to let you know what happened."

"Thanks, Lilly. Do you have the name of the police officer who had custody of Drew last night when he went to the hospital?"

"I have his card here somewhere. But Tom was with him. I'm sure you can call Tom and try to get some information out of him. Now that they have the killer in custody, he might be more willing to talk."

"Tom Toole was there? I thought he had been promoted to a desk job."

"I don't know anything about that. But he was definitely the one who responded to our 9-1-1 call."

"Okay, thanks. I'll give him a ring. Thanks for all your help, Lilly. It was nice getting to know you."

Lilly couldn't see that Celie really knew her at all, but it was a nice thing to say. On the other hand, Celie probably knew way more about Lilly than Lilly even realized. She was, after all, a private investigator. "You too, Celie. Take care."

When Lilly left for work the kids were still asleep. She didn't have the heart to wake them up. Harry was already at the jewelry shop. "Hi, boss. Wow, you look tired. Long night?"

His jaw dropped when Lilly told him what had transpired at her house the night before.

"Thank God you and the kids are okay. What if Tighe hadn't come home when he did?"

"I don't even want to think about that."

She and Harry spent several minutes carrying pieces of jewelry from the vault to the display cases in the front of the store, and it wasn't until everything was set up for the day that Lilly realized the morning routine had calmed her down.

"Feeling better? You don't look as tense," Harry said.

She smiled. "I am feeling better. It's good to be at work so I have something to do besides thinking about my problems."

She went back to her office to turn on the computer. While she waited for it to boot up, she leafed through several invoices on her desk. Her leg jiggled up and down. Something wasn't sitting right.

Harry poked his head into the office. "Boss, Mallory is here to see you."

Lilly followed Harry into the front of the shop. "Good morning, Mallory. What's new with you? How's Tisha doing?"

"She's doing much better. She and Tom had a talk and they're an item again."

"Don't tell me it was man trouble that caused her depression."

"I think that triggered it. You should have seen how she perked up once they decided to keep seeing each other."

Lilly refrained from shaking her head in dismay.

"I've tried telling her she has to be happy with herself before she can be happy with a man, but she doesn't listen," Mallory said.

"It's something every person has to learn for herself. Or himself."

And then out of nowhere, something clicked. Something Celie had said. Tom—he was up for a promotion. Could that be the same promotion Bill was hoping to get?

That changed things.

"Mallory, I've just thought of something I need to do right away. Could I come by the pottery shop later to chat?"

Mallory gave her a confused look. "Uh, I guess. I just wanted to run something by you, but it can wait. Sorry for keeping you."

"Oh, no, you're not keeping me. I just now remembered it as we were talking. Sorry I have to run."

Mallory waved goodbye and Lilly rushed back to the office. She dialed Celie Wolf. "Celie? It's Lilly. Listen. Did you tell me Tom Toole was up for a promotion at work?"

"Yes."

"Do you happen to know what that position would be?"

"I think so. Let me check my notes. I write everything down, just in case ... yeah, here it is. He's up for deputy lieutenant."

Same as Bill. So they were competing for the same job.

"Okay, thanks."

"Mind if I ask why you want to know?"

"I was just wondering. He and Bill are up for the same job, that's all."

"Oh, I see. Well, if that's all you need...."

"It is. Thanks, Celie. Talk to you later."

Lilly hung up. Her heart was beating fast. She wondered if there was a connection between Tom and Jeremy Folsom, Mallory's ex-husband. It seemed likely that the two men, both involved with sisters, would have met at some point. She needed to find out.

She needed to talk to Mallory. She hurried to the front of the shop. "Harry, I hate to ask you to do this, but can you watch the shop for me? I need to run down to talk to Mallory."

"Sure." Harry cocked his head. "You realize you just sent her out of here, right?"

"I know she was just here, but I've thought of something and I need to talk to her." This was an issue she needed to address in person.

Lilly raced out the door and down the block to the pottery shop. It wasn't open yet, but the front door was unlocked. She pushed the door open and rushed into the large, bright room, breathless from hurrying. She stopped short when she saw that Mallory had a customer with her. She was standing behind the counter and she looked up in surprise.

"Lilly! Are you all right? What's wrong?"

"Nothing's wrong. I'm just in a hurry, that's all." She leaned against the counter to catch her breath while Mallory waited for her to speak. "I'm sorry, I didn't know you had a customer."

"That's okay. What do you need?"

The man had turned around and was staring openly at Lilly who, after a few seconds, was breathing more slowly. "I came to ask you a question. It might seem weird, but I need to know. I'll wait until you're done."

Mallory cocked her head and gave Lilly a confused look. "It's okay—you can talk. I'll help you if I can. What is it?" She waited for Lilly to speak. Lilly was in no mood to spare niceties for the stranger who stood there.

"You told me about your ex-husband, right? Do you remember if he's met Tom Toole, by any chance?"

Mallory grimaced and her shoulders fell. She glanced at the man watching the conversation unfold.

"Lilly, I'd like you to meet my ex-husband, Jeremy Folsom."

Lilly remembered, too late, that it was rude to stare at someone with one's mouth open. She closed it as if she were a guppy and held out her hand. "Nice to meet you." Jeremy shook her hand without a word. Lilly cleared her throat. This was awkward. Should she wait for him to answer her question?

She didn't need to wonder for long, though, because a moment later the door to the pottery shop opened again. Mallory shot a look toward Lilly. "I was hoping you wouldn't put two and two together," she said. Lilly followed Mallory's gaze toward the door. Tom was standing inside the door, his arms crossed over his chest.

"Jeremy, Mallory," he said. "Lilly." He nodded toward her.

Lilly looked from Mallory to Jeremy to Tom and back to Mallory again.

"I came into your shop this morning because I needed to talk to you," Mallory said. "I wish you hadn't had other business to attend to."

CHAPTER 91

"What's going on here?" Lilly asked. Her hackles were raised. Something in Mallory's tone set alarm bells ringing in her head.

There was a *click* and Lilly spun around. Tom had locked the front door. Her heart skipped a beat. He pulled his service revolver from his holster and held it at his side, pointed down. "All of you, in the office." He jerked his head toward the office in the back of the pottery shop.

Mallory stood aside as Lilly came around the counter and went first into the office. She whispered to Lilly as they shuffled forward. "I was trying to warn you—"

"Mallory, would you shut that big trap of yours just once?" Tom said in a gruff voice. "My God, no wonder Jeremy left you. You never stop talking."

Mallory grumbled something that Lilly couldn't quite hear, but it sounded like something that wouldn't be repeated in polite company.

Tom wasn't polite company.

Once all four were in Mallory's office, Tom closed the door

behind him and leaned against it. He passed a hand over his eyes, as if the crew in front of him had frustrated him to no end.

"Tom, listen—" Mallory began.

"No, you listen, Mallory. I'm not going to ask you again to keep your mouth shut. I need to think." Jeremy remained silent, scowling at Tom.

Lilly was desperate to know what was going on, but all she could think about was a way to get out of there. A quick glance around the room revealed the back door, which probably led to the alley behind the store where employees parked. If she could make a dash for that....

But she couldn't outrun a bullet from Tom's gun.

Was there something she could throw at him to distract him?

Not likely. He was a police officer, highly trained to deal with situations similar to this one. Of course, when he trained, it was probably assumed that he would be the good guy.

But Lilly knew what happened when people assume.

Mallory had made a comment about putting two and two together. What did that mean? Jeremy Folsom was the man Celie suspected of piloting the plane that buzzed Bill and Noley's reception. Mallory, whose sister was dating Tom, was Folsom's ex-wife. Tom had acknowledged Jeremy when he came into the pottery shop, so the men had obviously met. This was the connection everyone had missed.

Furthermore, Celie had learned that Jeremy Folsom owed money to someone, and that he had likely piloted the plane as a favor to that person.

Now Tom was in here, waving his gun around at Mallory and Jeremy. Could Tom be the one who had hired Jeremy?

Then Lilly remembered the reason she had come to see Mallory—Tom and Bill were up for the same promotion at work. Could this whole thing have had something to do with the promotion?

Tom was still glaring at his captives, not bothering to hide his disdain. Lilly could see him clenching and unclenching his jaws.

She could only assume this was not going to end well.

She was definitely never planning another wedding for anyone.

"Tom, it's not too late to do the right thing," Jeremy said.

"And you're the expert on doing the right thing, I suppose?" Tom sneered at Jeremy.

"No. But I can see that if you go through with this, there's no turning back."

"Shut up." Tom waved the gun toward Jeremy. Lilly flinched.

The silence grew in tandem with the tension in the stuffy room. Lilly and Mallory cast sidelong glances at each other several times, but if Mallory was trying to communicate something, Lilly had no idea what it was.

Tom started pacing in front of the office door.

"Folsom, you couldn't do one simple thing, could you?" Tom asked.

"Tom, you should probably keep it to yourself right now." Jeremy inclined his head toward Lilly.

Lilly couldn't keep quiet any longer. "No need to keep it to yourself on my account," she said, addressing Tom and Jeremy. "I know what happened."

Tom raised his eyebrows and fixed his mouth in a cruel twist. Lilly couldn't believe she had welcomed him into her home. "Oh, really? And what happened?"

Lilly gestured toward Jeremy. "Jeremy here buzzed my brother's wedding reception with a plane that you hired him to fly." She gazed steadily at Tom, almost daring him to contradict her, but hoping he couldn't hear her knees knocking together.

"I see Bill isn't the only goody-goody in the family," Tom said. "You seem to know everything, too. You must get it from him."

Lilly kept her lips pressed tightly together. *Don't let him get to you, Lilly. Keep the focus on the problem at hand.*

"All right, Tom. That's enough. We've all had enough," Mallory said. Lilly looked at her in confusion.

"I'm sorry, Jeremy, Tom. I just can't do this anymore. Lilly is my friend."

Lilly whirled her head toward Mallory. "What are you talking about?"

CHAPTER 92

"Mallory!" Tom barked. "That's enough out of you!" He took a step toward her, but Jeremy placed himself between them. Lilly noticed he walked with a limp, probably from the plane crash. He put his hands out toward Tom, palms facing forward.

"Tom, give me the gun. It's over. Too many people know what happened. You have to turn yourself in. We both do. In fact, I'm in just as much trouble as you are."

Tom retreated until his back was against the office door. "Wrong thing to say, Folsom. I am not turning myself in, and I am not going to be in trouble. No one in this room is going to say a word to anyone because no one is going to live to talk about it. I'll just be the hero who happened to come into the pottery shop when there was a deadly fight taking place." He grinned again.

Jeremy, who had been taking one slow step after another toward Tom, stopped. Lilly couldn't take her eyes off Tom, but she could sense Mallory's fear just a few feet away. She couldn't hear a thing over the pulsing of the blood in her own ears. Until her phone buzzed in her pocket.

"What's that?" Tom asked, pointing the gun from one person to the next.

"It's my phone," Lilly said.

"Give it here." Tom held out his hand.

"I'm not throwing my phone."

"I said, *give it here!*"

Lilly didn't know if it was the tone of his voice or the gun in his hand that frightened her more, though it was probably the gun. She threw the phone to Tom, who let it clatter to the floor.

What a jerk. Now I'm probably going to need a new phone screen. If I live through this.

She wondered who was calling. Tom glanced at the phone, which had landed screen-side up. "Who's Harry? Your boyfriend?"

"None of your business."

"He works for Lilly," Mallory said. "He's probably wondering where she is. When she doesn't answer, he'll call the police. Tom, give Jeremy the gun and turn yourself in."

"Do you call the police every time someone doesn't pick up the phone?" he asked with a sneer.

Lilly blurted out a response. "I told him to call the police if I didn't answer the phone. He knew I was heading over to the pottery shop."

Tom's eyes narrowed and he looked at her skeptically. "You're lying."

"No, I'm not. I came over here to confront Mallory with what she knows about what happened at the wedding reception and I thought there might be trouble. I told Harry to call me at a certain time and then to call the cops if I didn't answer. This is the prearranged call."

Tom looked doubtful as the phone continued to buzz on the floor. Finally he kicked it over to Lilly. "Answer it. Tell him you're fine."

She picked up the phone with trembling hands, her eyes never leaving Tom's face.

"Hello?"

"Lilly? I just called to let you know that Beau called here. He tried texting you but didn't get a response. He's on his way to your mom's house to help Nikki with her."

Oh, no. Something must be wrong with Mom. I need to get out of here.

"No, I'm fine, Harry. Turns out I was wrong. Don't worry about a thing."

"Um, that's good. Glad to hear it. Did you ... did you hear what I said?"

"No, everything is fine. I'll be back soon."

"Okay. I mean, I guess. Are you all right, Lilly?"

"Nope."

"What do you want me to do?"

"All right. Talk to you soon."

She hit the button to end the conversation, placed the phone on the floor, and slid it back toward Tom, whose gaze flitted from one captive to the next. She hoped Harry would understand that she needed him to call the police. Quickly.

"If the cops show up here, you're going to be the first one I shoot," Tom said, pointing his gun at Lilly. She flinched. Maybe Harry calling the cops wasn't the best thing.

CHAPTER 93

"Tom, this is nuts. You'll never get away with this."
Jeremy was advancing toward him again.

"Stay back!" Tom brandished the gun, waving it around like a madman.

While Tom's arm was in the air and the gun was pointed toward the ceiling, Jeremy rushed at him clumsily, wrapping his arms around Tom's waist and pulling him to the ground. Mallory screamed and threw herself on top of Jeremy. Lilly was momentarily rooted to the spot with surprise and fear, but she quickly recovered herself and grabbed the first thing her hand touched—a stapler on Mallory's desk. A stapler wasn't much of a weapon against a gun, but she could throw it if necessary. She launched herself in the direction of the back door; then jerked to a stop when she heard a loud *pop*.

It felt almost surreal as she looked down at her body to make sure she hadn't been shot. No blood. Good. She spun around in the direction of the three people on the floor and saw immediately that blood was seeping across Mallory's shirt.

Forgetting her need to get outside as quickly as possible, Lilly ran toward Mallory.

Jeremy saw her approaching and yelled to her. "Get out!"

"But she's hurt!"

The two men were struggling for possession of the gun, and it went off again. This time the bullet ricocheted off the back door, right where Lilly would have been if Mallory hadn't been shot, and hit the ceiling. Motes of dust and bits of ceiling plaster rained down on the foursome as Jeremy and Tom continued to tussle. Finally Jeremy landed a punch right in Tom's face and Tom hit the back of his head on the floor. Jeremy used the momentary distraction to grab the gun and fling it away from them, then punched Tom again as he tried to reach for Jeremy's neck.

"Get help!" Jeremy roared at Lilly. She searched the floor for her phone, which had been kicked around by the men fighting, and saw it under Mallory's desk. She scrabbled for it and was just wrapping her fingers around it when Tom landed a kick on her elbow. She gasped in pain as tears swam before her eyes. But she blinked them away and reached again for the phone.

Once it was in her hand, she ran back to the door leading to the alley behind the pottery shop, yanked it open, and stumbled into the sunshine. She blinked and hit the numbers 9-1-1 before noticing two police cars bearing down on her, one from each end of the alley. She ended the call and bent over with one arm dangling and the other on her knee, sucking in deep breaths of air.

One of the officers ran up to her and assessed the situation rapidly. He radioed for an ambulance.

"Not me," she insisted. "There's someone inside who's been shot."

Immediately every officer drew his or her service weapon and moved toward the back door of the pottery shop in an almost reflexive formation. Upon seeing their response to the danger, she felt a sob erupt from her throat. She was safe now.

Her phone rang. She looked at it dumbly, then answered it.

"Hello?

"This is 9-1-1 dispatch calling back. Do you need assistance?"

The tears sprang from her eyes. "They're already here. Thank you." She leaned against the wall of the pottery shop and sank down to the ground, where she sat with her head on her knees, crying as if the world might end. It was relief, mostly, but the pain in her arm was excruciating. She could hear shouts and commotion coming from inside Mallory's office, and it wasn't long before two of the officers emerged with Tom between them. He was handcuffed and his nose was bleeding profusely. The officers said nothing, but looked on grimly as Tom ranted about being up for a promotion against Bill Merriweather, the one guy in the station who could do no wrong. She wanted to laugh, knowing Bill was a shoe-in for the promotion now and that Tom was sealing his own fate by yammering on and on in front of other police officers, but the tears kept falling and she couldn't even manage a smile.

It wasn't long before Harry appeared. He dropped to his knees in front of her. "Lilly, it's me, Harry. Are you all right? What happened? I called the police as soon as I knew you were in trouble, but I didn't know what to tell them. I called Hassan and he's on his way."

CHAPTER 94

That made her cry harder.

"Boss? Lilly? Are you all right?"

She finally lifted her head. Snot ran down her face and she wiped it away with her good arm. Finally her tears slowed and she managed a smile.

"I'm okay, Harry. I don't know what I would have done if you hadn't called when you did. You saved my life."

Those words jerked her thoughts back to the present. Mallory. Was she all right? Was she alive?

Her eyes must have looked frightened, because Harry put his hands on her shoulders. He looked into her eyes. "What is it?"

"Tom Toole shot Mallory in there. Is she okay?"

Harry stood up and ran toward the officers who were still standing quietly nearby with Tom between them. Lilly could hear him talking.

"Is Mallory okay? Lilly says she was shot."

"We have to wait for the paramedics to get here," one of the officers answered. And as if on cue, an ambulance roared up the alley. A woman and a man jumped out and the officers waved them inside. The man paused on his way in when he saw Lilly.

"Are you all right?" he asked.

"I'll be fine. Get to Mallory first."

He didn't need to be told twice. He raced after his partner and just moments later he was back outside, jogging to the ambulance. A police officer accompanied him. Together they retrieved a stretcher from the back and wheeled it into the office. Several minutes later they reemerged, this time with Mallory strapped to the gurney. They loaded her into the back of the ambulance just as an officer emerged from the back of the store with Jeremy in handcuffs. Another ambulance appeared on the scene, and moments later Lilly's arm was being examined. Harry stood by, watching and running his hands through his hair.

"Don't worry, Harry. I'm going to be fine. Do you know what happened to my mom?"

Harry shook his head.

"That's okay. I'll find out. I can't believe my cell phone still works."

"I think you need some X-rays, ma'am," one of the paramedics told her.

Lilly nodded. "Okay. Let's go so I can get it over with. Harry, can you take care of the shop?"

"Sure. I'll phone Hassan and reroute him to the hospital."

"Thanks, Harry."

By the time Lilly arrived at the emergency room, Hassan was already there, pacing. The paramedics had put Lilly in a wheelchair. They wheeled her through the lobby instead of going through the back door, so she was able to reach her good arm out to Hassan as she passed by. "Can he come with us?" she asked the paramedic.

"Sure."

Hassan followed the paramedic and Lilly into the labyrinthine emergency department. He pulled up a chair and sat down once Lilly was situated in an examination cubicle.

She closed her eyes and leaned back against the pillow.

"Are you really all right?" Hassan asked, holding her hand gently in his.

She opened her eyes. "I'll be fine. My arm hurts, that's all. Tom kicked it."

"What exactly happened?"

Lilly told him the story, ending with her gratitude for Jeremy knocking Tom off balance so she could make a break for the back door. "And Harry had called the police, as I hoped he would, so they arrived just as I reached the alley behind the pottery shop."

Hassan shook his head. "I can't believe Tom was behind the whole thing. No wonder the investigation has been going so slowly. He knew who did it all along."

*L*illy shifted uncomfortably.

"Are you sure you're all right?" Hassan asked.

She nodded.

"Thank God." He gazed at her, his dark eyes intense.

"My arm isn't my main concern right now. I need to know what's up with Mom. Beau was trying to get ahold of me to say that he was going over to her house to help Nikki with her. Can you hand me my phone?" She gestured toward a table near the bed where the paramedic had placed her phone.

Hassan complied and Lilly dialed Nikki's number. Nikki answered on the first ring.

"Hi, Lilly."

"Hi. I heard Beau called looking for me. Is Mom all right?"

"She burned herself on the stove. We brought her into the emergency room to have her hand checked out and bandaged. I felt she needed an antibiotic and a prescription for pain relief."

"Wait. You're in the emergency room?"

"Yes. I hope it's okay that we didn't wait for you."

"No, no. That's fine. I'm also in the emergency room."

"You're kidding. What happened? Are you all right?"

"It's a long story, but I'm fine. Where are you? I'll send Hassan out to find you."

"All right. I'll step out of your mom's room."

Lilly hung up and asked Hassan to pull her cubicle curtain aside and step into the passageway. He did so and waved his hand just a moment later.

"Nikki, we're over here," she heard him say.

It only took her a second to arrive at Lilly's bedside. "What are you in here for? Are you sick?"

"No, I hurt my arm. I'll be fine. Am I allowed to get out of bed to go see Mom?"

"They'll find you when they're ready," Hassan said. "Come on, I'll go with you."

He helped her off the bed and they accompanied Nikki back to Bev's cubicle. Bev lay back against the pillow, her eyes closed and a look of pain across her features. Beau sat on the chair next to her bed, holding her hand as Hassan had done for Lilly.

"Mom? It's me, Lilly. How are you doing?"

Bev's eyes fluttered open and she looked around in obvious confusion. "What are you doing here, Lilly?"

"Nikki told me you were here and I wanted to check on you. I hurt my arm and I'm waiting to see a doctor. You burned yourself?"

Bev nodded, closing her eyes again and wincing. Beau gave her a tender look. "Bevvy's going to be fine, aren't you?" He squeezed her hand.

I can't stand it when he calls her that. But Lilly had to admit that he was being very kind and she appreciated it.

Bev nodded slightly.

The doctor appeared in the cubicle a couple of minutes later. "I'll go back to my cubicle and as soon as I talk to the doctor, I'll be back," she told Nikki.

She was returning to her own bed when she heard a voice calling out weakly.

"Lilly? Lilly Carlsen? Is that you?"

She stopped short and looked at Hassan in surprise. "Did you hear that?"

He nodded, his brow furrowed. "Who was it?"

"I don't know. Hello?" She raised her voice a little so the other person could hear her.

"Lilly? It's me, Mallory."

"Mallory? Where are you?"

"In this room." The voice seemed to come from behind the curtain that separated Lilly's cubicle from Bev's cubicle. Lilly wiggled the curtain just to be sure. She didn't want to mistakenly bumble into the wrong room.

"In here?" she asked.

"Yes."

Lilly drew back the curtain and drew in a sharp breath. Mallory lay on the bed, her features ashen and her eyes sunken into her skull. "Thank God you're all right! I was so worried, wondering what had happened to you. Where's the doctor? Why isn't someone in here with you?"

"The nurse went for more pain meds and the doctor said she'd be right back."

"Where are you hurt?"

"The bullet grazed my side, but I'll be okay."

"I'm so glad."

"Are you all right? Is your arm broken? You didn't get hit with a bullet, did you?"

"I'm fine, I don't think my arm is broken, and I didn't get hit with a bullet. I'm just waiting for a doctor."

At that moment Mallory's doctor appeared behind Lilly. "Excuse me, please. And who are you?"

"It's okay, Doctor. This woman was with me when I was hurt," Mallory said.

"My bed is right next to yours, Mallory. I'll come back when I've been cleared to get out of here." Lilly turned around and Hassan followed her back to her own bed.

CHAPTER 96

She waited a while for a doctor to show up, since there were far more urgent cases than hers in the emergency department. When he did arrive, it was the same doctor who had examined Bev. He examined Lilly's arm gently. "Looks like you've dislocated your elbow. I can get it back into place for you."

"Good. How long will it take?"

"We'll give you some medication for the pain and a light sedative before we do it, so it'll be just a little while."

"Why a sedative?"

"The procedure is simple, but can cause some pain."

That turned out to be a grand understatement. Even with the medication and the light sedation, the pain caused by the procedure caused Lilly to become nauseous and light-headed.

Once the doctor had gotten Lilly's elbow back in place, Lilly lay back and closed her eyes. "Can I just rest for a few minutes? Then I'll go see Mom and Mallory."

"Sure. I'll send you home with a prescription for additional pain relief, but you should be back to normal before too long.

You'll need to keep it in a sling for a few days, too. Is that your mom a few doors down?"

Lilly nodded. "Is she going to be all right?"

"Burns are very painful, as I'm sure you know if you've ever suffered a burn. But I think she's going to be all right. The greater concern, obviously, is her mental state."

"I know. She's been in here several times just in the past couple of weeks."

"I saw that in her chart. I know she has a nurse with her all the time, but it might be time to start thinking about nursing care in an environment with greater resources. I know Nikki from other patients we've had in here, and she's the best. But there's only so much she can do without a team of doctors and nurses to help her."

Lilly looked down at her elbow, which was encased in a soft ice pack. "I know. It's a conversation I've been dreading, but I think it's time I talk about it with my brother."

"Make sure you include her regular physician in the discussion. That person will obviously have a lot more information than I do. All I know is what I've seen in her chart here."

"Thanks, Doctor."

When the doctor left, Lilly and Hassan gazed at each other. "I hate to think about it," she said.

"I know. But you have to do what's best for your mom."

"I want her to go back the way she used to be," Lilly said quietly.

"We all do. But you're not alone. You have me and Bill and Noley and the kids, and even Beau and Nikki, behind you. If you ask Nikki, she'll probably tell you she agrees with the doctor."

Lilly nodded, suddenly unable to speak. She swallowed and the lump in her throat hurt. She reached for the Styrofoam cup next to her bed and took a sip of ice water. "Do you think I can go see her now?"

"I'm sure you can, but let's wait until the doctor comes back with a script for pain meds. Then we'll get you discharged."

"Okay."

They waited at least a half hour before the doctor returned. "I've already sent the script to your pharmacy. You can pick up the medicine on your way home. The nurse will be in with some forms to sign and then you can get out of here. Do you want to go see your mom?"

"Yes."

"That's fine. I'll tell the nurse to find you in there."

The doctor left and Hassan helped Lilly into the cardigan sweater she had been wearing. She winced. "My arm hurts more now than when I came in here."

"Maybe so, but it will start feeling better soon, I'm sure."

Before going to stay with Bev, Lilly peeked into Mallory's cubicle. A nurse was bustling around the bed, checking tubes and machines hooked up to Mallory. "How are you doing?" Lilly asked gently.

"I've been better. But the doctor says I'm going to live." She smiled. "Lilly, I owe you an apology."

"Not now, Mallory. You rest. When you're better, we'll talk."

Mallory nodded and lay back against the pillow. Then Lilly left and pulled back her mom's curtain.

CHAPTER 97

"*D*id you hurt your arm? Are you all right?" Bev eyes were focused on the sling Lilly was wearing. Her words were hard to understand; her voice was soft and strained, no doubt due to the pain caused by her burn.

Lilly smiled at Bev. "I'm fine, Mom. How are you doing?"

"I hurt, but I want to go home."

Lilly glanced at Nikki, who gave her a rueful look. Lilly had a feeling Nikki knew what she and the doctor had discussed.

"We'll get you out of here soon, Mom, I promise."

"Okay." Bev closed her eyes and was sleeping just a few minutes later.

Nikki, Beau, Lilly, and Hassan stood around Bev's bed, talking quietly, while they waited for her to be discharged. Nikki and Beau couldn't believe what had happened at the pottery shop, and expressed their relief that Lilly was okay. Finally, after what seemed like hours, a nurse appeared with the paperwork to show Bev's regular doctor, a prescription for more pain medication, and some extra bandages for Nikki to use when she changed the dressing on Bev's burn.

As afternoon turned to early evening, they all bade the

nurses farewell and drove in a convoy back to Bev's house. Hassan drove Lilly in his car. "What are you going to say to Mallory when you talk to her again?"

"I don't know. Something strange was going on, and I have a feeling Mallory is going to tell me that she knew all along who was behind the plane incident at Bill and Noley's wedding reception." She sighed. "I had her figured all wrong. Here I was thinking she and I might end up good friends, and she was keeping this awful secret from me."

"Maybe she had a good reason for keeping it from you."

"I can't think of one. Anyway, I think I'm just going to have to wait and see what she says, and then play it by ear."

Hassan covered Lilly's hand with his own. "You've been through a lot. After we get your mom situated at her house, why don't you and I go have dinner at the diner and I'll take you home? You need a long soak in the tub and a good night's sleep."

She squeezed his hand. "That sounds good. I'll call the kids and let them know what's been going on."

Even though it was early, Lilly and Nikki helped Bev change into a nightgown once they got her in the house. Hassan and Beau cleaned up the mess that had been left in the kitchen when Nikki and Beau had taken Bev to the hospital all those hours ago. Then, while Nikki prepared a small plate of scrambled eggs for Bev, Lilly called Laurel and Tighe at home to let them know what had transpired during the day. The kids couldn't believe Lilly had been in such danger or that their grandmother had been hurt. They were relieved to hear that both women were all right.

"When are you going to be home, Mom?" Laurel asked.

"Hassan and I are going to the diner for dinner, then I'll be home right afterward. Is everything all right there?"

"Yes. Vanessa asked if she could spend the night. I think she can't deal with her parents right now. Would that be okay with you?"

"Sure. She's welcome anytime. What happened with her parents?"

"They met her boyfriend and they disapprove."

"I'm sorry to hear that. I don't think of Vanessa as the type of person who would choose a boyfriend she can't take home."

"She isn't. He's coming over, too. You'll see why her parents disapprove. But don't worry—he's not spending the night. He'll leave once you get home."

"All right. I'll see you soon, honey."

"Bye, Mom."

Wait. How will I see why they disapprove? But that wasn't Lilly's concern just then.

Everyone sat in the living room talking while Lilly helped Bev eat some of her scrambled eggs. When Bev had eaten a few bites, she indicated that she was ready for bed.

Lilly and Hassan left and drove to the diner. Lilly leaned her head against the headrest and let out a long breath.

"Would you do something for me?" Lilly asked, keeping her eyes closed. "Would you try to find out what happened to Tom and Jeremy after they were taken into custody this morning? I'm dying to find out."

"Consider it done."

CHAPTER 98

At the diner Lilly ordered the Salisbury steak and Hassan ordered a Reuben sandwich. "This is comfort food at its best," Lilly said between bites. "It really hits the spot."

They were almost done eating when they saw Nikki and Beau come into the diner. They didn't see Lilly and Hassan, and Lilly didn't wave to them or acknowledge them.

"Aren't you going to say hello?" Hassan asked.

"No. They need some time to themselves. Nikki's been running ragged with my mom in the past few weeks. I have a feeling she and Beau haven't seen much of each other."

"Beau was really good with your mom today."

Lilly nodded. "He was," she agreed. "He and Mom have always gotten along really well. I'm grateful to him for helping Nikki today."

She thought back to the days following Beau's return to Juniper Junction after being away without so much as a phone call for fifteen years. "You know, a couple of years ago I couldn't have imagined myself being grateful to him for anything."

"I'm glad you're friends," Hassan said. He took her hand and held it in his. "I think I need to get you back to your house. Are you ready to head out?"

Lilly nodded and they left. Nikki and Beau had their heads together talking, so Lilly didn't say anything on the way out.

As they pulled up to Lilly's house, Hassan noticed a strange car in the driveway. "Whose car is that?"

"Probably Vanessa's boyfriend's. Laurel said he would be here when we got back from dinner. Why don't you come in and meet him?"

"Sure."

They went inside and found Laurel, Vanessa, and Cyrus sitting around the kitchen table. Lilly was surprised to see that Cyrus appeared to be of Arabic descent. He had dark olive skin and jet black eyes and hair. He was a handsome young man and he smiled as he stood to shake hands with Lilly and Hassan after Laurel introduced them.

"Thank you for being so kind to Vanessa," he said. "She needs someone who's accepting of her right now."

Lilly thought it a very grown-up thing to say. She smiled at Cyrus. "Vanessa knows she's welcome here anytime."

"I should get going. I have a long drive," Cyrus said. "I was just staying long enough to meet you." Vanessa stood up and walked outside with him after he bid everyone goodbye.

Lilly turned to Laurel. "He seems like such a nice guy. I mean, I've only known him for three minutes, but I get a good vibe from him."

"He's awesome. Can you guess why Vanessa's parents don't like him?"

Lilly and Hassan shook their heads.

"Because he's brown. Can you believe it?"

Lilly and Hassan looked at each other. They knew well the bigotry that existed even in this day and age. "Unfortunately, I can believe it. Suddenly I think much less of Vanessa's parents."

"And wait until they find out they're going to have a grand-child that looks like Cyrus," Laurel said. "They'll flip."

Suddenly Lilly was bone-weary. The harrowing experience of being held at gunpoint by a madman, the pain of her dislocated elbow, the stress over her mother's burn, the additional stress of the conversation she had had with the doctor about her mother's care, and finally, the revelation that Vanessa's parents were bigots, hit her like a steamroller. "I need a bath and my bed," she said. She wanted to cry, but she was even too tired to do that.

Hassan held her in a strong embrace and told her he'd wait for her to call him in the morning. "Laur, take good care of your mom tonight, okay?"

After Hassan left, the tears finally began to roll silently down Lilly's cheeks. Laurel hugged her and hurried upstairs to fill the tub with hot water. When the bath was ready, Lilly went upstairs. Barney had watched the whole episode curiously, and when Lilly told him to stay downstairs with Laurel, he complied. It was as if he knew she wanted to be alone.

After a good soak, Lilly crawled into bed. Tighe came in to see her just before she drifted off to sleep.

"Where have you been today?" she murmured.

"Working. And I talked to Sally Anne. She says to say hi."

Lilly offered him a sleepy smile. "She's a nice young woman."

Tighe smiled and kissed Lilly's cheek. "I'll see you tomorrow, Mom."

The next morning Lilly awoke feeling sore all over her body, but she got out of bed and managed to dress herself. She was glad it was Sunday and she didn't have to go into the shop. Harry called around mid-morning.

"Boss! How are you feeling?"

A feeling of guilt for not calling him once she was released from the emergency room washed over her.

"I'm fine, Harry. I'm so sorry I didn't call you yesterday. It turned out my mother was two beds down from me in the emergency room and—"

"What happened to your mom?"

"She burned herself in the kitchen."

"Is she okay?"

"She'll be all right. She's on pain meds, so I'm thankful for that."

"Thank God. So what were you saying?"

Lilly thought for a moment. "Oh, yeah. I was explaining why I didn't call yesterday. Anyway, after we got Mom back home and all situated, Hassan and I had dinner and I went home, where I had an overnight guest. Long day. Again, I'm sorry."

"Please don't be sorry. You've got a lot on your plate right now."

"I've got a lot on my plate all the time, it seems."

"How's Mallory? Have you heard anything?" Harry asked.

"Believe it or not, she was in the bed between me and Mom yesterday. She was in a lot of pain, but the bullet didn't hit a major artery or anything. But to answer your question, no. I haven't heard anything. Hassan was going to call me as soon as he found out what happened to Tom and Jeremy Folsom, Mallory's ex-husband, and maybe he can find out about her, too."

Harry hung up after a few minutes and Lilly sat down at the kitchen table with a second cup of coffee. It wasn't long before Hassan called with news that Tom had been arrested on a number of charges ranging from assault to false imprisonment to conspiracy to commit a federal crime. Jeremy had been arrested by the feds for his part in Tom's harebrained scheme.

"Thanks for letting me know. I wonder if there's any way to find out how Mallory is doing," Lilly said. "The hospital won't disclose any information to anyone who's not a relative."

"You know her sister, don't you? Can you call her?" Hassan asked.

Lilly smacked her forehead with her good hand. "I forgot. I can just call Tisha and ask her. I'll let you know what I find out."

Lilly called Tisha right away.

"Hi, Tisha. It's Lilly. I'm just calling to see how Mallory's doing this morning."

"Oh, hi. She's still in the hospital." Tisha's voice was flat.

"Any word on when they'll let her go home?"

"No."

"Are you okay?"

"Well, my boyfriend is in jail. But other than that, just fine."

And your sister is in the hospital having been shot by said boyfriend, Lilly thought. Where were Tisha's priorities?

"Yeah, I know. But I guess the important thing is that Mallory wasn't hurt worse."

"Yeah."

"Will you keep me posted about her?"

"Yeah."

Lilly hung up, frustrated and angry that Tisha couldn't even bother to be upset about her sister's injuries. She was struck by a sudden desire to know that her mom was okay. She was so lucky to have a caring and loving family, even if they did drive her mad sometimes, and she needed to know that Bev was all right. She dialed Nikki without saying another word.

"Nikki? How's Mom today?"

"She's okay, I suppose." Not exactly an enthusiastic response.

"Is the pain in her hand any better?"

"Actually, it seems to be worse today. But I've just given her some pain medication and she's napping. Hopefully she'll feel a little better when she wakes up."

"Okay. I'll try to stop by later."

She hung up the phone feeling miserable. No answer about Mallory, her mom was in more pain than yesterday, and her own arm was hurting more and more. She popped a half dose of painkiller and decided to take a nap herself.

CHAPTER 100

*L*aurel came into Lilly's room early in the afternoon to thank Lilly for letting Vanessa spend the night at their house. "She's been so sad lately, Mom. I think she just wanted to be with people. Isn't Cyrus nice?"

"He is. He seems to care about her, which is nice. A lot of guys wouldn't come around anymore if their girlfriend was pregnant."

"He's not like that. But he called her this morning to talk. He wants to meet her again today to talk about the baby and what they're going to do."

"What they're going to do about what?"

"I don't know. He just told her he wants to talk."

"Is she upset about that?" Lilly frowned. She was worried that Vanessa was under too much stress.

"I don't know. I'll let you know what happens once I talk to her. He had planned to go back to New Mexico last night, but didn't. He stayed in a hotel, so he's on his way back to Juniper Junction now."

"All right. Keep me posted."

Lilly was still exhausted by late afternoon, but she dragged herself over to her mom's house to see how Bev was doing.

Not well, it turned out.

Nikki met her at the door. "She's pretty lethargic, Lilly. I just wanted to warn you so you're not upset when you see her."

It was a good thing Nikki had said something. Lilly was shocked when she walked into the living room and saw Bev sitting in her favorite chair, her head lolling to one side and her eyes closed. Lilly stopped herself before gasping in surprise. She turned to Nikki.

"Is she okay? Is she going to be okay?"

"This is normal, Lilly. It's probably a good thing Bill's coming home. I think you two are going to have to have a long conversation very soon."

Lilly swallowed. She couldn't deal with this, not tonight. "Okay, Nikki. He'll be home tomorrow evening. We'll talk the next day."

Lilly's exhaustion, combined with her sorrow over seeing Bev like that, was too much for her to handle alone. She called Hassan when she got home and asked him to come over. Laurel and Tighe were already there and looked up at her in surprise when she walked into the kitchen with tears already streaming down her face.

"Mom! What's wrong?" Tighe had been slicing carrots and he threw the knife into the sink. He rushed over to her and put his arm around her shoulders while Laurel pulled a chair over.

Lilly couldn't talk for the sobbing. The kids looked at each other, their eyes wide, and waited for her to speak.

"I just came from Gran's house and she looks terrible. I just can't take it anymore. And my arm hurts and Bill's not here."

The kids each pulled up chairs and sat down next to her. Tighe had his arms around her and Laurel held her hands. Such was the scene Hassan encountered when he walked in.

"Lilly! Tighe ... Laurel! What's wrong?" He crouched in front of Lilly. "Tell me what happened, love."

That made her cry harder.

"It's Gran," Tighe offered.

Hassan's eyes widened. "Is she okay?"

"I think so, but Mom's upset about her. That's all we've been able to figure out."

After several long minutes, Lilly was able to explain how she had found Bev. "Bill and I have to talk. Soon. I don't know how long she's going to be able to stay in her own home," Lilly said between sobs. "I'm so sick of crying."

No one answered. How could they? They didn't know what was going to happen—no one did. Lilly hadn't expected anyone to speak or have any answers for her. It was enough that they had listened while she was upset.

CHAPTER 101

It was late when the four of them sat down to the dinner Laurel and Tighe had prepared. More comfort food: meatloaf, mashed potatoes, and glazed carrots. Lilly couldn't bring herself to eat, but everyone else was able to eat a little bit.

Hassan gave her an over-the-counter sleep aid shortly after dinner. He stayed to make sure she was okay until it was time to take Barney out. Then he settled the sweet pooch quietly on Lilly's bed before going home.

Lilly awoke confused and weepy the next morning. It wasn't even light out when she woke up, and she lay in bed watching the clock and stroking Barney's soft fur. She was startled when her phone rang. It was Tisha.

"She's dead!"

In her confusion, Lilly didn't realize right away who Tisha was talking about. "What? Who's dead?"

"Mallory!"

Lilly was stunned. Mallory was dead? "But she said she was going to be okay. What happened?"

"An infection in her blood. Septimus or something."

"Sepsis?"

"Whatever."

"How did that happen?"

"The doctor said that something on the bullet gave her an infection. She died from that. It happened so fast. I have to go. They need me at the hospital."

"Okay. I'm sorry, Tisha."

Tisha hung up without another word.

Lilly called Hassan next, thanked him for coming to her rescue the night before, and told him about Mallory.

"I'm glad you're feeling better this morning. We'll get through all of this, love. I'm sorry about Mallory."

"Me, too. You know, it would be so much nicer if you just lived here."

"All you have to do is say the word, love. Whenever you're ready to make it official."

Lilly smiled. She was getting to the point where making it official sounded pretty good, but she also knew it wasn't wise to make such a big decision when she had so many other things going on in her life.

"You'll be the first to know, I promise." She hoped he could hear the smile in her voice.

When she hung up she remembered Bill and Noley were coming home that day. She swung her legs around and got out of bed. Barney watched, seemingly annoyed that she was done petting him for the moment. "We've got stuff to do, Barn."

She got ready for work early and woke Tighe and Laurel before leaving the house. She told them she wanted to have Bill and Noley over for dinner so they wouldn't have to fend for themselves their first night home from Aruba. The kids were happy to prepare dinner, so they promised to do the cooking and the cleaning while Lilly was at work.

Celie called later that morning. "I've spoken to the police, Lilly. I have all the answers."

CHAPTER 102

"Good. I could use some answers. What did you find out?"

"Jeremy met Tom several years ago through Jeremy's ex-wife, Mallory Abbott. It is my understanding that you know her."

"Yes."

"Apparently Mallory and Jeremy visited Tisha on several occasions over the years, and Tisha and Tom have had an on-again, off-again relationship for a long time. So Tom and Jeremy knew each other. They didn't exactly hit it off. Tom did a background check on Jeremy and found out that Jeremy had a special place in his heart for games of chance. He's a pretty good poker player himself, so he figured he could win some easy cash from Jeremy.

"They played poker on a number of occasions, and Jeremy lost every time. Rather than just making him pay up, though, Tom kept a running tab for a rainy day. And that day came when he learned he and your brother were up for the same promotion at work.

"He obviously knew Jeremy was a pilot, and when Jeremy

couldn't pay Tom the money he owed him from the poker losses, Tom gave him an offer he couldn't refuse. He said he would forgive Jeremy's debt if Jeremy would just do this one little thing at Bill's wedding. You had passed around the event schedule, so Tom knew exactly what time the wedding party would be taking photos. He presented it as a prank so Jeremy wouldn't think it was that bad."

"Any kind of prank involving an airplane is bad."

"You know that and I know that, but Jeremy isn't the sharpest knife in the drawer."

"Well, he was smart enough to scratch the tail number off his plane."

"That's true. Maybe I'm not giving him enough credit. Anyway, you know the rest of the story. The prank went awry, Jeremy crashed the plane, and Tom was in charge of the investigation so it went nowhere."

"Why did Tom do it?"

"Easy. Apparently he's had it in for your brother for years. It goes back to jealousy from when they were growing up. Tom feels like he's always been in Bill's shadow. He hoped a prank like the one at the wedding would expose Bill for being a coward and Tom would get the promotion, but obviously it didn't work out that way."

Lilly shook her head in disgust. "Did you know that Mallory died yesterday?" she asked.

"Yes. In speaking to Jeremy, I learned that she knew what had happened because she and Jeremy remained good friends. He told her all about it. Tom threatened to harm Jeremy if she told anyone about it, so that's why she didn't say anything to you."

Lilly was silent for several moments. She felt sorry for Mallory, who had been keeping a secret she didn't want to keep. All because of Tom. And worse, she had a feeling Mallory had planned to tell her the morning she was shot.

"How did you manage to speak to Jeremy?"

"He already lawyered up and the lawyer happens to be a friend of mine. I tagged along to their first meeting.

"Oh, there's one more thing. Tom's now been charged with second-degree manslaughter in Mallory's death. What a waste." Celie's voice held a strong note of disgust.

"Any word about Drew?"

Celie scoffed. "The Hendersons paid their bill in full and I haven't spoken to them since the day Drew was arrested. But I have heard through the grapevine that his lawyer is working on a plea deal. In exchange for a lighter prison sentence, Drew will be required to get a job—in another state—and relinquish any interest he may ever receive in his parents' holdings. At least that's what I've heard."

Lilly heaved a sigh of relief. It was good to know the young man would be leaving Juniper Junction.

She stopped at her mom's house after work. She steeled herself before walking in, and so she wasn't surprised when she found Bev in much the same state as she had been the previous day. Nikki smiled sadly. "I'm glad you're going to have that talk with Bill soon. This is no way for your poor mom to live. I try to help her with gross motor skills and communicating, but there's only so much I can do here by myself."

Lilly hugged Nikki. "I know. We're so grateful for everything you're doing for her. Bill is on his way home now and we'll talk as soon as we possibly can."

She had texted Hassan earlier in the day and asked him to come for dinner, so he arrived at the house bearing a bottle of wine and a smile. He kissed her and held her away from him. "You are beautiful inside and out, you know that? I'm glad you're feeling better today."

"Gross," Laurel said. Tighe laughed.

"Like you and Drew didn't do that, but worse, in public."

"Ugh. Don't mention that name. And speaking of doing worse, how's Sally Anne? Hmm?"

Tighe sobered.

"What's wrong, Tighe?" Hassan asked.

"Sally Anne and I had a long talk and we've agreed to take things very slowly from now on. I won't see her as often as I had planned this summer. I think the whole thing with Vanessa has me spooked."

"As it should," Lilly said. "I'm proud of you. There's nothing wrong with taking things slow. Mistakes happen when you move too quickly."

The doorbell rang and Barney launched himself into the living room. Lilly followed, laughing. "They're here!" she called.

Everyone crowded into the foyer as Lilly opened the door and Bill and Noley, tanned and smiling, stepped inside. There were hugs all around, back slaps, cheek kisses, and a jumble of voices as the Carlsens and Hassan welcomed the Merriweathers back to Juniper Junction. They all trooped into the kitchen, where Lilly poured wine for the adults. She lifted her glass in a toast to the newlyweds.

"To Bill and Noley Merriweather. Welcome home. We've missed you!"

Glasses clinked around the kitchen and Bill put his arm around Noley. "I was surprised I didn't hear a word from you while we were gone, Lil. I'm glad we didn't miss much."

THE END

LAUREL'S CHICKEN POT PIE

You'll notice this recipe calls for refrigerated pie crusts. Laurel, of course, makes her own. Feel free to use your favorite pie crust recipe in place of the store-bought ones!

1 qt. warm water

¼ c. salt

4 boneless, skinless chicken breast halves

2 T. olive oil

½ t. each ground pepper, garlic powder, and paprika

2 boxes refrigerated pie crust (enough for two covered pies)

5 c. chicken broth

2 T. Better Than Bouillon chicken paste

12 T. butter

¾ c. flour

1 glug/splash heavy cream

3 medium carrots, peeled and diced into ¼ inch pieces

1 14-oz. can green beans

1 8-oz. can yellow corn

1 10-oz. bag frozen peas

Preheat oven to 450 degrees.

Place qt. warm water in a large bowl. Add ¼ c. salt and stir until salt is almost dissolved. Add chicken breasts and soak for 15 minutes.

Pat chicken breasts dry and place on rimmed baking sheet coated with cooking spray. Brush oil onto each breast, flipping to get both sides. Mix pepper, garlic powder, and paprika in a small bowl, then sprinkle mixture on each chicken breast, flipping again to get both sides.

Bake for 12-15 minutes, depending on size of chicken breasts. When a thermometer inserted into the thickest part of the breast reads 165 degrees, take the chicken out and set aside on a plate.

Lower oven temperature to 425 degrees.

Take the pie crusts out of the fridge to come to room temperature.

Place chicken broth in a pan and heat over medium heat. Swirl the bouillon paste into the broth and simmer.

While that simmers, parboil the carrots for two minutes in a pan of boiling water. Drain and set aside.

Place butter in a Dutch oven and heat over medium heat until melted. Add flour and stir constantly for 2 minutes. Add hot chicken broth mixture to the butter and flour and cook, stirring constantly over medium-low heat, for 4-5 minutes or until thickened. Add a glug/splash of heavy cream and stir until blended.

Once the gravy is thickened, add chicken (with juices from the plate), carrots, beans, corn, and peas to the Dutch oven. Stir until combined and turn off heat.

Roll out pie crusts to fit two 9" or 10" pie plates. Place bottom crust in each pie plate. Fill each pie plate with one-half the chicken mixture, then top with top crusts. Crimp to seal and cut three or four slits in the tops to allow steam to escape.

You can cook both for a crowd, or you can cook one and freeze one. If you're going to freeze one, allow to cool, cover tightly in plastic wrap and then foil, and place in freezer.

Bake pie(s) for about 30-35 minutes.

HASSAN'S MEDITERRANEAN VEGETABLE SALAD

Dressing:
    1 clove garlic, minced
    3 T. red wine vinegar
    1 T. lemon juice
    1 t. Dijon mustard
    ½ t. dried oregano
    ½ c. olive oil
    Salt and freshly ground black pepper

Salad*:
    4 plum tomatoes, seeded and coarsely chopped
    1 yellow pepper, diced
    ½ red onion, thinly sliced
    1 handful Kalamata olives (without pits)
    1 can chickpeas, rinsed, drained, and patted dry
    1 medium cucumber, peeled, seeded, coarsely chopped, and
patted dry
    ¼ c. sun-dried tomatoes in oil, thinly sliced
    Crumbled Feta cheese

Make the dressing: In a large jar, combine all dressing ingredients. Shake vigorously. Set aside.

Make the salad: In a large bowl, combine all salad ingredients except for the cheese. Toss very gently. Shake dressing one more time and pour it in a slow stream over the vegetables in the desired amount. Toss very gently again. Pass crumbled feta cheese separately.

This is excellent with naan.

*Don't feel constrained by these ingredients, and don't be afraid to switch up the amounts of vegetables. Choose whatever sounds good to you!

LAUREL'S SHORTCUT MEATLOAF

1 ½ lb. ground chuck or meatloaf mix from the butcher
1 small onion, finely chopped
½ t. salt
1 8-oz. can tomato sauce
2/3 c. breadcrumbs
1 t. dried basil
Pinch celery salt
1 can cream of mushroom soup
Preheat oven to 350 degrees.

Using your hands, mix all ingredients in a large bowl just until combined. Do not overmix.

Place mixture in a greased loaf pan, being careful not to pack too tightly. Spread approximately ½ can of cream of mushroom soup, undiluted, over top of meatloaf.

Bake for one hour. Allow to sit for a few minutes before eating, to allow the meatloaf to set up a bit.

JOIN MY VIP GROUP!

I invite you to join my VIP Group by visiting www.amymreade.com.

VIP Group Members are treated to exclusive content, news of upcoming releases, and free goodies in The Secret Room of my website.

ABOUT THE AUTHOR

Amy M. Reade is a USA Today and Wall Street Journal best-selling mystery author who practiced law until she realized it was way more fun writing fiction.

She writes cozy and Gothic mysteries under the name Amy M. Reade and historical mysteries under the name A.M. Reade. She lives in New Jersey with her family and loves reading, cooking, traveling, playing with the dog, quilling, counted cross-stitch, chocolate, wine, and cheese, though not necessarily in that order.

If you're looking for her and she's not in her office, check the kitchen. If she's not there, then she's definitely in the laundry room.

To find out when her next book is coming out and to grab some fun freebies, sign up for her mailing list at www.amym-reade.com.

9 781735 522135